SEASON *of* WATER *and* ICE

Donald Lystra

Donald Lystra (signature)

SWITCHGRASS BOOKS   NORTHERN ILLINOIS UNIVERSITY PRESS   DeKalb

Published by the Northern Illinois University Press, DeKalb, Illinois 60115
Printed in Canada using postconsumer-recycled, acid-free paper.

Library of Congress Cataloging-in-Publication Data
Lystra, Donald.
Season of water and ice / Donald Lystra.
   p.   cm.
ISBN 978-0-87580-628-0 (pbk. : alk. paper)
1. Fathers and sons—Fiction. 2. Michigan—Fiction. 3. Domestic fiction. I. Title.
PS3612.Y74S43 2009
813'.6—dc22
2009017671

Chapter 1 of this book appeared in a slightly different version entitled "Family Way" in the Fall 2006 issue of Cimarron Review.

Chapter 10 of this book appeared in a slightly different version entitled "Excursion" in the Fall 2009 issue of Natural Bridge.

Acknowledgments

I wish to express my appreciation to the National Endowment for the Arts for its generous support during the preparation of this work. Appreciation is also given to the MacDowell Colony of Peterborough, New Hampshire, for granting me a creative writing fellowship in the fall and winter of 2008 and for honoring me with its Gerald Freund award for 2008–2009. Grateful thanks are also given to the University of Michigan for making its library facilities available to me during the preparation of major portions of this work.

I would like to thank the staff of Northern Illinois University Press, especially Sara Hoerdeman, Linda Manning, and Tracy Schoenle, for selecting my book for inclusion in its new fiction imprint, Switchgrass Books, and for their enthusiastic support and expert assistance throughout every step of the publishing process.

Alex Glass of Trident Media Group is owed much thanks for his tireless work and wise counsel on behalf of this book.

I am grateful to my wife, Doni, and my children, Margot and Brad, for the encouragement they provided as their husband/father embarked on the new enterprise of writing.

Finally, heartfelt gratitude is given to the many individuals who have assisted me with their support and expert commentary, not only in the writing of this novel, but also with the writing craft in general. Writing is a solitary activity, but it helps to have good people standing with you and encouraging you on. I am fortunate to have family and many friends who did this for me. I owe them all a great debt.

This book is for my family.

PART / ONE

Chapter One

IN THE EVENINGS MY FATHER quizzed me. Standing at the kitchen sink with his hands in soapy dishwater, the sleeves of his white shirt turned up above his elbows, he would ask me to explain the principles of science and mathematics and history that I'd learned that day at school. A good answer earned a brief smile and a stiff nod of his head. But if my performance was sloppy, or I acted disinterested, or sullen, he would cross-examine me until my lack of knowledge was exposed and then tell me to prepare a better explanation for the next evening.

"I understand that you've memorized the Gettysburg Address, Danny," he said to me one night. "But tell me its significance. It was more than a bunch of high-sounding words. Lincoln had a practical purpose in mind."

This was in the fall of 1957, the year I turned fourteen, the year the Russians sent their Sputnik into outer space and proved that they were way ahead of us. My father and I were living in a rented cabin on the shore of a large lake in northern Michigan, just outside the Manistee National Forest. The previous winter he had left his foreman's job in a General Motors' factory in Grand Rapids to take over a sales territory for a company that made power hand tools. Being a salesman was a different career for him, but he understood tools and how to work with your hands and he believed that explaining things to people—explaining good products that were durable and well manufactured—was all you needed for success. Selling, he'd told my mother the previous December when he announced his brave plans to her, was the perfect outlet for his independent spirit, and he believed he'd make a great deal of money doing it, and we would have a fine life.

He handed me a plate. I held it under the running faucet. "I guess it meant the country was going forward with the Civil War," I answered. "There would be no turning back."

"That's part of it," he said. "But what else?"

I let a long silence fill the room, knowing that the lack of a quick answer would irritate him. After a moment he glanced in my direction.

"It meant we were all the same country," I said. "We had to stay together, even if it caused a lot of pain."

He grunted, then pinched a burning cigarette off the counter's edge and took a deep drag. He was silent for a long time, staring out the window at the lake glistening in the setting sun, and I thought that my answer must have reminded him of some fact that needed to be considered. My father was not well educated but he liked to read, and he had read many books about Lincoln. Possibly he identified with the rail-splitter president: his struggle to transform himself from a backwoods bumpkin into a pillar of society; his difficult marriage; the bad luck that haunted him throughout his life.

"Okay, Danny, but what about the Negro?" He set the cigarette back on the counter. His hands went back into the dishwater. "What was the black man's role in all this violence?"

I thought about his question, but it made no sense. The word Negro didn't even appear in the Gettysburg Address, and I told him so.

"Well that's a question you need to think about, then," he said. "Just because something isn't mentioned doesn't mean it's not there. See if you can find an answer, and we'll talk about it tomorrow."

My father believed in the infinite possibilities of self-improvement. *His* father had been a Dutch immigrant who had worked all his life as a housepainter and had died under the wheels of a tramway car when my father was just fifteen. When they opened the General Motors factory in Grand Rapids in 1936, my father got a job on the production line, and in time he made it into the tool-and-die trade, which he was good at, and then into the lower ranks of management. But he hated working for a corporation and he hated the changes that were happening in the world—what he called "the gradual slide toward conformity and anonymity"—and his real love was the outdoors. He'd learned to hunt and fish during the Depression from a man named Harry Sherwood, an elder in the Methodist Church, and he loved those things still, loved the freedom they gave you, the sense of being in control of things. Living on a lake was his idea of the perfect place for us, even though the weather turned cold after Labor Day and most of the other cottages stood boarded-up and empty. But for me it was different. I rode a bus to school in McBride, a town of run-down stores and empty grain elevators nine miles away, and I attended classes with the children of lumberjacks and farmhands and Indians from the nearby Chippewa reservation. In the afternoons I spent countless hours alone, casting for bass from the end of a rickety wooden dock or reading books about the military academy at West Point, where I wanted to be a cadet one day.

"I've got to drive to Grayling tomorrow," my father said. He had drained the sink and was putting away the dishes I had just dried. "There's a man in the Western Hardware there who wants to talk about moving his account. It ought to be an easy sale, if my instincts are good for anything."

He looked at me as if he expected a response. But this time it was my turn to give a grunting, inarticulate reply. I was tired of the games he played to keep alive the fiction that everything was fine. Six months into his new career I knew he was failing. I'd seen the letters on a closet shelf demanding back rent on the cabin and I'd heard his late-night telephone calls to my uncle Glenn in Lansing, asking for a loan. Three weeks ago my mother had reached her limit. She'd gone off to live at her parents' house in Oak Park, Illinois, explaining that she needed a respite from the pioneering style of life. It was hard for me to blame her. The small summer cottage we lived in was cramped and smelled of mildew. The only heat came from a kerosene stove that you lit each morning with a wooden match. On nights when the wind blew up from the lake you could feel the walls shake and watch the curtains tremble like restless ghosts around the window frames. Worst of all, there seemed to be no end in sight. The blueprints for the house my father planned to build in town—a brick ranch style that he and my mother had selected one high-spirited night from a *Good Housekeeping* magazine—lay neglected in a drawer.

"I talked to your mother this afternoon on the phone," my father said.

"Is she coming back soon?" I was looking out the window where a gray heron was wading in the reeds along the lakeshore.

"I don't know. She didn't say."

"Didn't you ask her?"

"I did. But she didn't favor me with a response."

The heron lifted a leg and planted it slowly out in front, pausing to look for some movement in the water.

"I'm afraid she's angry with me," he continued, after a moment.

"About what?"

"For leaving my job with General Motors, I suppose, and casting my lot with the minions of the highway."

I didn't know what "minions of the highway" meant, and I didn't really care. But I knew that my mother had not wanted my father to leave his job with General Motors. *Her* father had been the treasurer for the Hudson Vacuum Cleaner Company in Chicago and as a girl she'd known a comfortable life, even during the Depression years. She understood the advantages that came from working for a large corporation and she assumed that my father would follow that path. In the months before we left Grand Rapids she'd taken to her bed with terrible headaches. More than once I'd missed a day of school to stay home and take care of her, boiling water on the stove to make hot compresses that she held against her forehead and reading to her from the poetry books that she loved—even though I barely understood what I was reading.

"She's going to call back later tonight," my father said. "She wants to talk to you."

"About what?"

"Just to say hi, I imagine." He sat down at the kitchen table and placed a mug of coffee on the oilskin tablecloth. "And to remind you that she loves you. She said she's afraid you'll forget that important fact if it's left unspoken for too long."

"I know she loves me," I said.

"Well, that's good" he said. "It's a fait accompli, as the French would say." He took a sip of coffee, then stared at the steaming liquid as if something was not entirely to his liking. "Why don't you tell her how good life is up here in the wilderness?" he said. "Maybe that'll entice her to come back and join the fun. Tell her your father is still managing to keep a roof over your head."

Out on the water the heron's head shot forward so fast that I didn't even see it happen. One moment he was standing still and the next he was holding a struggling bluegill in his beak.

I set the last dish on the counter. "All right," I said. "I can tell her those things."

After we finished the dishes we went outside to practice golf. This was a routine my father had insisted on since we'd come to live on the lake. He'd started playing the year before on a dusty par-three course in Grand Rapids, and he was anxious to master the fine points of the game and show he could be good at it. Golf, he'd told me more than once, was an integral part of the selling formula. On a golf course you got to know a man in ways that were impossible in an office, and you could demonstrate your character without being threatening or offensive.

Now, in the fading October sunlight, he bent over the small white ball, his hands wrapped lightly around the club shaft. As he prepared to take his shot he talked out loud, giving a summary of the thoughts he used to guide his stroke: the position of his feet, the angle of the clubface, the speed of the takeaway. All of this talk, I knew, was for my benefit, a continuation of the never-ending learning process in which he put such store.

He made his shot. The ball arced beautifully through the twilight air and dropped within a couple of feet of a Hills Brothers coffee can.

"Now it's your turn, Danny." He straightened up, a tiny smile on his face. "Just remember to hit through the ball. That's the secret of a good golf stroke."

I positioned myself over the ball and brought the club back in a long looping arc, then came down hard. The ball took off like a shot. But instead of heading for the coffee can, it sailed over a row of cedar trees that bordered the property.

"That was a worthy effort, son," my father said. "But now you get to learn the dark side of the game: how to recover from disaster."

Without a word I dropped the seven iron onto the grass and went off to retrieve the ball, grateful to have a break from my father's lessons. Turning my back, I pushed through the tangle of cedar branches. When I came out on the other side I saw a girl standing in a grove of pine trees. She was a tall skinny girl of about seventeen, and she wore red shoes and a white dress that the breeze whipped around her legs.

"Is this yours?" She held up the golf ball.

"Yes." I put out my hand for her to throw it to me.

"You need to be more careful." She tossed the ball up into the air and caught it coming down. "I should probably throw it into the lake. That would teach you a lesson." She looked in my direction. "There's people around that you could hurt, you know, hitting wild like that."

"I don't see any people."

"There's me, for one," she said. "You could have hit me."

I took a couple of steps in the girl's direction. She had dark hair that fell around her shoulders and large brown eyes that seemed to look right into you. The breeze from the lake folded the white dress up tight against her body.

"Where'd you come from?" I asked.

She pointed to a small tar paper–sided house on the far side of a narrow inlet. From this distance, it looked more like a hunting shack than a place where a family would live.

"You're the people who're renting the Michaelsons' place," she said. She threw the ball up into the air again, following it with her eyes. "But you don't look like what I expected."

"What did you expect?"

"I don't know. Some Italians from Detroit, maybe. Or hillbillies with a herd of goats."

Just then I heard a noise behind me. I turned around and saw a group of small sailboats headed toward a red buoy anchored about a hundred feet offshore. The boats were heeled far over in the breeze, their sails stretched tight. They seemed to struggle to make headway toward the buoy.

"That's the Wednesday night sailboat race," the girl said. "The rich people drive out from town to use our lake for a little while. Then they go home and give it back to us."

"They don't look rich to me," I said. Out on the water, men in flannel shirts and blue jeans were shouting back and forth. The sails flapped wildly as they came around the buoy.

"Well, maybe you know more about it than I do," the girl said.

We stood for a moment without saying anything. Then from the other side of the cedar hedge I heard my father's voice call out: "It's getting too dark to see the ball, Danny. You better come inside." I heard the door of our cabin open and close. Then a light came on in one of the windows.

I turned back to the girl. "Why are you living out here on the lake after Labor Day?" I asked.

"This is where we live all the time." She turned and looked across at her dilapidated house. "My stepdad does handyman work for the cottage owners, like fixing leaky roofs or hauling trash. He does taxidermy, too, when he can get it."

"So are you going to give me the golf ball?" I asked.

"I'm still thinking about it," she said, and she threw the ball up into the air again, high this time, drifting to one side to make the catch. Then she started walking in my direction, taking slow, graceful steps like she was in no particular hurry. Seeing her like that, with the breeze blowing out her dark hair and pushing the dress up tight against her body, I decided she was pretty and that other people would think so, too.

"Why, you're only young," the girl said when she got close. "You looked older from back there. I guess because you're so tall."

"I'm eighteen," I said.

"Sure you are. And I'm twenty-five." She grinned a crooked smile. "Anyway," she said, "I guess there's nothing wrong with being young. Nothing that time won't cure." She held out her hand with the golf ball. "And I didn't mean what I said about throwing your golf ball in the lake. That was a comment meant for an older boy."

I reached forward and lifted the golf ball from her hand.

"Now you'll have to do *me* a favor someday," she said.

"All right," I said, although I couldn't imagine what I could do that would help her in any way.

She tilted her head back and looked at me through slightly narrowed eyes. "I don't suppose you know anything about geometry?" she said.

"I'm pretty good at math," I said, which was a true statement, although I didn't always like to admit it. At school in Grand Rapids I'd been told I had an aptitude for the subject—"a natural inclination to organize the world according to the unforgiving logic of numbers" was how one of my teachers had put it—and I'd been given special assignments and had worked all the way ahead to trigonometry. But being good with numbers sometimes made me feel strange, as if I saw the world differently from other kids and couldn't connect with them.

"Well I'm an idiot in that particular category," the girl said. "That's why I'm taking geometry for the second time."

"Why don't you get help from your teacher?"

"I don't go to school this year," she said. She was so close that I could see little flecks of lipstick on her mouth. "I take my classes at home." She paused, still looking into my face, as if her statement had a special meaning that I should understand. It didn't, though, so I just stood there waiting for her to continue.

"They think I'll corrupt the other kids," she said with another crooked smile. Then she pressed her hands against the front of her dress and smoothed the fabric over her stomach. "I'm in the family way," she said, looking down at the tiny bulge that the tight fabric revealed. She tossed her head to get a strand of hair out of her face. "That's a high-class way of saying you're pregnant, in case you don't know about such awful things."

"I know what it means," I said and I did, because my father had explained those things to me the year before during a Sunday afternoon walk through Garfield Park. He'd told me about love and explained how men and women copulate and how it was a thing that people did but not something you talked about. And then he'd explained how a girl kept from getting pregnant by keeping track of her cycles, and he said that when I was older I should be careful not to get a girl in trouble, but that if I did it would be my fault and I shouldn't expect help from him or anyone else.

"Does it shock you?" the girl asked. "My shameful condition."

"No," I said. "It's all right." Although it *did* shock me. It shocked me very much to have a pregnant girl standing close and to hear her speak so calmly about a thing I knew to be a terrible sin. For a moment I tried to make it seem less strange by picturing her in bed with a boy, both of them in love and grabbing and holding each other under a blanket. But it was a hard thing to imagine, so I stopped.

During all the time that I was thinking, the girl had remained silent. She just stood and stared at me, her head cocked a little to one side, as if it was my turn to say something important and she was waiting to hear what it would be. But I didn't know what to say, so I just repeated "It's all right" again and then turned and looked out onto the water.

It was almost dark now and hard to see much of anything. But then I spotted the sailboats on the far side of the lake, a cluster of dim gray triangles rocking slowly over a great flatness, heading in the direction of a larger boat decked out with colorful flags. Suddenly a puff of white smoke appeared like magic in the air above the larger boat, followed a second later by the crack of a pistol shot reaching us across the water.

"That's the end of the race," the girl said, following my gaze. "Now they know who the winner is." She turned back to me. "Well anyway, what you said was very sweet. Too bad my boyfriend didn't feel the same way. He joined the army when he found out he'd knocked me up." She looked at me and grinned. "That's another way of saying it."

"That's too bad," I said.

Suddenly the girl's expression hardened and she shot me an angry look, as if I'd said something stupid. But then she shrugged and smiled in a way that made her look sad. "I cried at first," she said. "I cried quite a lot. But now I'm reconciled to it. You can reconcile yourself to almost anything, you know. The main thing is that I love my baby and will take good care of it." She looked down at her stomach again, and I knew she was thinking about the baby growing there and how she would take care of it. "You don't need other people so much," she continued. "Not as much as they say you do. You don't need a husband, that's for sure. Whether or not

I'm a good mother is the important thing."

I still didn't know what to say, although it seemed like a terrible thing that her boyfriend had done to her, and I wished I knew words that would help.

"What about *your* mother?" the girl said, looking up. She tossed her head again to get the strand of hair off her face. "I haven't seen any woman around your place."

I thought about how I should answer. All her talk about getting pregnant and losing her boyfriend and having to take her classes at home had made me feel sorry for her, and I wanted to say something that would make her life seem better. And then I thought about my mother at her parents' house in Oak Park, and I wondered what *she* was doing that very minute, whether she was out in the backyard talking to a stranger about her life or whether she was listening to music on the radio or whether she was getting ready to call to tell me that she loved me. All of these thoughts ran together in my head so that I didn't have a single thought to say to the girl, only a lot of half thoughts that added up to nothing.

"My mother's dead," I said. "She was killed last year in an automobile accident."

A shocked expression came onto the girl's face, and she took a half step backward, as if what I'd said had been a sort of blow.

"Why that's terrible," she said. "You must feel awful."

"I did at first," I said. "But you get used to it. It's like what you said about your boyfriend going away."

Just then a voice called out. We both turned and looked across the inlet where a woman in a blue dress stood near the shore. The girl walked down and waved across.

"I'm talking to our new neighbor, Momma," she yelled. "I'll be there in a minute."

"You come in right now, Amber," the woman called out.

"Oh, Momma," the girl said. "He's only a boy."

"You heard me," the woman called back.

The girl—Amber—turned and walked back up the bank to where I was standing. She put her hand on my arm and leaned in close. "I've got to go," she said in a kind of hushed voice. "Momma's been crazy ever since I got pregnant. She thinks all you boys have got only one thing on your mind."

I looked at Amber, surprised she would think about me in this way. She started to turn away, but she stopped with her hand still resting on my arm. "I'll tell you something," she said, and she leaned in so close that I could feel her hard stomach press against my arm. "If you ever get lonely for your own momma, you can come over and talk to me." I felt her hard stomach and I felt the ends of her hair whipping my face in the breeze. "I'm a momma, too, so it'll be practically the same thing. Just come over anytime you want." She smiled and squeezed my arm. Then she turned and walked off through the pine trees, walking in that graceful way.

When I got back to the cabin, my father was sitting in an upholstered chair next to the kerosene stove. All around him on the floor were the things he called his peddler's gear—boxes of steak knives, key chains, ballpoint pens—things he gave to people he wanted to sell to.

I sat down at the kitchen table and got out my books and started to work on the Gettysburg Address. I wanted to find the answer to my father's question so I'd be ready for the next night's examination. But after talking to Amber, it was hard to concentrate. I couldn't stop thinking that she was pregnant and didn't have a husband or a boyfriend to help her out, and how, in spite of that, she was still looking forward to being a mother. Then my thoughts went in a different direction, and I began to think about my own mother. I'd told Amber that she was dead when she wasn't, which seemed like a terrible betrayal, and I decided I'd make up for it by the things I said to my mother that night, words that would express my hope that she would soon come home.

Just then the telephone rang in the back of the cabin and my father got up to answer it. I heard him laugh softly and say my mother's name. Then I heard him talk in a low steady voice I couldn't understand. He talked like that for several minutes, then called my name. I went back and took the receiver from his hand.

"Hello, Danny boy," my mother said. "How's life in the woods?"

"It's good," I said. "It's fine."

My father headed back toward the living room.

"Your mother misses you, Danny. Tons and tons."

"I know, Mom. I miss you, too."

"Are you making lots of friends at your new school?"

"I haven't made too many friends yet, but there are some kids I talk to."

"What about the girls, Danny?" She spoke in a teasing voice. "Have any of the girls caught your eye?"

"No," I said. "No girl has caught my eye."

There was a pause then, as if my mother didn't know what to say next. Then I asked her: "Is Oak Park nice?"

"Oh, yes, it's lovely. There are beautiful gardens everywhere, and the people are very friendly. Most of them are comfortable, Danny. Comfortable with money, I mean. And in Chicago there are wonderful libraries and a natural science museum that I know you'd just love."

"When are you coming home?" I asked.

"Oh, Danny, that's a subject we need to talk about."

I felt something go hollow inside of me.

"Your father and I have been talking," she went on, "and we've decided it's best to continue like this for the time being. He's working very hard, you know, and of course he's going to be a great success eventually. But in the meantime it's probably best if I stay here." She stopped talking and after a moment I realized she was waiting for me to say something. But I couldn't think of anything. I still had that hollow feeling, and it seemed to take up all the space where words would come from.

"Your mother isn't very good at living out in the country," she went on, after the silence grew uncomfortable. "In the beginning I thought I could do it, but then I found out I couldn't. The country's a wonderful place for men and boys but it's not a place for a woman, Danny. So I'll just stay here until your father builds our new house in town. You remember the house we selected?"

"Yes."

"Your father thinks he'll be able to get it started soon, maybe in the spring. So it won't be very long. And in the meantime you can come and visit me. You can come for Thanksgiving. We can go to the museums and have lunch in the Palmer House dining room."

I leaned back against the wall. Then I noticed I was gripping the telephone very hard and I forced my hand to relax. At my mother's end I heard a radio playing softly in the background.

"I love you, Danny boy," my mother said, after we'd been silent for a very long time. "I love you tons and tons. That's the important thing. Always remember that. It doesn't matter if we're together as long as we love each other."

"I love you, too, Mom," I said.

"Oh, Danny," she said, and there was a catch in her voice. "I'd better go now. Otherwise I'll start to cry, and it'll be just terrible. Good-bye, sweetheart."

"Good-bye, Mom."

"Remember that I love you."

"I will. Yes. I will."

And then we both hung up.

I went back into the kitchen and sat down at the table. I still had that hollowness inside of me and I couldn't think of any words to make thoughts from. And then for some reason I remembered a day last spring when my mother and I had driven up north to meet my father, who was going to show us the land where he planned to build our new house and give us a glimpse of the brilliant life that lay in store for us. We met him in the parking lot of the motel where he'd been living since he'd started his salesman's job in March. It was a sunny day, and he was sitting on a metal lawn chair reading a newspaper and smoking a cigarette. When we drove up he smiled and folded the newspaper and came over to the car.

"There's a pretty sight," he said, looking at my mother.

"Hello, Jim," my mother said. "Are you taking a sunbath?"

I got out of the car to move into the backseat. As I was standing on the gravel parking lot, my father came around and draped his arm across my shoulders. We both understood that this was as close to an embrace as he would ever come.

"Hello, bub," he said. "Have you been taking good care of your mother?"

"Yes, sir," I said.

"He's been my guardian angel, Jim," my mother said, leaning across the passenger seat and looking out, and I believed she was thinking about her headaches and how I'd stayed home from school to read poetry and make hot compresses. "I could go to the moon and back and be safe with him," she added.

My father got into the passenger seat. Then he leaned over and kissed my mother on the mouth, putting his arm around her shoulder and holding her tight for a very long time.

"My goodness," my mother said. She laughed and made a fanning motion with her hand. "That's a nice how-do-you-do." And then she looked back over her shoulder to where I was sitting in the backseat. "Now you know what love looks like, Danny," she said, and she smiled at me in a way that made her look pretty.

Outside the cabin, the wind moved a tree branch against the windowpane. It made a rough scratching sound, as if some burrowing animal were trying frantically to get inside. I closed my book, got up from the kitchen table, and stood in the doorway to the living room. After a moment my father noticed me standing there and looked up.

"Did she give you the amazing news?" he asked.

"She said she's going to stay in Oak Park."

"That's what I meant."

"She's going to stay there until you build the house."

"That's what I understand, too. Or until hell freezes over, whichever happens first."

I looked quickly at my father. He stared back with an odd expression. And then he shook his head from side to side, as if he wished he could cancel out the last words he had spoken.

"I have an answer to your question," I said. "The one about the Negro slaves."

My father blinked a few times, like he didn't know what I was talking about. But then he set aside the box of steak knives and looked up at me and smiled.

"Well, let's hear it, bub."

I didn't know exactly what I was going to say any more than I knew why I'd told Amber that my mother was dead when she wasn't. *That* was just an idea that had come out of my mouth without any thought behind it, a feeling that had arisen in me and been released. Something I'd said to make Amber feel better and not a thing to worry or feel ashamed of.

"They couldn't do anything," I said. "Not then. They just had to wait." I put my hand up on the doorjamb. "But they could do something later."

My father stared at me with a perplexed expression, as if I were a stranger who had walked in out of the night. His gaze drifted back to the box of steak knives. Then it came back to me.

"You said it differently than I would've," he said. "But I guess that's what I thought, too."

I turned away then and went back into the kitchen and sat down at the table where I'd been working on the Gettysburg Address.

I thought about the conversation I'd had with my mother. I was able to do that now. She had told me she loved me, because she was afraid of leaving those words unsaid, afraid of what that lack might mean. But even though she'd spoken the words, I knew she did not mean them, not in the way Amber loved the baby that was growing inside of her, which involved some loss, some giving up.

Outside, the wind moved the tree branch against the side of our cabin. And I thought about the sailboats out there in the darkness. And I tried to imagine how it would feel to be out there with them, on the open water, jostled by waves and with spray coming over the side and everything dark and moving and never settled. And for a moment I actually made myself dizzy, confused, and off balance, as if I'd been cut off from something important and was alone in a wild and unforgiving place. And then I had to close my eyes until my breathing steadied and my heart stopped pounding and I felt calm again and at peace. Settled and composed. Strong. Unafraid of what lay ahead.

Chapter Two

AFTER THAT NIGHT IN EARLY OCTOBER, things seemed to change in our lives. Changed for me and for my father, too, in ways we probably didn't expect. My father began to spend more time on the road, trying to make more sales. On many nights he didn't come home at all. I would get a telephone call in the late afternoon asking if I was all right or needed anything, and he would suggest some dish to make for dinner: a piece of chicken he'd put away in the refrigerator in waxed paper or a can of stew or Spam and fried potatoes—something simple that a boy could make. Always, though, he would leave the number of the hotel or boardinghouse where he was staying, with instructions to call if I had trouble with anything or needed help with my homework or just wanted to talk.

All of this was fine. I was alone during the long afternoons and evenings, but I saw people during the day at school—children and teachers—enough people to satisfy me. And I was beginning to enjoy the solitary things you could do on a lake—fishing for bass in the weed beds along the shore or exploring the shallow bays and inlets in an old wooden rowboat I'd found propped up against a tree. Sometimes I would take the rowboat into other lakes—there were four altogether, linked by narrow channels clogged with reeds and lily pads—and I would imagine I was Samuel de Champlain or René La Salle coming down from Canada to explore uncharted lands. And sometimes in the late afternoon, just as the sun was going down, I would hike out into the forest and find a clearing and sit on a stump or fallen log and wait for animals to come by: black squirrels or raccoons or porcupines or wild turkeys or deer—almost always something interesting would come by. And in the evenings, after dark, I liked reading my books about West Point and mathematics by the kerosene stove or listening to a baseball game on the radio from the station in Traverse City. All of this was fine.

It was, I will admit, an odd time for me: a time of watching and waiting. My life had changed in many different ways, but I guess I wanted to deal with the changes slowly and in private. I missed my old friends from Grand Rapids—the kids I'd grown up around— but I wasn't in a hurry to make new ones. I think I was trying to hold myself apart so that I wouldn't react to things too much, stand at the side until I knew which thoughts or feelings were the right ones to have—the ones an adult would have, I suppose—and I could commit myself to wholeheartedly. And maybe, too, I felt threatened in certain ways, threatened by the idea of how you think the world is supposed to be and the kind of person you are—and what you actually see.

My mother called every few days. We would have long conversations about the exciting things she was doing in Oak Park and the interesting people she was meeting, and she would ask me what I'd done that day at school and tell me how terrible she felt to be away. But it was different from before, because I knew now that she would not be coming back for a while. And I guess I was satisfied with that, satisfied that she understood what was best for her—and satisfied that she would be back eventually.

And so being alone and living on a lake and being without a mother didn't seem so bad—even though most people would probably tell you it was. Or maybe I was merely getting used to it. In any case it was all right. Not really such a bad life.

At school one day in algebra class we listened to the broadcast of a rocket being launched down in Florida. But at the last minute something went wrong, and the rocket fell over and exploded. I remember hearing it on the radio, the voice of the announcer counting down the seconds, the roar of the rocket engine starting up, and then the even bigger roar of the explosion.

Mr. Horak, our algebra teacher, had come over from Latvia after the war, and he'd spent time in a Russian refugee camp and knew the brutality of Communism. You could tell from his expression that the exploding rocket had upset him as much as if a close friend had died or he'd seen a terrible accident along the highway. Then someone laughed, and a boy said he guessed it was just a matter of time before the Russians would be in charge of us. For the next fifteen minutes Mr. Horak lectured us about how we needed to take life more seriously and become better students and how we especially needed to study science and mathematics, because those were the subjects that led to the technical breakthroughs needed to defeat Communism.

That afternoon after school I walked through the pinewoods to Amber's house. I had decided I would tell her about the rocket blowing up and ask what she thought about Communism, which I believed she would have an opinion about. I also wanted to begin tutoring her in geometry; I had gotten the crazy idea that if she became good at mathematics she could go to the university and get a job and be able to take care of her baby by herself. Riding home on the bus that afternoon, I had pictured her working in a laboratory in a white smock, holding a beaker of smoky chemicals up to the light or standing over a machine and taking readings off a dial, a clipboard cradled in her arm. They were crazy thoughts—completely insane considering the circumstances of her life, and I suppose I knew that even as I was thinking them. But it was enough to give me the courage to make the walk around the inlet to her house.

Up close, the small one-story structure looked even more decrepit than it had from a distance: curling strands of loose tar paper hung from the outside walls like flags of surrender; plastic sheeting covered the windows; a rusted screen door, broken from its hinges, lay propped up against a maple tree. The woman who answered my knock on the door looked haggard.

Her stringy brown hair was arranged in no particular style, and she wore a shapeless gray housedress, tattered at the edges. She held the door partly open and peered out suspiciously.

"What do you want?" she asked.

"I want to talk to Amber about geometry. We had a conversation about it a few days ago."

"Geometry." The woman spoke as if the subject were distasteful in some way.

"I live over there." I turned and pointed across the inlet.

"You're the boy who lives at Michaelsons."

"That's right. I live there with my dad. My name's Danny DeWitt."

The woman stepped out onto the tiny cement-block stoop and I stepped down to make room for her. She peered at me as if I were a curiosity. "I'm Mrs. Dwyer," the woman said. "I'm Amber's mother."

"I'm pleased to meet you, ma'am."

"Are you a Christian?" she asked.

"I think so," I said. "My family's Methodist."

"Then you must go to Reverend Thatcher's church in McBride."

"I guess we will eventually. We haven't gone anyplace yet."

"But you've been here for a while."

I didn't know what to say so I just stood looking back at her with no particular expression. In Grand Rapids we'd gone to church almost every Sunday, but since coming to live in the country we hadn't gone a single time. I thought it was because we didn't feel connected to things in the way we'd felt in the city. Or possibly it had something to do with my father's new plan for his life, which was to get free of things that complicate your life and limit your opportunities.

Amber's mother gave me a tiny smile. "What was it you wanted to see my daughter about?"

"Geometry," I said.

She stared at me, as if she were trying to figure something out. "You know Amber's carrying a baby?" she said next.

"Yes, ma'am. She told me that."

"She let a boy take some liberties with her. Then he ran away."

I didn't say anything. Amber's mother stood and watched me.

"What would you do with a girl who did a thing like that?" she blurted out suddenly, as if my opinion might count for something. "A girl who'd been given a good Christian upbringing."

"I don't know, ma'am," I said. "I guess you'd know better about that than me."

"That's right," she said, and she nodded her head emphatically. "Her stepdaddy beat her within an inch of her life. That's what happened."

Her lips tightened, and she looked at me in a stern way, as if she wanted to emphasize the hard point she had just made. I held her gaze as long as I could, but then I had to look away.

"Well, just so you know the kind of girl she is," she said. "In case you want to try something."

She turned around and went back into the house. After a couple of minutes I heard muffled voices; then the door swung back and Amber was standing in the opening. She wore blue jeans and a red plaid shirt. A yellow ribbon held her hair back in a ponytail.

"What are you doing here?" she asked. "Did you lose another golf ball?"

"I thought I could help you with geometry," I said. "Like you asked me."

Amber blinked a few times, and I noticed that her eyes were red and watery. Then she shook her head as if she were trying to shake some thoughts out of it, the thoughts she'd had before coming to answer the door, maybe, whatever those had been. Then her eyes came back to me and she smiled. "I didn't think you'd take me seriously," she said.

"Didn't you mean it?"

"Well, yes. I meant it all right. But I guess I didn't think you'd take me seriously. A lot of people don't these days."

I didn't know what to say so I just stood there silently. Then I said, "I can probably help you out some."

Amber looked at me as if she was still uncertain about something. Then she turned and looked back into the house. I could hear her mother working in the kitchen, pots and pans rattling, water running from a faucet, a radio playing a song by Dinah Shore. I leaned a little to one side and looked into the dim interior. Above a stone fireplace a gun rack held a rifle and some shotguns. Next to that was a picture of Jesus praying in Gethsemane. A pair of muddy boots sat on a newspaper near the door.

Amber turned back and stepped out onto the stoop, drawing the door closed behind her. "As a matter of fact I could use some help just now," she said. She smiled at me. "I have a test tomorrow on something called a parabola."

"I know about those."

"Well, if you know anything at all, it'll be more than me," she said, and she laughed in a sort of bitter way. Then she stepped over to the edge of the cement-block stoop and looked down along the side of the house. "I suppose we could use my stepdaddy's workshop," she said. "Out back where he does his taxidermy. It's kind of creepy in there but it's got a workbench and it's quiet." She looked at me. "He's gone off for a couple of weeks to work on a roofing project in Mancelona, so it's not being used right now."

"That sounds good," I said.

"Give me a minute to get my book, and I'll meet you there."

I went around and stood next to the shed and waited for Amber to come out. It was a bright fall day: spots of sunlight moved over the ground beneath swaying tree branches. A battered green Chevy pickup sat beneath a hemlock tree, the truck bed filled with soggy, decomposing leaves. A Standard Oil thermometer nailed to a tree read fifty-nine degrees.

From inside the house I heard Amber's voice; it sounded like she was continuing a conversation that had already started. "He's only a boy, Momma," I heard her say. "It's not like he's going to rape me."

"Don't get smart with me," Amber's mother said in a loud voice. "I'll throw you out in a minute if you get smart with me. Just like Ray wants me to do. You're lucky to still have a place to stay."

There was a long silence, and then I heard Amber say, "Please, Momma, don't be this way. You didn't used to be this way."

Then Amber's mother said, "Well, you've already got yourself pregnant, as far as that goes. So I guess there's no more damage to be done."

After another minute Amber came out carrying her books and a pad of paper and pencils. She used a key to unlock the padlock on the door to the shed. When she inserted the key into the little opening, I noticed that her hand was trembling.

Inside, two long workbenches held animal heads and skins. The air was heavy with chemicals and the faint tinge of rotting flesh. A single lightbulb dangled from the ceiling. Amber pulled the chain and it came on.

"This'll be a good place to work," she said. She went over to one of the workbenches and moved some raccoon skins off to one side to make a little open space. "There's light coming in from the window."

We sat down on stools and I began to tell Amber what I knew about parabolas. I explained it using diagrams to show how the different equations look on paper. But when I looked up I could tell she hadn't been listening.

"Pay attention," I said. "It takes concentration."

"Okay," she said. She blew out a stream of air so that her cheeks puffed out. "Go over it again."

I went over it a second time and then I worked a couple of problems. Then I had Amber work a couple of problems by herself. Even though she wasn't really interested, I could tell she understood what I had told her. She worked the problems quickly, even spotting a trick in one of them.

"Okay," she said, after she'd finished. "I think I've got it now."

"Some are more complicated. You should probably work a few more."

"No," she said. "I think I've got it."

She closed the book and pushed her stool back from the workbench. Then she picked up a pencil and started to draw on the pad of paper, her hand moving in quick little jerks.

"We should work some more problems," I said.

She smiled. "Geometry's not going to be that big a factor in my life, Danny. I'm actually going to be an artist."

I leaned over and looked at her drawing. It showed a girl in a long flowing dress standing on the edge of a cliff.

"You're pretty good," I said.

"There's a lot more I need to learn." She kept working on her drawing, adding flounces to the girl's dress and making it look like the wind was blowing. "You've got to know about composition, for one thing. That's how you arrange things in a picture. And about paints: what kinds there are and which colors work together and which ones don't."

"Where do you learn about that stuff?"

"There's some schools, but they're mostly in big cities." She held the picture out at arm's length and examined it with a little frown. "There's a good school in Montreal that'd let me in. But you've got to know how to speak French to live there."

Amber tore off the page and wadded it up and threw it into a corner. Then she started working on another drawing. This one showed a deer running through the forest.

"A rocket blew up yesterday in Florida," I said. "Did you hear about that?"

"No," Amber said.

"It was on the radio."

She was concentrating on her picture, bending low and squinting.

"Do you think we've got a chance to catch up with the Russians?" I asked.

"I suppose so," she said. She shrugged. "I don't know. Maybe."

"Aren't you afraid of Communism?"

She smiled, still working on her picture. "I've got other things to worry about," she said with an odd smile.

I remembered I had planned to ask Amber about the Cold War. And I also wanted to tell her what Mr. Horak had said about science and mathematics. But I could see she wasn't interested, and so instead of saying any of those things I said something else, and not for any reason I understood.

"Why were you crying when you came to the door?" I asked.

"Oh," Amber said. "Was I crying?" She spoke in an offhand way.

"You looked like you were. Your eyes were red and swollen."

She finished the picture of the deer and held it out and studied it like she'd done with the other one. Then she crumpled it up and threw it into a corner of the shed; it bounced down next to the first.

"I was having an argument with my momma," she said. She turned and looked into my face.

"What about?"

"The same old thing. About being pregnant and what to do with the baby." She took a deep breath and held it for a moment. When she let it out I felt it rush against my face. "My parents say I've got to let somebody else take the baby when it comes. Some family who's got money. They say I can't be the mother if I'm not married."

"That's too bad," I said.

Amber turned and looked at me with a hard expression, and for a moment I thought I'd said something to make her mad. But then she gave a small tired smile. "I won't let them do it, though. I'll run away if I have to."

She smiled again, but this time in a sort of inward way. Then she looked over at a snarling black bear's head lying next to us on the workbench, and she reached out and touched a white tooth with her index finger, delicately, as if she were testing it for sharpness. Then she put her hand on top of the bear's head and worked her fingers into the thick mat of black fur.

I watched Amber staring at the bear's head, a calm expression on her face, and I believed she was thinking about her baby and how she wasn't going to let anyone take it away from her, even if it meant running away. And then I noticed how the light from the window was playing off her face, making highlights and shadows that showed the shape of her mouth and the curve of her cheek. And I thought she looked very beautiful, and for a moment I felt the urge to tell her that—that she was a pretty girl—because I didn't think she heard it very often and would like to know it. But I had never said those words before—not to my mother or to any girl I had ever known—and I was afraid I'd say them wrong and end up feeling foolish.

"You remember what I told you about my mother being dead?" I said instead.

Amber stopped working her fingers into the bear's fur. She turned and looked at me. "Yes. Of course."

"That wasn't true," I said. "She's only gone away for a while."

Amber frowned. "Where's she gone to?"

"To a city near Chicago."

"Chicago," she said. "That's odd. Doesn't she love your daddy?"

"Of course. She only wanted to go away for a while."

Amber looked at me with a disbelieving expression. "But it doesn't make any sense. Why would she go away if she loves your daddy?"

"She just did," I said.

Amber stared at me. She stared at me for a long time. And I think she was trying to decide if it was worth the trouble to ask more questions about my mother. But then she looked down at her lap, where she'd put her hands.

"So why did you say she was dead?" she asked, and she used a different tone of voice this time. "Why'd you tell me a lie?"

"I don't know," I said. "I guess I thought it would make you feel better about your boyfriend being gone."

"I don't get it," Amber said. She shook her head slowly, still looking down. Then she stood and walked over to the other side of the little room so I had to turn around in my chair to see her. "What would your momma being dead have to do with my boyfriend?" She crossed her arms and stared at me, her eyes small and hard, like little chips of black granite. I wanted to return her stare but my gaze kept sliding off.

"It made it seem like we'd both lost somebody," I said, staring into the corner. "Like we'd both been hurt and could understand each other."

I tried to look at Amber's face, but my gaze slid off again. This time it fell on her stomach, where the tiny bulge cast a shadow across the front of her plaid shirt.

"I don't like being lied to," Amber said in a trembling voice. "If you're going to lie to me, I don't want anything to do with you. I don't care if you teach me geometry or do anything else."

"I won't do it again," I said, still staring at her stomach.

"Too many people lie," she said, and she sounded slightly hysterical now. "Pretty soon it's what you expect."

"I understand," I said again, although I was confused and didn't exactly know what she was getting at.

Amber kept looking at me with those granite-hard eyes. I thought she was going to say something else. But then she suddenly burst into tears.

"Goddamn you," she said. "I thought I could trust you, but you're no different than anyone else." She covered her face with her hands and turned away. "You're just a goddamned liar."

I went over to where Amber was standing. I felt terrible about making her cry. I had never made anyone cry before and I was surprised that I could do it.

"I'm sorry," I said. I reached out to touch her, but I didn't know where to put my hand. Then, without even thinking about it, my hand settled on the place where her waist tucked in on the side, the little recess above her hip. And I remember thinking that it felt all right for it to be there, like it was a natural place for a hand to be, and so I left it there.

Amber took her hands away from her face. Tears were streaming down her cheeks. Suddenly she stepped against me and pressed her face into my shoulder. I felt her warm tears on my neck.

"Oh, Danny," she said and she spoke in a small trembling voice. "You need to take better care of me. Won't you do that?"

I didn't know what to say. I'd never had a girl put her arms around me or ask me to take care of her. It frightened me.

"Yes," I said. "Of course."

"My life is very difficult," she said. "You have to understand that."

"It's all right," I said, and I sort of stroked her ponytail where it hung down the back of her neck. "Don't worry. Everything will be all right."

That was all either of us said for a while, maybe for two or three minutes. We just stood together, Amber with her head resting on my shoulder, me with one hand on her hip and the other one stroking her ponytail, feeling her faint breath against my neck and the dampness from her tears.

Finally Amber stepped back. She sniffed a couple of times. With the back of her hands she wiped the tears from her cheeks.

"I guess I had a little episode," she said in a husky voice. She smiled, and I could tell she was embarrassed. "A moment of craziness."

"That's all right," I said.

"When you're pregnant you go a little nuts sometimes." She stepped over to the workbench and began to gather up her books and papers. "The chemicals in your blood are out of kilter. The doctor told me that. Things aren't completely normal with how your brain works."

I stood watching Amber gather up her books.

"Do you think you'll do all right on the parabolas?" I asked.

"I guess so." She spoke in a distracted way, as if her mind was already on something else.

I thought we should study more about parabolas, but Amber reached up and pulled the light chain. We went out through the door into the twilight evening where crickets were starting to chirp. She handed me her books while she put the padlock on the door clasp. Her hands weren't shaking anymore.

"Do you want to study tomorrow?" I asked. Out on the lake I heard the buzz of a motorboat. It sounded loud in the still evening air.

"You know what I think?" she said, and she spoke as if she hadn't even heard my question. "We *are* sort of the same. You were right about that. We're both outsiders."

I wasn't exactly sure what she meant about being an outsider— even though that was sort of how I felt about myself. But it was nice to hear her say we had something in common—some connection— because I didn't feel connected to much of anything right then. In any case, we stood looking into each other's face for a long time, just staring at each other with no particular expression, as if something important had just happened and we wanted to burn the memory of it deep into our brains.

"Okay," she said, after the long moment had passed. "I guess I'll see you sometime."

"Okay," I said.

And then she turned and went back into her house, and I went back to my house, too.

Chapter Three

THAT EVENING MY FATHER was late coming home. I remember thinking it might be a sign that he was making progress as a salesman, and I pictured him spending a long afternoon in the stockroom of some hardware store, filling out order cards for all the products the owner wanted to buy from him—electric drills and saber saws and routers—and then afterward taking the man out for drinks and talking about golf or telling jokes to him, which he'd told me was another part of being a salesman.

But when he came through the door I knew right away that I was wrong. He had the look I was seeing most nights now, the look of being slowly ground down by things he couldn't control. I was standing at the stove, cooking fried potatoes and beans and bologna slices. He threw his coat over the back of a chair and loosened his tie and rolled up the sleeves of his white shirt. Then he went over to the cupboard where he kept a bottle of scotch.

"How's it going, bub?" I could tell he was making an effort to sound cheery.

"Good," I said. "I'll have some beans and potatoes ready in just a minute."

"No need to hurry. I'll just sit here and enjoy my drink."

I wasn't used to seeing my father drinking whiskey, even though he'd been doing it for a while now. In Grand Rapids we'd been taught that drinking was a sin, something done by people who lacked ambition and were careless about their lives. Once, my father's car had broken down in a strange neighborhood, and he'd gone into a bar to use a telephone to call a tow truck, and I remember it'd become something of a joke in our family that he'd actually set foot in such an awful place.

I stirred the beans in with the fried potatoes. After a minute the mixture got hot and bubbles started rising up in the pan, big heavy bubbles that oozed up slowly and made a lazy plopping sound. I turned down the gas so it wouldn't burn.

"Did you hear about that rocket?" I asked.

"Yes, I did."

"Do you think they'll get things back on track eventually? Get a satellite up?"

Behind me, I heard my father pour some more scotch.

"I think they will, bub. I expect our scientists will get on top of this."

"Do you think there'll be an atomic attack?" I asked next, because the Russian president had recently said that they would bury the U.S., and some people thought that meant an attack was coming soon.

I heard ice cubes rattling in my father's glass. Then he said: "I don't know, son. The world's gone crazy, as far as I can tell. So I wouldn't be surprised at anything."

I turned around. My father was sitting in a kitchen chair, his legs out straight, his glass balanced on one knee. When he saw the look on my face he smiled reassuringly.

"There's no need to worry," he said. "Ike says he's not concerned, so I guess we shouldn't be either. He says the next rocket will work better." He sat up straighter in the chair. "When the U.S. gets ready to do something, it usually means it's going to happen, Danny. I saw it during the war. Your father helped make the Sherman tanks, you know, up until I was drafted in '43. We turned them out by the thousands."

"I remember you told me that," I said.

"And how about polio? That's another great triumph."

He was talking about the Salk vaccine that had been announced two years ago at the university in Ann Arbor. My class had been in the test group that had gotten the vaccine early, before they knew if it was any good. I remembered going down to the gymnasium and standing in a long shuffling line to wait my turn to get the shot, one among hundreds of kids who didn't know what was happening but who assumed it was all right, somehow, because adults were in charge. That amazed me now—thinking about it in the cabin outside McBride—that utter trust, and I wondered if I would feel that way now, and I thought that I probably wouldn't.

I got down two plates and filled them with food, beans and potatoes on one side and two pieces of bologna on the other. Then I balanced two slices of bread on top of the bologna and carried the plates over to the table.

"You seem to know your way around a kitchen pretty well," my father said.

"It's not hard."

"You could probably qualify as a sous-chef at one of the finer restaurants. The Durant Hotel in Flint, for example. That'd be a good one."

"What's a sous-chef?"

"That's a chef in training. An assistant chef, if you will." He took a bite of bologna. "*Sous* means under in French. So sous-chef means an under-chef."

"That's interesting," I said, and I thought I'd try to remember the word and tell it to Amber the next time I saw her, because of what she'd said about wanting to know French so she could live in Montreal.

We ate for a while in silence. My father took sips of scotch now and then between bites of food.

"Not that I want you to be a chef, Danny," he said, all of a sudden, as if it was something, he'd been thinking about all along. "That was just a little joke. I expect you're destined for better things than that. At least I hope so."

We finished eating. I started to pick up the plates to carry them over to the sink.

"Hold on, Danny," my father said. "Why don't you just sit here at the table for a while and relax. You've done enough. Your father's not a helpless soul." He picked up the plates and carried them back to the sink. I heard him put the plates into the sink and run some water. Then I heard the snap of a Zippo lighter and smelled smoke.

"I talked to your mother last night," he said. I heard him blow out some smoke; then I saw a drifting cloud of it come over to my side of the room. "She called after you were in bed."

I didn't say anything.

"She seems to think it'd be a good idea if you stayed with her for a while. What do you think about that?"

"You mean live with her in Chicago?"

"That's right."

"How long would it be for?"

"I don't know. Maybe just a week or two." The water stopped running. I heard him exhale more smoke. "Or maybe through the school year."

I turned around. "What would you do?"

"What do you mean?

"What would you do up here all by yourself?"

He was leaning back against the counter, his arms crossed, the cigarette held off at an odd angle, like a girl. He brought the cigarette up to his lips and took a deep swallow of smoke. "I suspect I'd do what I'm doing right now, Danny, try to scratch out a livelihood in the north woods of Michigan." He started to raise the cigarette up to his lips but he stopped halfway. "Which may be another way of saying I'd try to tilt at windmills."

I didn't know what "tilt at windmills" meant and I didn't really care. But I was beginning to understand that my father could sometimes use words to keep the truth away, rather than to bring it closer.

"How are things going in that department?" I asked, looking straight at him. This was not a question I'd ever asked my father before, nor the words I normally used to talk to him, and he looked at me with a slightly surprised expression, as if he recognized the difference, too. Then his expression changed, and I could tell he was trying to make up his mind about something—whether or not to tell the truth, probably.

"Not too good, Danny," he said finally, "since you've broached that delicate subject." He turned on the faucet and held his cigarette under the stream of water. "It could be the case that your father isn't cut out for this line of work."

"That's too bad," I said. Then I said: "Why don't you give it up and go back to your job in Grand Rapids?"

"It's not that easy," he said. "I had some words with the supervisor when I left. I got a few things off my chest, you might say. So I don't think he'd exactly welcome me with open arms."

"You could try," I said.

"And, anyway, this is the life I've chosen. This is what I want to do. That counts for something, doesn't it?"

"Why does it matter so much?"

"I guess you could say I got tired of working in a factory and wanted to try my hand at something different. Something where I could be out on my own. Does that make any sense to you?"

"Yes. I guess so."

"It's a kind of adventure, really, if you look at it in the right way. It's a kind of adventure that's fading away. I'm not sure it'll be available to your generation, Danny, though it makes me sorry to say that. In the future the world will be run by corporations and the unions. There'll be no room for the little man to shine."

I heard what my father said but I didn't completely believe him, even though I wanted to. I knew he didn't like working in a factory with a thousand other men, and I knew he didn't like it when he'd been forced to join the union. But I had never heard him talk about wanting an adventure before. He had taken his new job because he believed he'd be good at it and could make money and have a good life in the country: that's what he'd said before. But now he was explaining it in a different way. And I thought it was because it was turning out to be a mistake and he felt trapped and wanted a better reason for having done it in the first place. Better than just money.

"Of course none of this helps solve the situation with your mother," my father said. "That's your main concern, isn't it?"

"I miss her," I said. "I miss having her around."

"I do, too, son," he said. "She's my wife, after all. I love her."

And then I had to turn away and look out the window so my father wouldn't see my face. He was trying to be brave about the things that were going wrong in his life right then: his decision to become a salesman and my mother's decision to go away until he built the house in town. And so I felt I should be brave, too, to help him out and make him feel better.

"And of course I love you, too," my father said. I could feel him looking in my direction. "That's not unimportant."

"Thank you," I said, still looking away.

He came over and sat down across the table from me. He lit up another cigarette. "Maybe I could learn to rob banks," he said, the cigarette bouncing between his lips. "Maybe that'd be a better occupation for your father."

"I don't think you'd be any good at that," I said.

"Maybe we could do it together, then. Be a father-and-son team."

He smiled again, and I smiled back, even though I didn't think what he'd said was funny. We were quiet for a while.

"So what do you think about Chicago, son?"

"What?"

"About going to live with your mother in Chicago."

I turned and looked out the window, in the direction where Amber's house stood across the inlet, and I wondered what was happening there between Amber and her mother. But it was dark, and all I could see was the faint reflection of my father and me sitting there at the kitchen table, a man and a boy living together in the woods of northern Michigan, our own life coming right back to me.

"Can I think about it for a day or two?"

"Sure. Take all the time you want."

He rubbed the tip of his cigarette against the edge of the ashtray until only a glowing point of light remained. Then he got up from his chair and walked out of the cabin into the dark outside, where he stayed for a long time, thinking whatever thoughts were on his mind.

Chapter Four

AS I WAS GETTING READY to leave for school the next morning, my father told me he would be late coming home that night.

"I'm driving over to the eastern side of the state," he said. "Around Bay City and Saginaw. We'll see what your father can accomplish over there." He was standing at the kitchen sink, pouring a cup of coffee. When I came in he got another cup and poured it for me.

"That's a good idea," I said.

"If your mother happens to call, tell her I've gone into town or that I'm out fishing. Whatever good lie you can think of."

"All right," I said, surprised to hear him speak that way. I turned on a stove burner and placed a slice of bread on the wire rack to make some toast. "Isn't that somebody else's territory?" I said. "Those cities."

"Yes," he said.

"Won't you get in trouble if you start selling in someone else's territory?"

"Maybe," he said. "But it's a free country, Danny. If I can sell the merchandise better than someone else, why shouldn't I be allowed to do it?"

"I guess that makes sense," I said, although I knew the sales territories had been set up for a reason and ignoring the boundaries could get you in trouble.

"Sometimes you've got to bend the rules a bit," he said, which was a phrase I'd heard him use before, when he was doing something for his own private reason. He came over to where I was standing waiting for the toast and put a hand on my shoulder. "It's time to kick this operation into high gear, Danny," he said. "We don't want to be poor forever, do we?"

"No," I said, "I guess not," and I smiled at him, even though I didn't feel good about what he was doing.

"Well, all right then." He took a last long swallow of his coffee and turned toward the door. "I'll be home about nine," he said. "See if you can learn a couple of interesting facts at school that we can talk about."

"You bet," I said, and I forced myself to smile again.

School that day was a regular day except that in the morning, when classes were changing, I saw Amber standing in the principal's office. She was behind a glass partition staring down at the floor and biting her lower lip. In one arm she held the geometry book we'd studied from the night before. For a moment I thought about going in and asking if there was any little fact or detail about parabolas she wanted to have explained again. But then the bell sounded and I had to pass on to my next class.

When I stepped off the school bus that afternoon Amber was waiting for me in the green Chevy pickup I'd seen parked behind the taxidermy shed. She was parked along the edge of the gravel road with the engine running. As I came over she smiled and rolled down the window. Rock-and-roll music poured out from inside.

"I've got an appointment with the baby doctor," she said. "Do you want to come along?"

"You want me to go with you to the doctor?" I said, because it seemed like a strange request.

"That's what I just said." She gave a short laugh. "No one else wants to."

I didn't know what to say. Going to the doctor with Amber sounded kind of strange, like I would be invading her privacy—or she would be invading mine. It brought to mind things I didn't particularly want to think about—the features of a girl's anatomy that were fascinating to consider in a general way but not in too much biological detail.

I looked around, uncertain about what I should tell her. I think I was actually hoping that I might see something that could serve as an excuse. But we were out along a country road and there was nothing to see—nothing that could serve as an excuse—just the school bus disappearing into the distance behind a roiling cloud of dust.

I looked back at Amber. She was staring at me with a hopeful expression, as if my going with her would actually make a difference in some way. And I thought about her mother standing on the cement-block stoop in her shapeless gray dress and about her stepfather stretching raccoon skins on a rack. And then I thought about myself, sitting in a clearing in the woods, waiting for an animal to come by.

On the radio, the singer said something about his girlfriend and how much he loved and needed her.

I shrugged. "Sure. Why not?" I said.

"Good," Amber said. "I need all the moral support I can get."

Amber made a U-turn, and we started down the gravel road, heading back in the direction of McBride, kicking up a trail of dust that I could see in the side-view mirror.

"I'm always nervous when I go to see the doctor," she said. "I'm afraid he'll find out something's wrong with the baby." She reached over and turned down the radio, which had started to play a different song.

"What could go wrong?"

"A lot of stuff. It could be misshapen or its insides could be all mixed up. Like if the organs didn't fit together right." She reached up and adjusted the rearview mirror. "Or it could be retarded. You know, not be completely right in a mental way. That'd be the worst thing of all."

"Does that kind of thing happen very often?" I asked.

"Sure. Sometimes. You don't hear about it much because the kids it happens to end up in special homes or hospitals. Some live with their families, but they don't let them out where people can see them."

"I don't think you should worry," I said to Amber. "I bet those things don't happen very often."

"Maybe," she said. "But I heard our preacher say that when it does happen it can be because a baby's been conceived in sin. And I guess mine qualifies." She glanced over at me with a nervous smile. "He said it's how God dispenses justice."

I thought about what Amber had said, because I wanted to understand it. And I tried to think about it like I thought about a problem in mathematics—so that all the separate parts had to match up and be true at the same time—and I decided it didn't make any sense. Why would God punish a baby for something the parents had done? What good would that do? And what if the parents decided later on to get married but the baby had already been damaged? That wouldn't be fair, either. None of it made sense.

"That can't be right, Amber," I said. And then I told her the reasons why I thought that way.

"Do you really think so?" she said after I'd finished talking. She sounded doubtful.

"Of course," I said. "It's only logical."

"Who says God's logical?" she said.

"He has to be," I said. "Because logic's the same thing as being true."

Amber glanced over at me a couple of times, as if she expected I had something more to say on the subject. But I just stared straight ahead, as if the matter had been settled and my thoughts had already gone on to other subjects. But I realized, too, that what I'd said about God felt right, and that truth could be counted on the same way people wanted you to count on God.

"I saw you today at school in the principal's office," I said, because I thought it was time to talk about something else.

Amber didn't say anything.

"Were you taking that math test?"

Amber kept staring at the road ahead, as if driving the pickup required all of her attention. Finally she glanced over. "I was *supposed* to take the geometry test," she said. "Only I was a little late, and they said I couldn't take it." Her gaze flicked up to the rearview mirror where a car was coming up behind us. "They gave me an F," she said. The other car flew past in a swirl of dust and gravel.

We drove along for a while in silence. I didn't want to say anything because I was afraid if I opened my mouth the words would come out too strong and show that I was mad at Amber for wasting all the work we'd done. I remembered my idea about Amber working in a laboratory, and I realized now how crazy it was. She was just a country girl, I thought, careless about her life and unconcerned about the future. Getting herself pregnant without having a husband was one sign of that. Being late for the geometry test was another.

Finally said, "That's too bad. You knew that stuff real well."

"I know I did," she said eagerly. "I even studied it some more after you left. Before I went to bed." She threw a nervous glance my way. "They make it hard for me, Danny," she said. "That's why they wouldn't let me take the test. They want me to drop out of school and stay away until the baby comes. I guess they think all the other girls will start getting pregnant if they see me."

Up ahead, the 4-H fairground, a big grassy field divided by white fences, was coming into view. Beyond that I could see the grain elevators looming up in downtown McBride.

"I'm sorry," Amber said, and her voice sounded small and scared. She looked over. The white fences of the 4-H fairground flashed by outside.

"What about?" I said.

"For getting an F on the geometry test. I let you down."

I looked at Amber. Her eyes were filled with tears, and she had a kind of pleading look on her face. And suddenly I realized how much she wanted me to like her. And connected to that wish, she had another: to be a normal girl again, a girl who went to school and took tests and got treated like everybody else.

"You didn't let me down," I said. I looked across at Amber. I kept looking until she looked back at me. "It wasn't your fault," I said. "It was the people who wouldn't let you take the test."

Amber squeezed my arm where she was still holding on to it, and I smiled at her and she smiled back. "Thank you," she said.

We drove past the houses on the outskirts of McBride, small one-story structures with garages set close to the street so the owners wouldn't have far to shovel when the heavy winter snows came. A few people were walking on the sidewalks or raking leaves into the gutters. We passed the redbrick school building that I'd left just an hour earlier. Some kids were hanging around the parking lot, smoking cigarettes and leaning against car fenders. A group of cheerleaders was practicing on the grass next to the gymnasium. I watched as they ran forward and threw themselves headfirst into the grass, then bounced over on their hands and came up clapping.

"I used to be one of those," Amber said. She nodded toward the girls in their pleated skirts. "But now those girls hardly even talk to me. I guess they think you can catch pregnancy like the measles." She laughed in a bitter way. Then, after another moment, she said, "Being a cheerleader was sort of dumb, but I liked it."

We went through the small downtown of McBride and over the railroad tracks and into the other side of town. Then Amber turned off onto a side street that led into a neighborhood I'd never been in before. After a couple of blocks she stopped in front of a house, bigger than the ones around it, with turrets and a large front porch. A sign hanging over the porch said Edward S. Gardner, M.D.

Inside we sat with some other women in the waiting room reading old magazines that lay scattered around on tables. After a minute I heard some muffled voices from back inside the doctor's office. I started to wonder what the doctor did when he examined a pregnant woman, whether he could see inside where the baby was or if he just felt around on the outside and could tell things from that—tell if the baby was going to be all right or if it had one of the problems Amber was worried about. And I realized I really didn't know anything about pregnant women, except a little about how they got that way, and I suddenly felt very strange sitting there in the doctor's waiting room, a boy surrounded by women who were going to have babies. And I wished I was someplace else, back in the school parking lot smoking cigarettes, maybe, and watching the cheerleaders do their flips on the grass, or at the lake casting for bass from the end of the wooden dock. Just about anyplace seemed better than where I was.

Finally the nurse called Amber's name, and she passed back through the swinging door, giving me a tiny smile as she went by my chair. One of the other women followed her with her eyes, then turned to another woman and said, "That's Marge and Ray's girl that got herself knocked up." The woman she was talking to, who had on a blue-and-white checked dress, said, "It's no surprise, the way she was carrying on." And then the first one said, "It was bound to happen, wasn't it?" And then they both laughed.

When I heard the women talking about Amber, I forgot about feeling strange. Their comments made me angry, and I wanted to defend her in some way, even though I didn't know what that way should be. I guess I felt responsible for her, as if the long glance we'd exchanged in the taxidermy shed had caused us to enter into a pact of some kind, and it was time for me to hold up my side of the bargain. So I looked over at the first woman and fixed her with a hard stare. After a while she glanced up and smiled weakly. Then, after another minute, she looked up and said, "Is something wrong, young man?"

"I don't like what you said about Amber."

"It's got nothing to do with you."

"Yes, it does," I said, which seemed right because of what had happened in the taxidermy shed.

"Well, if she's your friend you better watch out for yourself. She's carrying another boy's baby, you know."

"I know it," I said. "She fucked a boy and got pregnant. That's how it happens."

The woman glared at me, and right away I felt my heart begin to pound and my face get hot. I'd probably never said that word out loud before—I'm sure I'd never said it to an adult—but I wanted to shock the women, do something outrageous that would make them mad. Saying *fuck* was the only thing that came to mind.

The woman kept glaring at me. I forced myself to stand up to her stare. Finally, her eyes wavered and she looked over at her friend; they both shook their heads. Then they both went back to their magazines, and I went back to my magazine, too.

After a minute I felt all right again.

Chapter Five

ON THE RIDE HOME from the doctor's office Amber was in a better mood, relaxed and easygoing, joking about things, not worrying about the baby having problems. She let me shift the gearshift while she worked the clutch pedal. At first she held her hand on top of mine, but then I told her I knew how to drive already and she didn't have to bother.

"Where'd you learn how to drive?" she asked.

"My dad taught me. He lets me drive on back roads when there's not too much traffic around."

"That's just about every road around here," Amber said, laughing.

We drove along for a while in silence. It was a warm day. The windows were open and air streamed in, ruffling my shirt and mussing up my hair. Amber's hair was mussed up, too. Strands of it danced around her head.

We passed a couple of farms with broken-down barns and rusted farm machinery abandoned in the fields, as if the owner had gotten tired of being a farmer and just walked away one day. Then we passed some cornfields and then a herd of black-and-white cows grazing on a hillside.

"Here," Amber said. She reached up and pulled a stack of index cards from under the sun visor and handed them to me. "Make yourself useful."

"What are these?" I asked.

"They're French words. Remember I told you I needed to learn French if I'm going to art school in Montreal? Well, that's my allotment for today: ten new words. Read them off, and I'll tell you the meanings."

I looked down at the first card. *L'oeuf* was written on it.

"I don't know how to say this."

"Just try your best. I'll get the idea."

I said the word as well as I could, but I could tell that I'd mangled it pretty badly.

Amber laughed. "Maybe you better spell it," she said, and so I did.

Amber scrunched up her face in concentration. Then she said, "Luff. That's how you say it. It means an egg."

I flipped the card over to see what was written on the back. "That's right," I said.

"Try another," Amber said. "Do them all."

We went through the whole stack that way, all ten words, me spelling them out and Amber pronouncing them and giving the meanings. After a few words I began to see how you pronounced them, how the French sounds were different from English sounds.

"You want me to do it again?" I asked when we'd finished the last word. "I think I can say them right this time."

Amber didn't answer, and after a moment I looked over at her. She was staring up at the rearview mirror.

I turned around. Through the swirling dust cloud I saw a car. It was coming up fast.

"Christ almighty," Amber said, under her breath.

"What is it?" I said.

"It's Wayne," she said. "My old boyfriend."

The car came up right behind us and honked its horn. Then it pulled out alongside us. The boy who was driving looked over and grinned at Amber. He motioned with his hand like he wanted her to stop.

"Goddamn it," Amber said between clenched teeth. She kept on driving, looking straight ahead, as if she were trying to pretend he wasn't there.

When the boy saw that Amber wasn't going to stop, he swerved a couple of times, like he was trying to force her over. Then he sped up and pulled around in front. The cloud of dust he kicked up made it hard to see. Stones pinged the hood and fenders. Then he started to slow down, and Amber had to slow down behind him.

She pulled off into the weeds and coasted to a stop.

"Do you want me to do anything?" I asked her.

"No. Just sit there and shut up."

The boy got out of his car and came walking back, grinning, walking in a slow ambling way, like he knew Amber was waiting and he didn't need to hurry. He wore blue jeans and a T-shirt with the sleeves rolled up, and he was tall and muscular, like someone who lifted weights or did hard manual labor. His face was thin and angular, and he had small dark eyes and long hair combed back on both sides to make little waves.

I was afraid for Amber, afraid of what the boy might do to her. He was bigger than I was and older—twenty-one or twenty-two maybe—and I knew I couldn't do much to protect her. But I was tall, and I'd been in some school yard fights back in Grand Rapids—not serious fistfights but wrestling fights where people don't get hurt. So I knew how to throw someone to the ground and hold him there, and I thought that's what I would do with Wayne, if I had to.

"Who's your new boyfriend?" Wayne said to Amber when he'd come up alongside to the pickup. He still had that big grin on his face.

"He's just the neighbor boy who's helping me with geometry. He came along with me to town to see the doctor."

Wayne bent down and looked across Amber to where I was sitting on the passenger side. "What's going on, buddy? You trying to steal my girl?"

"No," I said. "I'm not trying to steal her."

"Well, just see that you keep your hands to home."

"Wayne, stop it," Amber said.

Wayne came up close beside the car and put his hand on the window ledge. "I need to talk to you, Amber," he said, and his voice sounded serious now.

"Well, I don't want to talk to you," Amber said, looking straight ahead through the windshield. "We did all our talking already."

"I just want to talk to you a minute, that's all."

"Well, go ahead and talk then."

Wayne glanced over at me, then back at Amber. Finally Amber turned and looked at Wayne. It was the first time she'd looked at him since he'd come up beside the pickup.

"I need to talk to you alone for a minute, Amber," Wayne said. "It's important." He reached in and placed his hand on Amber's arm, not in an angry way but only like he wanted to be touching her.

Amber looked up into Wayne's face for a long time. Then she pulled her arm back.

"All right," she said. "But only for a minute." She looked over at me. "Stay here, Danny," she said. "I'll be right back."

I watched through the windshield as Amber and Wayne walked down the road and out into a wheat field that had just been mowed. They stood and talked, standing face-to-face, the setting sun casting their long shadows out across the rows of stubble. At first Wayne did all the talking. Amber just listened, looking down at the ground, shifting her weight like she was anxious for Wayne to finish saying whatever he had to say. But finally she said something back, and I could tell from her expression that she was mad. Wayne stepped in close and put his hands on her shoulders. Amber tried to push him back, but he kept holding; finally she stopped pushing.

And then Wayne pulled her up against him and started to kiss her. And at first Amber acted as if she didn't care, like she just wanted to get it over with. But then something seemed to change, and she rose up and pressed back against him. One hand moved up and touched the back of Wayne's neck, and her fingers sort of worked into his hair, like they'd done the day before with the bear's head. Wayne's hands moved over Amber's body.

I looked away then and tried not to think about what was happening. Whatever was happening was between the two of them alone. It didn't have anything to do with me or anyone else. They were just two people together in the wheat field with the setting sun stretching out their shadows, just two people alone and no one else, kissing and holding on to each other. But there was one thing I couldn't help wondering about as I sat there in the car, and that was whether Amber liked what was happening and wanted it to keep on happening or if she was just going along with it for some reason that only she could understand.

Finally they stopped kissing and walked back to the pickup. Wayne was smiling, but Amber looked embarrassed. They were holding hands.

"I'll come around and get you tomorrow, then," Wayne said. "About five o'clock."

Amber stepped up into the pickup. "We'll see," she said. "I'm not completely decided."

"Well, think hard about it," Wayne said. He looked at me. "Tell her to do the sensible thing, buddy," he said. "Tell her it's like a geometry problem. There's only one right answer." And then he laughed out loud like he'd said something funny.

Amber put the pickup into gear, backed up, and pulled out around Wayne and his car. For a while she didn't say anything and I didn't say anything either. We just drove along kicking up dust. Then she said, "I guess you got to feast your eyes on a moment of real passion." She looked over at me for a second, then back out the windshield. "I hope you weren't too badly scandalized."

"No," I said. "It was all right if that's what you wanted to do."

Amber looked over at me again, only this time she held her gaze a little longer, as if I were some kind of puzzle she was trying to figure the answer to.

"Wayne's not going into the army after all," she said, after she'd stopped looking at me. "They found out he's deaf in one ear and they wouldn't take him. He didn't even know he was deaf. Isn't that funny?"

I said I thought it was.

"He said he wants to marry me now. Or he thinks he does. I'm not exactly sure which one it is. But anyway he's decided he loves me and wants to talk about getting married. Not right away, but maybe in a few months. She looked over at me again. "He's got a job down at Patterson's Lumber running a table saw. So he's earning money. That's a good sign, don't you think?"

I told her I guessed it was.

"He's a good boy," she said after another minute passed. "Nicer than he looked back there. You'd like him if you got to know him."

I didn't know what to say or what Amber wanted me to say, so I didn't say anything. But I didn't think I would ever like Wayne.

"I suppose you think I'm a nut," Amber said. She drew back a strand of hair and wedged it behind her ear, but right away the wind blew it out again. "A regular basket case."

"No," I said. "I don't think that."

"Well, even if you did, I wouldn't care," she said, and she spoke in a way that sounded cross. "Love's a harder problem to solve than your geometry things. You'll learn that someday. It's not like parabolas, where you just work it through and everybody comes to the same right answer and is happy."

"That's not what I think," I said.

"Well, I don't care if you do or if you don't."

I turned away then and looked out the side window. We were passing a forest of pine trees all lined up in straight hard rows. My father had told me they'd been planted during the Depression by Roosevelt's Conservation Corps and that someday they'd be cut down and used for telephone poles. I tried to count the rows, but they were flying by too fast. I got up to nine before I lost my place.

We passed on into a swampy area with cypress trees and water standing in a ditch next to the road. The water looked black and oily. I sat next to Amber and tried not to think about anything, not about Amber or about Amber's baby or about my own father and mother or about anything at all. I wanted the ride to be over so I could be alone. When I got home I'd go down by the lake and cast for bass. There were some big bass out in the weeds, and you could catch them if you were patient. That would be a good thing to do until my father got home. I'd just get out of Amber's pickup and walk down to the lake and start casting with my fishing rod.

"My parents told me I have to give the baby away," Amber said in a quiet voice.

I was thinking so hard about fishing that it took me a moment to come back and realize that she had spoken to me.

"They got some papers from the county and said I have to sign them."

"Oh," I said.

"Yes, *oh*," she said, mocking the way I'd said it. "They told me they won't have anything to do with raising a bastard kid. If I keep my baby I'll have to find some other place to live."

We were getting near the lake now. The forest was thicker, dark and shadowy, like it gets in the lowlands around water. Amber slowed the truck and turned onto the two-track road that led through the forest to her house. She followed the road for about a mile, then went up a shallow rise and stopped the pickup behind the taxidermy shed. She turned off the engine, and the pickup shuddered to a stop. Then she leaned forward and rested her forehead against the rim of the steering wheel, looking down through the spokes onto her lap.

"Not that this would be such a wonderful place to raise a kid," she said, as if she were talking to herself. "I guess I know that better than anyone."

"Then don't sign the papers," I said. "Find someplace else to live."

Amber turned her head in my direction, still letting it rest against the steering wheel. Her face had no expression. Her eyes were little glints of white in the dimness of the pickup.

"That's a brilliant idea," she said, her voice filled with scorn. "Why didn't I think of that?"

We got out of the truck. Amber walked up to the back door of her house, moving slowly, like moving was an effort. When she got to the back door she turned around. I couldn't see her eyes now, but I could feel her gaze.

"Thanks for coming with me," she said in a weary voice. "It helped to have you along." She smiled—at least I thought she did, because I couldn't really see her. "I'm sorry for what I said to you," she added.

"That's all right," I said, looking away in the direction of the lake, where the sun reflected golden off the dead calm water.

"No," she said. "It isn't. You deserve better. But you'll have to learn to live with what you get and make the best of it. Just like we all do."

She turned and went into the house and closed the door behind her, and I was left there standing all alone.

That evening my father was late coming home, just like he had said. It was after midnight before I heard him coming into the cabin. He came into the bedroom where I was sleeping and turned on the light. I could tell he'd been drinking.

"What's tonight's lesson, Danny?" he asked me in a slightly slurred voice. He sat down heavily on the side of the bed. The mattress sagged under his weight. "Tell me what you learned today in school."

I propped myself up on one elbow, rubbing my eyes. I was still wearing the clothes I'd worn that day at school. I'd fallen asleep on top of the blankets reading a book about West Point.

"I didn't learn too much today," I said. My mind was still foggy from being asleep. "It wasn't a remarkable day."

"Well, you must have learned something," he said, and he sounded cross. "Some little thing that made the day worthwhile."

I looked at him then and saw that one of his eyes was blackened and he had a cut along one cheek. The collar of his shirt was torn; it flopped at a comical angle.

"What happened?" I asked.

His hand went up and touched the cut on his cheek. "I had a bit of an altercation," he said.

"What's that mean?" I said.

"Don't they teach you anything at that school, Danny? An altercation is a violent disagreement. A fight."

"With who?"

"A gentleman named Frank. That's all I know. I'm afraid in the confusion I neglected to get Frank's last name. He seemed to think I had no business selling my wares in Bay City. It was," he said, and he looked at me in a cunning way, nodding his head and squinting slightly, "exactly as you predicted, Danny. Evidently there is no allowance in this company for extra effort."

"Do you want me to get something for that cut?" I said.

"No, no, no," he said, waving one hand. Then his expression sharpened. "I just want you to tell me one goddamned thing you learned today. Is that asking for too much?"

For an instant I felt like saying something angry back to him—"Go to hell" or "Why don't you get a good job." But those were thoughts that came out of my feelings, and I knew I couldn't trust them. They might be too strong or too weak for the situation, or come from a mistaken way of thinking—some fact I didn't understand that adults did. So instead I thought back over the day that had just passed. My strongest recollection was of the trip to McBride with Amber, and for a moment I tried to think of some way I could put that into one of the lessons my father was looking for. But it was all jumbled up, just a mass of feelings and impressions, and so instead of telling him that, I told him about some other things—the quadratic equation and how Thomas Jefferson had bought Louisiana from the French in 1803. But those were things I had learned before and not things I had learned on that particular day. In any case, they seemed to satisfy him.

"Okay," he said, and he smiled in a resigned sort of way. "Good night, then." He leaned forward and for a moment I thought he was going to kiss me, but instead he merely touched my shoulder. Then he stood and walked unsteadily out of the room, one hand reaching out blindly to touch the doorjamb as he passed through the doorway. After a minute I heard the rattle of metal hangers knocking together on a rod, then the squeaking of a mattress being compressed under his weight.

I lay on my back looking up into the darkness. I could feel my heart pounding in my chest and the rush of air flowing in and out of my lungs. I felt the rough fabric of the blanket against my hands. All of my sensations seemed stronger than normal.

I thought again about the day that had just passed and how I hadn't been able to tell any of it to my father. How I hadn't known the words to give it meaning. At least not the meaning he was looking for, those neat, well-organized lessons. And then I thought about my father and all the troubles he was facing. And then I thought about Amber and the pact that we had made.

"I've decided about Chicago." I said suddenly. I called the words out into the darkness. My heart was still pounding.

There was a long silence. Then my father's voice came back, sounding uncertain and confused. "What?" He sounded half asleep.

"I've decided I'm not going to go to Chicago. I'm going to stay here. I'll go for a visit, maybe, but not to stay."

There was another long stretch of time when nothing happened. Then I heard my father say, "Good." Then, a moment later, he said, "Don't worry, son. Things will work out."

And that was all either of us said that night.

Chapter Six

WHEN I AWOKE THE NEXT MORNING I was sick. My head ached and I had a fever and sore joints. My father said that if I wanted, he would call my mother, and she would probably come back and take care of me. But he didn't want her to come back in that way, he said—in a forced and guilty way—unless I really wanted him to call her.

"That's all right," I said. I was lying in my bed in the little lean-to bedroom in the back of our cabin. The room was in partial darkness because the window shade had been drawn to keep the daylight out. In the next room the kerosene stove fought back against a late October frost. I could see the flame through the little mica window. "I'll be all right by myself."

My father stood in the doorway looking in at me, as if he didn't know what to do.

"Do you think it's the Asiatic flu?" I asked, because there was an epidemic that fall, and many people had been hospitalized, and some of them had died.

"I don't know," my father said. "We'll have to be careful." Then he said, "Doggone it, bub, I feel terrible leaving you alone in this condition."

"That's all right," I said. "I'll probably just sleep, anyway."

"If I could I'd stay home with you myself. But I've got appointments all day long. You know I'd stay with you if I could, don't you?"

"Sure," I said. "I know that."

He stood a while longer in the doorway, looking in at me in the partial darkness, rubbing his cheek with one hand. I thought he might say something about what had happened the night before, but he didn't. Possibly, I thought, he didn't even remember, like the forgetful drunks you saw on TV comedies.

"Give me a day to figure something out, bub. Maybe I can get someone to come by and check up on you from time to time."

"I'll be all right," I said again. "I can listen to the radio."

"I'll leave some orange juice in the refrigerator. Try to drink as much as you can."

"I will."

"And there's some eggs, too. You can fry up some eggs if you get hungry."

"All right," I said.

After my father left I slept for a while. Then I half woke and heard the wind whistling around the cabin. Then I slept again.

When I awoke the second time the clock on the bedside table said one o'clock. I was still feeling feverish; a film of clammy sweat covered my chest and arms. Outside, the wind was still blowing, maybe stronger than before. I propped myself on one elbow and lifted the corner of the window shade. Tree branches were bending in the wind. Across the lake a gray sky was streaked with black, angry-looking clouds. I let my gaze travel along the shoreline; in most places dense forest grew right down to the water's edge, but here and there you could see a clearing where a cottage or a cabin had been built, and in one spot there was a small abandoned resort hotel that I wanted to explore someday. I noticed some movement in front of our cabin. Looking closer, I saw that it was Amber and Wayne. They were walking together along the shore. Amber had on the white dress I'd seen her in that first night, and over that she wore a heavy mackinaw jacket with long sleeves that covered her hands. They stopped walking for a moment and Wayne leaned in close and said something in Amber's ear. Amber stared down at the waves pounding up against the bank, a blank expression on her face. Then Wayne took her arm and pulled her around so that she had to look at him. Amber stared up into his face, her hair whipping wildly in the wind.

I lay my head back down on the pillow. For a while I tried to distract myself from how miserable I felt by not thinking about anything, just letting my mind go completely blank, like when you erase the writing on a blackboard and are left with gray smudges. But it was hard to keep my mind blank. Thoughts kept creeping in. I kept picturing Amber and Wayne lying together in the backseat of Wayne's Plymouth or in a grassy meadow, having sex and getting her pregnant. And then I began to think of all the girls I'd known in Grand Rapids, and for a while I tried to imagine the sort of girl who would be right for having sex with. I hadn't had sex with any girl or even seen one naked, so it was hard to imagine exactly how it would happen, what the sequence of steps would be, how you would go from having a conversation or walking together along a lakeshore to having sex. And finally I decided that none of the girls I'd known in Grand Rapids had been right for sex. They were good for other things, maybe, but they were not right for having sex. But then, suddenly, I thought about things in a different way and I decided that maybe they were *all* the right kind, only I just didn't know it yet.

I raised my head again and lifted the corner of the window shade. Rain was coming down, big drops pelting the windowpane, rolling down in lazy jagged patterns just inches from my face. I looked up and down the shore; there was no sign of Amber and Wayne. They had probably gone somewhere in Wayne's car, I thought, back into McBride, maybe, or to a deserted back road. I imagined Wayne leaning in close and talking to Amber in a calm steady voice. Trying to convince her to have sex with him again.

I lay my head back down. I didn't want to think about Amber and Wayne anymore. That had nothing to do with me. If Amber wanted to take Wayne back, that was up to her. And if she wanted to have sex with him that was okay, too. They had done it once to get her pregnant, so doing it again wouldn't really matter. Like Amber's mother had said, the damage was already done.

I began to feel like I was going a little crazy, thinking about Amber in this way, so I forced my thoughts to go in a completely different direction. I thought about the Asiatic flu and how so many people had died from it. But then I began to wonder if *I* might die, too. I didn't feel like I was going to die, but I was feverish and headachy, and for all I knew that was how you felt before you died. Then for a while I tried to picture myself being dead—my body perfectly still, my eyes fixed and sightless, my mind empty of thoughts—and suddenly a kind of panic swept over me, as if thinking about being dead were a kind of sin or a way of inviting it to happen. And then I closed my eyes and prayed for God to forgive me and to understand that I didn't really want to be dead, and that thinking about it had been a sort of joke, a terrible joke but still only a joke. And then I must have become delirious, or possibly I fell back asleep, because I remember my thoughts going on and on and on, and I remember praying and thinking and dreaming about many other things that afternoon: about my mother coming back to Michigan, and about Amber keeping the pact we had made and not turning on me, and about having sex with a girl I couldn't imagine, and about America getting a satellite into outer space so the Russians would not bomb us, and about God being the same thing as truth. I thought or dreamed or prayed about these things during that entire afternoon. But not in a clear, practical way that gets you somewhere, only in the incomplete half-feeling way of being sick.

At four-thirty my mother called. "How is everything, Danny?" she asked me. I stood in the kitchen in my pajamas holding the phone.

"Everything's all right," I said.

"Your voice sounds a little hoarse. You don't have a cold, do you?"

"No," I said, remembering what my father had said about not wanting her to know that I was sick. "I'm fine. I ran in gym class today. They had us run the quarter mile and timed us. I think I got hoarse from breathing hard."

"Did you have a good day at school? Did you learn a lot of new things?"

"Yes," I said. And then I told her the same things I'd told my father the night before, about the quadratic equation and how Thomas Jefferson had bought Louisiana from the French for twelve million dollars.

"Oh, Danny," my mother said after I'd finished, and there was a new sound in her voice now, sort of plaintive and lost. "I so much wish I could be there with you. You're learning all those wonderful things, and I'm not there to share them with you." She paused, and I knew she expected me to say something, but I didn't have anything to say, nothing that would come out right. Then at her end I heard a noise in the background—like a car going by—and I pictured her standing in a telephone booth on a busy street corner, though I didn't know why she would be there or what she would be doing.

"Do you think your mother has abandoned you?" she said next. "Do you think I'm a terrible person?"

"No. Of course not," I said, because I didn't want her to feel angry or upset.

"Well, maybe someday you'll understand and forgive me, Danny. It's just something I have to do for a while. Being away, I mean."

"But why?" I said.

"Oh, Danny," she said, after a long pause. "I don't know if I can explain it. But sometimes things turn out different from what you expected. You feel like you're losing yourself. And so you just have to try something else for a while and hope that it saves you."

I waited, expecting she would say something more, because I didn't think what she'd said so far had been enough. But then I realized she was finished.

"Okay," I said, finally, because I knew I had to say something. "I guess I understand."

We were silent then, my mother and I, each thinking our own thoughts. I moved as far as I could in the direction of the kerosene stove, as far as the telephone cord would let me. I felt cold standing there in my pajamas.

"I wish you'd come to Chicago, Danny," my mother said. "We could have so much fun here." And then she talked for a long time about Chicago and the museums and the parks. And I understood that she wanted to see me in Chicago, where she could live the kind of life she wanted to live and have bright conversations with people who had gone to universities and were comfortable with money, but she did not want to see me on a lake in northern Michigan. A lake in Michigan was not a place where she could be with me, evidently, although she loved me terribly and wanted nothing more than to be together again.

"I'm afraid I've got to go now, Danny boy," my mother said. "There's a get-together tonight and your grandparents want me to go along. I guess it's a sort of cocktail party."

I didn't say anything, although I wondered what a cocktail party was like, and for a moment I tried to make a picture in my mind of a roomful of people standing around with drinks in their hands. I had been to potluck dinners at the Methodist church in Grand Rapids, which I thought were parties, and my parents would sometimes have another couple in for dinner on a Saturday night, and there would be conversation and joke telling. But I had never seen a cocktail party.

"Good-bye, sweetheart," my mother said. "I love you so terribly much it hurts. Please think about coming to visit me. Promise me you'll think about that, Danny boy."

"I will," I said. "I promise. I love you. Good-bye."

That evening my father brought a woman to the house. The two of them stood together in the doorway of my bedroom, the woman in front and my father behind, looking over her shoulder.

"This is Harriet Walker, Danny," my father said. "Miss Walker has consented to stay with us for a few days and take care of you. She does some nursing in her workaday life. At least that's what she tells me."

Harriet Walker turned and looked back at my father and smiled.

"So she'll know how to make you feel better," my father continued. "The little hospital in McBride has decided it can get along without her for a day or two, so she's available to help us out."

Harriet Walker came over to my bed. She was a tall brown-haired woman with large dark eyes. The green dress she wore was cinched at the waist by a shiny black leather belt. I remember thinking that the dress seemed out of place in our cabin, although it was a nice dress and would have been fine almost anywhere else. For some reason I had the impression that she and my father had come from a restaurant, although I didn't have any particular reason to think that, and then I thought that maybe my father had taken her out to dinner to talk about coming to stay with us and to convince her of doing it.

"Hello, Danny," she said. "How are you feeling?"

"I'm feeling all right," I said. "Maybe a little warm."

She reached forward to touch my forehead. Her hand felt smooth and cool.

"Oh my," she said. "You are running a fever, aren't you?" She looked back at my father. "But it's normal, Jim. It's the flu, after all. It comes with the territory."

She turned back and smiled down at me. Her eyes were calm and steady, like she wasn't afraid to look at things. "Let's get some cool cloths in here, Jim," she said. "We'll see if we can break Danny's fever. Once you break the fever things start to get back to normal."

"Aye-aye, captain," my father said, and he went off in the direction of the kitchen.

Harriet Walker stood next to the bed, smiling down at me with her steady-gazing eyes. Her long hair was pinned back with two plastic clips, but a strand had gotten loose and dangled along one side of her face. She walked over to the bureau and picked up a raccoon's skull that was lying there. She examined it with an interested expression, then set it down. Next she picked up a photograph of my mother in a silver frame; it was a picture my father had taken the year before, showing her smiling in front of a lilac bush with one hand raised to shield her eyes from the sun. Harriet Walker tilted the picture toward the window so she could see it better, then she set it down.

She came over and stood beside my bed again. "What's this?" she asked. She picked up the book lying on the bedside table.

"It's a book about West Point," I said. "It explains the traditions and the rules you need to know to be a cadet."

"Rules?" she said. She began flipping through the pages.

"Like duty, honor, and country," I said. And immediately I felt foolish, because it sounded like a silly thing to say in a cabin in the woods.

"Don't tell me you want to be an army man, Danny," she said. "Am I going to rescue you from the flu just so you can become cannon fodder?"

"I've thought about going to West Point when I get out of high school," I said. Then I said: "What's cannon fodder?"

"That's what you are after a bomb falls on you. Like my high-school sweetheart, Eddie Gilbert. He got blown up in the Battle of the Bulge. They sent him home in a bronze casket. Only it wasn't really Eddie. It was just little pieces of him wrapped up in a canvas bag."

She went over to the bureau and opened the top drawer and put the book into it. "There," she said, closing the drawer. "Out of sight, out of mind."

Just then my father came back with a basin of water and a stack of towels. "Is this what you had in mind, captain?" he said to Harriet Walker.

"Perfect," she said. She sat down on the edge of my bed and pulled back the covers. She unbuttoned the tops of my pajamas, then worked them over my arms. I felt the cold air against my skin.

"Are you wearing underpants, Danny?" she asked me.

"No," I said.

"Then I suppose you don't want me to take off your pajama bottoms?"

"I don't care," I said. Then I said, "No."

Harriet Walker laughed. "I'll assume the second answer is the one you want to leave on the record," she said. Then she began to put wet towels on my chest and arms, dipping the towels into the cool water and wringing them out before laying them carefully on my body. The wet towels felt cold against my skin, like I was encased in a watery cast. For a minute I thought I was going to be sick.

"You'll have to trust me, Danny," Harriet Walker said. "I've taken care of plenty of folks who were a lot worse off than you are."

"I trust you," I said, and that was true, even though I'd only known her for a few minutes.

"Okay," she said, after she'd finished covering my chest and arms with the wet towels. "Now your dad can do the interesting part." She smiled down at me. "You'll feel terrible for a while but then you'll start to feel better. Unless you're really sick, in which case you'll just feel terrible." She looked at me. "I'm just kidding, Danny," she said. "That's a bad joke. Strike it from the record."

Harriet Walker went out of my bedroom, drawing the door closed behind her. My father helped me out of my pajama bottoms. Then he finished putting the wet towels onto my legs and around my waist and hips and thighs. He worked very seriously, as if he had been given an assignment he wanted to do well on.

"I think we've had a stroke of luck, Danny," he said, glancing up at me. And I understood he was talking about Harriet Walker coming to help us out.

I lay in my bed in the darkness under the cool watery towels, waiting for my fever to break. I wanted to sleep but I was too uncomfortable. I hadn't had anything to eat all day and my stomach felt like it was drawn up into a hard little knot. My muscles still ached. I felt cold and hot at the same time.

In the kitchen I could hear my father and Harriet Walker talking, the murmur of their voices. Once I heard my father say, "I'm not likely to see it in my lifetime, Harry," and once I heard Harriet Walker say, "Being right is little consolation when it comes to feelings, Jim," and once I heard them both laugh out loud at the same time. Then the radio came on and played a song by Frank Sinatra, and then I heard a chair scrape across the floor, and then I heard some dishes clanking. Then I didn't hear anything because I went to sleep.

When I awoke it was the middle of the night. The band of light beneath my door was gone and the house was silent. The only sound was the rush of wind through the treetops and the gentle rattle of my bedside window.

I lay still, wondering what time it was and where my father and Harriet Walker were. The wet towels were gone. I was lying under the blanket with no clothes on. And then I realized that my fever had broken just like Harriet Walker had told me it would. I felt warm and comfortable. The vague cobwebby feeling had left my brain. My muscles did not ache.

I threw back the blanket and got out of bed. My pajamas were draped over the back of a chair. I put them on and opened the door and walked out into the living room, the floorboards creaking under my weight. The living room was dark except for a faint light coming from the kerosene stove. The tiny yellow flame cast a wavering light onto objects in the room, making everything seem to vibrate, like the way leaves tremble in the wind before a summer storm.

Harriet Walker was asleep on the sofa, a blue blanket bunched up around her waist. She wore a white slip with thin satin straps across her shoulders and a lacy pattern along the top. Her green dress lay over the back of a wooden chair, folded neatly.

I stood next to the sofa watching Harriet Walker sleep. Her hair was loosened from the plastic clips, and it fell in a confused way around her face. Her mouth was slightly open, and she breathed in and out in little sighs. Tiny beads of sweat glistened on her upper lip.

Watching her, I thought about her boyfriend, Eddie Gilbert, the boy who had been blown into little pieces and come home in a canvas bag. I wondered how much she had loved him and if his death was a terrible loss that she still thought about every day or if it was just something she had felt for a while and then forgotten. There are different ways of losing people, I realized. There is death, and there is leaving, and there is the end of the love you had felt for someone. All of those were possible.

Harriet Walker moved a little on the sofa. She drew in a deep breath, then let it out in a long ragged sigh.

Standing there, I wondered how it would feel to be blown up into little pieces, the way it had happened to Eddie Gilbert or the way it would happen in an atomic attack. So that you were just gone in an instant, wiped away completely, with no chance to know what was happening or to say good-bye to the people you loved or to brace yourself against the terrible jolt of pain. And then I suddenly began to feel afraid, and I tried to hold the thought of death away and only let it come into my brain for a moment of time—the moment I could stand to think about it—and then push it back before it became too strong to bear.

I went over to the door to my father's bedroom and pushed against it. It swung inward with a slight protesting squeak. A slow rhythmic snoring came out of the darkness. I thought about going in and telling my father that my fever had broken, because I wanted to be near someone when the feeling of death was still in my brain, and I thought he would like to know that I was well again and out of danger.

"Hello, sweetheart."

I turned around. Harriet Walker was watching me from the sofa.

"Are you feeling better?" she asked.

"Yes," I said. "I think my fever broke."

She smiled and reached out her hand. I went over and sat on the edge of the sofa. She touched my cheek.

"You feel cool, sweetheart," she said, sounding half asleep. "You're a normal boy again." She smiled drowsily.

"I think so, too," I said.

"Do you want to lie down with Harriet for a moment?" she asked. "You can share your sweet dreams with me."

I didn't know what to do because it seemed like a strange request, but I liked the idea of being close to someone when the thought of death was still so strong, and I liked the idea of being close to a woman.

Harriet Walker started to draw back the blanket, but then she stopped. "On second thought, I suppose it's not such a good idea," she said. "Scratch that notion, young man." She looked up at me and smiled again, then closed her eyes. "But just sit there for a moment, will you? You can do that. Sit there and be close."

She put her arm around my waist and drew me up against her side. I placed my hand on her shoulder. Her skin was warm and slightly damp.

"Were you in love with Eddie Gilbert?" I asked, after some time had passed, because it was the thing I had been wondering about before she had awakened.

"Yes," she said, without opening her eyes. "At least I think I was. It's hard to say now. So much has happened since."

"Do you miss him? Knowing he's never coming back."

Harriet Walker was silent for a long time. And I began to think she had not heard my question or had fallen back asleep. But then she suddenly answered, as if no time had passed at all.

"At first it was the thought of missing him that hurt most," she said. "More than the actual thing. Like a sadness you're supposed to feel and so you do." She moved a little, as if she was trying to arrange herself more comfortably on the sofa. "But I miss him, yes. I miss him terribly."

I turned and looked at the yellow flame burning deep inside the kerosene stove. For a moment it rose and cast a brighter glow into the room. Then it flickered and became smaller, and the room slid back into the wavering half darkness.

"You can go back to bed now," Harriet Walker said. Her mouth was close to my hand where it rested on her shoulder, and I felt the rush of her breath as she spoke the words. Then she said "Eddie" in a whispery voice, a voice I could barely hear, and then she whispered the name again—"Eddie"—as if she didn't even know she was saying it. Like it just escaped.

I sat looking at the wavering flame bathing the room in its unsteady glow. I felt the breath of Harriet Walker moving over the back of my hand where it lay on her warm shoulder. And then I felt her body relax—just suddenly in an instant of time—as if she were letting go of something or giving something away. And I knew she was asleep. And I knew she still loved Eddie Gilbert. And I believed my mother still loved me.

PART/TWO

Chapter Seven

HARRIET WALKER STAYED WITH us for two more days. During the first day I slept most of the time, which she said was normal after a fever has broken. On the second day she listened to soap operas on the radio—*Stella Dallas* and *The Guiding Light* and *Search for Tomorrow*—and then she made a pot roast and tapioca pudding for dinner. I didn't talk to her much because there wasn't anything I wanted to know. Nothing more than I already knew—that she was a nurse, that she was a single woman, that she'd loved a boy who'd been killed in the war, that she was willing to take care of me for a while.

When I left to catch the school bus on the third morning, I believed I would not see her again. Standing next to the door with my schoolbooks under my arm, I thanked her for taking care of me. She asked if she could kiss me good-bye, and I said she could, and she came over and kissed me, quickly on the mouth. Then she hugged me, and I hugged her back with my free arm, feeling the hard curve of her ribs beneath her soft skin. It reminded me of hugging my mother, from the days when she had lived with us and we had hugged each other.

"I think you've made a conquest there, Harry," my father said. He was sitting at the kitchen table in his white shirt and tie, eating some scrambled eggs.

"I guess it helps when you have a middle-of-the-night rendezvous," Harriet Walker said and laughed, and I understood that she had told my father about that. "Not that that's in your future, Jim," she said and she looked at my father and wrinkled her nose at him.

I waited for the school bus near the island of pine trees at the end of the two-track road that ran out to the county highway. It was a good place to wait because often there were animals to see—birds and squirrels and foxes and wild turkeys and sometimes a hawk circling lazily overhead—and you could stand behind the pine trees and be sheltered from the cold wind. Not many cars came along, but when a car or a truck *did* come along it was an interesting experience. First you heard a far-off rumble, like heat lightning before a summer rainstorm, except it was not summer and the air did not feel right for it, and then you saw a tiny speck approaching in the distance, a dark speck trailing a furious cloud of dust, the dust getting closer and the rumble becoming louder and the speck becoming larger. Then suddenly the car or truck was there, and then it was past and you were in the dust cloud, submerged in it, and everything was brown and choky and confused, and your clothes fluttered furiously from the windblast.

I was watching a car approaching in the distance when I heard the beep of a horn behind me. It took me by surprise and made me jump. When I turned around I saw Amber in the green Chevy pickup.

"I haven't seen you for a couple of days," she said, smiling at me as she cranked down the side window.

"I was sick," I said. "I had a fever and had to stay home from school."

"Was it the Asiatic flu?"

"I think so. But it wasn't so bad."

"That's good," she said. "The Asiatic flu can be dangerous."

Just then the car I'd been watching rocketed past, and there was a moment of noise and dusty blindness. Amber turned her head and squinted, and I turned and hunched my shoulders against the blast of air. Then everything calmed down.

"Come on," Amber said. "I'll drive you to school. I'm headed to town to deliver a mounted deer head for my stepdaddy." She motioned toward the back of the truck where something with sharp angles was covered by a canvas tarp. "You can read my French words to me."

For a moment I thought about telling her I didn't want a ride to school, but I couldn't think of how to say it without sounding rude, so I got up into the truck, and we started off, and I began to read the French words to her. It was a different group of words this time, and I tried to learn them as I read them off to Amber.

"I saw you and Wayne walking down by the lake when I was sick," I said after we'd gone through the words a couple of times.

"Oh, did you?" she said.

She was quiet for a while, staring out at the road ahead. Then she told me in a serious voice that she'd decided to forgive Wayne for going off to join the army. Wayne felt terrible about running off, she said, and he'd only done it because he was afraid of the responsibility of being a father. He'd always loved her, he said, and he believed things would work out between them if they gave it another chance, and they'd find the love they'd had before and be married. And that would be wonderful for her, Amber said, because then the baby wouldn't be illegitimate, and she wouldn't have to give it up for adoption.

"Anyway," she said, glancing over at me, "that's the latest news. Hot off the presses. Amber and Wayne are back together again."

"That's good," I said, even though I wasn't sure it was. "Are you going to get married soon?"

"Well, yes," she said. She pursed her lips and frowned. "I think that's understood. But not right away. Wayne says he wants to earn some money first. As long as it happens before the baby comes, that's all I care about." Suddenly she reached over and turned up the volume on the radio, as if she didn't want to talk about Wayne anymore and wanted me to know it. The sleeve of her coat rode up her arm, revealing a tiny bruise. It looked like the place where Wayne had grabbed her when they'd been walking down by the lake.

"Listen to this," Amber said. She started to move her head to the song, which was a Buddy Holly song about how love is like being on a roller coaster.

"It's true," she said. "Love is dangerous."

We came into town, past the grain elevators with their long metal chutes and the railroad tracks with lines of empty gondola cars waiting to be loaded with soybeans and corn. As we crossed the iron bridge over the Muskegon River, the wooden planks banged under the tires. I peered over the side and saw the water swirling lazily down below, clear water you could look through and see the gravelly bottom. We drove onto Main Street and passed the old Chippewa Hotel and the Kresge five-and-dime and the Majestic movie theater.

At LeRoy Street we turned and drove down a couple of blocks to the school, a squat two-story redbrick building with fluted columns, wide front steps, and a big lawn. Other kids were starting to arrive, kids who lived in town and didn't have to take the bus. I saw a couple I knew: Eddie Buchanan, whose father ran a funeral parlor, and Jimmy Sowmick, who was an Indian. Amber pulled over to the curb.

"Well, here you are, Mr. Einstein," she said.

"Do you want to study some geometry this afternoon?" I asked. I had the door open and one foot down on the pavement.

"I don't need to study any more geometry."

"What are you talking about?"

"I dropped my classes."

I turned and looked back at Amber. She stared at me in a slightly belligerent way, as if she knew I'd be disappointed but wanted to show that she didn't really care.

"I was failing most of them anyway," she said. Then, after a pause, she added: "Nobody thinks a pregnant girl should be going to school, Danny. That seems to be everybody's opinion. I guess they finally convinced me, too."

"*I* thought you should."

"Well, unfortunately your vote doesn't count for much," she said, sounding angry, like she was mad for having to explain something I should already know. "Neither does mine, as far as that goes. Some people have bigger votes in life. That's a fact you might want to get used to."

We were both quiet then, just staring at each other across the front seat of the pickup. Amber had a tiny smile on her face, but her lips were pressed together in a thin tight line.

"Don't worry," she said finally, and she spoke now in a regular voice. "We can still get together for other reasons than geometry. Just to talk. When Wayne's not around."

"Sure," I said, even though I didn't entirely believe her. "That'd be great."

I stood up and stepped out of the pickup.

"Or even if he is around," Amber added suddenly, and she leaned across the seat and grabbed my sleeve. "You'll like him once you get to know him, Danny." She stared up at me from inside the pickup. "He's nicer than how he looked the other day. You could be good friends."

I didn't say anything.

"In fact, why don't you come with us this afternoon? We're going to drive over to Granite Falls. Wayne's got something he wants to do there."

"Okay," I said, because I didn't have anything else to do that afternoon, and it seemed to be important to her.

"We'll pick you up right here at four." She smiled again, and this time it felt all right.

I closed the door, and Amber put the pickup into gear and pulled away. At the corner she stopped to wait for some kids crossing the street. While she waited she raised her hand and waggled her fingers at me in the rearview mirror. Then the pickup moved forward, leaving a trail of white smoke hanging in the air.

Chapter Eight

AT SCHOOL I STAYED BEHIND after every class to get the assignments I'd missed from being sick. In biology I had to make a diagram illustrating Mendel's law of genetics and show how traits are passed down through generations. In English I'd missed a debate about free will versus predestination, so I had to write a four-page paper about it, giving my opinions and supporting them with quotations from authoritative sources. In algebra, Mr. Horak explained the binomial theorem and gave me some problems to prove that I understood it.

Sitting in my algebra class after doing the problems, waiting for school to end, I watched through the window as the red and yellow leaves drifted down onto the school lawn. I thought about Amber and tried to figure out why she still wanted to see me, now that she was back with Wayne and didn't need help with geometry. It seemed odd that she would want me to hang around with her and Wayne, though it seemed odd, too, that I had agreed to do it—to tag along like that—and I wondered what it said about me, the kind of person I was. I'd been going to school in McBride for two months already but I hadn't made any friends, just a few kids I could say hello to. I didn't feel the *need* for it, I guess, and the country kids seemed different from the ones I'd known in Grand Rapids, less interesting somehow, or at least less interested in the things that interested me. But I didn't want to be an outsider forever—someone who is not attractive to other people—so

I decided it was time for me to *make* some friends. And then I tried to think of all the things I was good at, which were mathematics and fishing and reading books, and to imagine myself doing those things with other people. But none of the images came together in my mind, and I was left with a picture of myself standing alone in a clearing in the forest, waiting for a deer or a wild turkey to come along.

Later that afternoon I stood in front of the school waiting for Amber and Wayne. Most of the kids had already left. Off in the distance I heard the football team practicing on the field behind the parking lot, the coach's whistle and the sound of running feet and the crash of bodies coming together in pads. I'd played football in Grand Rapids—pickup games in Garfield Park and one season with the Gray Y—and I'd been good at it, like I was at most sports. If we were still living in McBride next year, I'd decided I would try out for the varsity team. I was bigger than most boys my age and I could run fast, and I thought I would be good at playing the end position where you get to catch the ball and score some touchdowns.

After a while a boy I knew from algebra class, Norm Decker, came by. He asked if I had seen any good algebra problems lately, and I grinned and said I hadn't but that I'd seen some pretty good ones in geometry. We talked for a while about baseball, and then we talked about a girl named Carla Cross, who was blond and had big breasts.

"I heard that for five dollars she'll let you look at them," Norm said. "Do you want to do it sometime? We could pool our money."

I wasn't really interested in seeing Carla's breasts that way, although I liked the *idea* of seeing a girl's breasts and would have done it under the right circumstances. But I didn't want to tell that to Norm, because I knew he would be glad to see a girl's breasts under any circumstances and figured that was how it was for everyone.

"Are you sure she'll do it?" I asked, just to have something to say. "For two people instead of one?"

"Why not?" Norm said. "What difference does it make?"

"It just seems like a different deal, that's all. Two instead of one."

"I'm telling you, it'll be all right. Anyway, she's just a bitch. She won't care."

"Let me think about it."

"Well, don't think too long. She might find herself a boyfriend, and then we'd be fucked."

Norm looked off into the distance, then turned back to me. "What're you standing here for?" he asked.

"I'm waiting for some friends to pick me up."

"Who?"

I started to answer, but I realized I didn't want to mention Amber's name. And I knew it was because of what Amber had said about the cheerleaders not wanting to talk to her and about what the women in the doctor's waiting room had said about Amber getting knocked up, and about what Norm had said about Carla Cross being a bitch.

"Just some friends," I said.

"So it's a big mystery," Norm said, grinning. "That means it must be something good."

Just then I saw Wayne's Plymouth coming along in the distance. Through the windshield I saw Amber sitting next to Wayne.

"Are those your friends?" Norm said, sounding surprised.

"Yes," I said, heading for the car.

Amber leaned across and pushed open the passenger door. "Did you think we'd forgotten you?" she asked.

"No," I said. "I trusted you."

I got into the front seat, and Amber scooted over closer to Wayne. As I reached back for the door handle, I glanced at Norm. He was grinning. Then he nodded his head, like he'd figured out some deep dark secret. I closed the door.

"Now I'm sandwiched in between my two favorite men," Amber said. "I'm in heaven." She batted her eyes in a comical way.

Wayne reached around behind Amber and put his hand on

my shoulder. "How's it goin,' buddy?" he said. He squeezed my shoulder hard.

"Fine," I said. I looked across Amber to where Wayne was sitting behind the wheel. He grinned and winked.

"His name's Danny," Amber said. "I told you that. You ought to call him by his real name."

"Sorry," Wayne said, and then he spoke my name—"Danny"— just a single word that he dropped out into the air.

Wayne drove through McBride and headed out of town, driving south along the river, past the cemetery and the power dam and the Red Arrow motel. The road hugged the river for a while, and I looked out at the broad glassy surface broken by swirls and ripples and eddies and at the tall sandy bluff rising up on the far shore, topped by pine trees. My father and I had fly-fished in this section of river one day last summer, just after we'd arrived from Grand Rapids, and I remembered the strong current that pulled against you like it wanted to suck you under and the rocky bottom that made it hard to keep your footing.

"Where are we going?" I asked, because no one had told me that yet.

"There's a man I've got to see at the Texaco station in Granite Falls," Wayne said. "He owes me some money that I'm going to collect." He turned and looked across at me. "It'll be fun. You'll enjoy it."

Amber reached into a little black purse and took out a package of Old Gold cigarettes. She shook one out and lit it with a Zippo lighter. Then she held the package out to Wayne and he took one, too. She held the flame under his cigarette. "Thanks, baby," he said, the cigarette bouncing between his lips. She snapped the lighter shut.

"What about me?" I asked.

"No can do," Amber said. "You're too young. It'll stunt your growth. Don't you know that?"

"I've smoked cigarettes before," I said. "And I'm pretty tall already."

"Well, I won't be a party to your corruption," she said. "Wayne and I have been corrupted already, so it's too late for us."

I took the package of cigarettes from Amber's purse and shook one out and lit it. I handed the package back to her.

"All right," she said. "Have it your way."

We drove on, the road rising up from the river and going into farm country, past orchards where Mexicans were picking apples from tall ladders. They put the apples into large canvas sacks that hung from their shoulders, then emptied the sacks into wooden crates lined up on the ground.

"What a job," Wayne said. "No better than beasts of burden." Then he started to talk about the kind of job he wanted to have one day. He said he had a lot of different ideas for making money and that anyone could make money if they just used common sense. One idea he had was to bring cigarettes over from Canada, where they cost less, and sell them for a big profit in Michigan. There were places that would buy them, he said, gas stations and grocery stores, and he knew which ones they were and the people who ran them. He said that he and another man had already done it once and that a person could make a living from it if they went about it like a steady job. Then he said he might also start a fishing guide service someday because he knew all the lakes and where the best fishing spots were, especially for muskellunge, which was a fish that downstate people would pay big money to catch.

"You're full of ideas," Amber said. "I'll be satisfied if you just give this baby a daddy. That'd be a good idea to start with."

Wayne laughed and put his hand on Amber's knee. She put her hand on top of Wayne's and they sort of laced their fingers together.

The road took a gentle curve and passed some billboards and then we were in Granite Falls. We drove through a neighborhood of small wooden houses and then into the downtown, three blocks of stores with cars angled up to the curb on both sides. The stores were like the ones you saw in all the little towns of northern Michigan, brick two-story buildings with fancy woodwork along the roofs. At the end of Main Street the road split and ran around a grassy square with a tall domed courthouse. In front of the courthouse a statue of a Civil War soldier stood on a marble column, gazing out at the horizon.

Wayne pointed an imaginary handgun at the statue with his thumb cocked back. "*Ka-pow,*" he said. "You're dead."

We circled the courthouse and headed back in the direction we had come from.

"We're early," Wayne said. "My friend doesn't come to work until five." He turned onto a road that headed down toward the river. "Why don't we go to the park for a few minutes?"

The park was just a mowed area along the riverbank with picnic tables and a playground. Wayne and Amber walked off in the direction of the river, holding hands, while I headed over to the playground where a woman was pushing a small boy on a swing. The woman was young, not too much older than Amber, and as she pushed the little boy she sang a song about flying in an airplane.

The song seemed familiar to me, as if I'd heard it a long time ago. I tried to remember the words but they were just out of reach in my memory. And for some reason it bothered me to realize that there was something in my life that I'd forgotten, as if a part of me had already been lost, even though I hadn't lived that many years. And then I wondered if that's what life is like in general, losing things you don't know about until something happens to remind you that the place they'd been is empty, like a song you've forgotten.

I began to feel strange and a little depressed, and so I walked over to the path that led down to the river. I guess I wanted to distract myself from my thoughts about the song and about forgetting things. As I came up near the riverbank I heard a noise. It was something like a moan but not exactly. Then I saw Amber and Wayne lying together in the tall grass along the river. They were kissing and holding each other and making those sounds. Amber's dress was bunched up around her waist and Wayne's hand was slipped inside her underpants. Then they stopped kissing and just held on to each other for a while, and then I heard Wayne tell Amber in an urgent voice that he loved her, and then I heard Amber say she loved him, too.

I stayed crouched down in the tall grass, not knowing what to do next. Part of me was glad that Amber and Wayne were back in love again—glad for Amber's sake, because that's what she wanted so that she could keep her baby—but I hated seeing them there on the ground like that. If Wayne wanted to kiss her I thought he should have found a better place for doing it—his car, maybe, or a dark street corner, or in the back row of a movie theater. Almost anyplace would be better than the weeds along a river.

I turned and walked back up to the car, trying not to think about what was happening between Amber and Wayne. When I got to the car I turned on the radio and heard a news report about the Negroes going to school in Arkansas and how the president had called in the National Guard to calm things down. Then a man sang a song about a girl named Diana and how much he loved and needed her, and then there was another song, and that was about love, too. And suddenly I realized that all the favorite songs were about love, and I began to wonder if *I* was a person people could love or if there was something wrong with me, some coldness or lack of interest. I remembered a girl I'd been friends with in Grand Rapids—a girl named Cheryl Hibson—and for a while I tried to remember her face and the exact color of her hair, and I tried to imagine us being in love and doing the things that Wayne and Amber were doing. Then—after I'd thought this way for a minute or two—I decided that I should try to find a girl in McBride and fall in love with her. But I realized I didn't know what I would do with a girl even if I had one, other than the sexual things you think about. And then I remembered what Amber had said about me being one of her favorite people, and I thought that maybe that was close to being in love and counted for something.

After a while Amber and Wayne came up from the river. Wayne's shirt was loose and sort of twisted around his waist. When he got up to the car he unbuckled his belt and worked the shirttail back inside his pants. Then he came over and put his arm around my shoulder. I could smell Amber's perfume.

"Have you ever had a girlfriend, Danny?" Wayne asked.

"No," I said, even though I'd known Cheryl Hibson, who I thought was a kind of girlfriend.

Wayne looked over at Amber. She was leaning back against a tree trunk, her face turned up toward the sun, her eyes closed. Her lipstick was smeared and a purple bruise showed from under her collar.

"Why don't you fix him up with someone, Amber?" Wayne said.

"Danny doesn't need a girlfriend," Amber said, keeping her face toward the sun. "Besides, he's got me. I'm halfway to being in love with him already."

She opened her eyes and looked over at me and smiled so that the corners of her eyes crinkled. Then she closed her eyes again.

"Maybe I've got something to say about that," Wayne said. "Maybe we'll have to fight to see which one of us gets you." He squeezed my shoulder to let me know it was a joke. "Anyway, I think it'd be a good idea if Danny had a girlfriend. Someone he could get his fingers sticky with."

"Oh, Wayne," Amber said. "Stop it now."

I looked over at Amber. The sun was on her face. She looked peaceful and happy and about as pretty as any girl I had ever seen, even though her lipstick was smeared and she had that little bruise on her neck. It was hard to believe that just a few minutes ago she had been back in the weeds with Wayne, kissing and making noises and pulling at his shirt.

The Texaco station sat on a gravelly space next to the railroad tracks. It looked like the kind of gasoline station that was used by trucks and farm machinery and not so much for pumping gas into cars. Two maintenance bays had pickup trucks up on hoists, but no one seemed to be around to work on them. A mound of old tires sat off to one side.

Wayne drove slowly into the parking area, his tires crunching on the gravel. He circled around behind a shed and stopped next to a tall board fence. Inside the shed, a man was sitting on a stool, reading a newspaper. He wore greasy overalls and a baseball cap. His back was toward us.

"Stay here," Wayne said in a kind of fierce whisper. He got out of the car, his eyes fixed on the shed, and began walking toward it, crouching a little and moving quickly. Halfway to the shed he tossed his cigarette onto the ground.

"What's he doing?" I said to Amber.

"I don't know." She sat up a little straighter. "All he told me is that he had to see a guy who owes him some money."

Wayne stood in the doorway of the shed looking in at the man, a strange twisted smile on his face. He spoke some words, just two or three, and the man looked up. When the man saw Wayne his body jerked.

Wayne said something else and the man stood up and started to back away. At first Wayne just looked at him and smiled. Then he stepped into the shed and followed the man across the little room. When Wayne had him backed up against the window he grabbed the front of his overalls.

"Jesus," Amber said. "What's going on?"

"Should I go and see if Wayne needs help?" I said.

"No." She put her hand on my arm. "Just stay where you are."

All of a sudden Wayne struck the man. It seemed to happen like slow motion in a movie: first Wayne made a fist and drew back his arm; then his fist came forward against the man's face; then the man's head jerked back, smashing against the windowpane so that cracks webbed out and a large piece of glass tilted and shattered onto the ground.

Wayne dragged the man over to the other side of the shed and hit him again. I could see the man's face now. Blood streamed from his nose, and his face was twisted in pain.

"Let me out," Amber said. She pushed against my arm. I opened the door and stepped out onto the gravel.

Amber ran up to the shed and shouted for Wayne to stop. She stepped inside and grabbed his arm. I heard her say that if he didn't stop he would be arrested. Then she asked if that was what he wanted to happen with a baby on the way, his own baby who was helpless and depended on him.

Wayne held the man by the front of his overalls. He sort of smiled at Amber. Then he hit the man one more time, just a quick short punch, and the man slumped down to the floor.

Wayne walked over to the cash register, punched it open, and took out a wad of bills. He stuffed them into his shirt pocket. Then he stepped past Amber and walked out of the shed.

Amber stood looking at the man. She took an uncertain half step in his direction. But then she turned and followed Wayne back out to the car.

On the drive back to McBride, Wayne explained that he and the man had had a deal to bring cigarettes over from Canada, which was the deal he'd told us about earlier, only the man had claimed that some of the cigarettes had gotten ruined from being left out in the rain, and he had not paid Wayne his share of the money.

"I was just collecting what was owed to me, honey," Wayne said to Amber. "It was the deal we'd agreed on."

"I don't care," Amber said. She was sitting in the front seat between Wayne and me. Her hands were folded on her lap, and her arms were tucked in against her sides, like she wanted to stay as far away from both of us as she could get. "You don't go around beating people up. That's an ignorant way to settle things. I guess I know that better than most."

"But you're the one who's always saying how we need money if we're going to get married. I was doing it for you." He took the wad of bills out of his shirt pocket and dropped it onto Amber's lap. "Here," he said. "Count it. I think it's a lot."

"I don't want to count it," Amber said. She brushed her hand over her lap so that most of the bills fell onto the floor. "It doesn't belong to us. It's stolen."

"Hey, Danny," Wayne said. He glanced over at me. "Pick those up, will you?"

I leaned down and gathered the bills up off the floor. Some had gone back under the seat, and I had to crouch down and reach far back to get them. Some had blood on them. They made a big handful.

"Get the other ones, too," Wayne said, glancing down at the bills still on Amber's lap. "Only don't try any funny business with Amber. I'll be watching."

"Jesus Christ," Amber said disgustedly. She folded her arms and looked out the windshield. Wayne laughed.

We drove back to McBride, past the apple orchards with the Mexican workers and the river with the high sandy bluff and the deep, fast, hard-wading current. Nobody said anything. Not a single word. I looked out the side window and thought about what had happened at the Texaco station. I had never seen a man strike another man before, and I was surprised how simple it was and how fast it could happen, how it could be a thing you saw on a normal day and not something that seemed remarkable or that you had to get prepared for. Wayne had kissed Amber in the tall grass along the river, murmuring that he loved her, and ten minutes later he had struck a man and taken his money. That was something I wouldn't have guessed to see in a million years, that smooth change from normal life to violence. And then I thought about my father and how he had come home the other night bruised and bleeding, and I wondered if *he* knew how to fight, knew the ways to force a man onto the ground and make him give you something. In Grand Rapids we had watched the Friday night boxing matches on TV, and once he had taken me to see the Golden Gloves matches at the civic auditorium. But I didn't think my father knew how to fight. At least not that I knew about.

When we got back to McBride the streetlights were just coming on. We drove through the center of town and turned and went past the high school. The football team was just coming in from the practice field. The players walked slowly in the twilight, carrying their helmets, their heads bowed. It seemed like a long time since I had stood by the side of the road and listened to them shouting and crashing into each other.

Past the high school Wayne turned onto the road that went out toward the lake. I sat holding the money in my hands. From time to time I looked over at Amber. She was staring ahead through the windshield, an odd expression on her face—not sad or angry or confused but more like she was resigned to something. Trying to feel all right about the way her life was at that moment, maybe, even though she didn't entirely like it.

"At least you could wipe the blood off your hand," she said to Wayne, as we were leaving town. Wayne reached around and got a handkerchief out of his hip pocket. Then Amber took the handkerchief and did her best to clean the blood off. She held Wayne's hand as if it were an object—an ashtray or a porcelain figurine—and cleaned it very carefully, spitting on the handkerchief and wiping each knuckle and down between the fingers. Then she folded the handkerchief into a neat square and gave it back to Wayne.

"Thanks, baby," he said. "But now you're an accomplice to my misdeeds."

"Shut up," Amber said in a vicious way that surprised me. And then she started to cry, big wracking sobs that shook her body and made her gasp for air.

"Baby," Wayne said. He reached over and took her hand. She let him take it, lacing her fingers into his like they were making a fist together.

When we drove up to Amber's house nobody said anything. Amber got out and started walking toward the back door while I stood off to the side and watched Wayne back his car around. He headed out the dirt road, back toward the highway. I watched his red taillights bouncing off between the tree trunks.

"Do you have to go in right away?" Amber said. She was standing outside the back door. The glow of a bare lightbulb shone down so that her eyes were just black holes.

I looked across the inlet to our cabin. Through the bare tree branches I saw lights in the windows. I knew that my father would be wondering where I was. But I was already very late, and it didn't seem like a few more minutes would really matter.

"Let's walk down by the lake," Amber said. She held out her hand. I walked over and took it.

"I'm sorry you had to witness that insanity," she said after we'd walked partway down the slope that went to the lake. "It must have been shocking to you. It certainly was to me."

"No," I said, because I didn't want her to think that what Wayne had done had shocked me. "I've seen fights before."

"Have you?" she said. I could feel her turn and look at me. "I'm surprised."

"I've seen kids fight," I said. "And I've seen boxing on TV."

"This was different, though."

"Yes," I said after a minute. "I guess it was."

Along the shore an overturned rowboat lay across two logs. We sat on it and looked out at the water. Amber was still holding my hand. She held it tight in both of hers.

"Wayne's not so bad, I guess," she said after a while. "He was trying to get the money that belonged to him. That makes sense. That's fair."

I felt her looking at me in the darkness, as if she was studying my face for something, some sign that she would recognize when she saw it but that she didn't know about ahead of time.

"Yes," I said. "I think so, too."

"He's trying to make some money," she said, still looking at me.

"That's all. Trying to make money so we can have a start in life."

I didn't say anything because I had already agreed with her and didn't know what else I could do. But I didn't think Wayne had taken the money because he wanted to get a start in life. And I didn't think he loved Amber—not the way you're supposed to love a person you're going to marry.

"I think he'll be a good father once he comes to terms with it," she said.

We were quiet for a while. Amber leaned her head on my shoulder and brought my hand onto her lap, holding it between both of hers. I felt her hair against my neck and I smelled her perfume. Then I smelled something else, a kind of sourness, like rotten apples, and I realized it was from Wayne.

I remembered what Amber had said about being halfway in love with me, and for a crazy moment I wondered what would happen if I tried to kiss her. But I didn't know how she would react—whether she would sit there and let it happen or kiss me back like she'd kissed Wayne that afternoon or pull away and tell me it was wrong and slap my face.

"Do you ever think you'd like to have a girlfriend?" Amber asked me.

"I think about it sometimes." I pulled my thoughts back from kissing her.

"Maybe Wayne's idea wasn't so bad. There are some girls I know. Nice girls that you'd like."

I didn't say anything.

"We could do things together. You and me and Wayne. It'd be easier if there was another girl."

She raised her head up from my shoulder. I felt her turn and look at me in the darkness. "I think you and Wayne could be good friends, once you got to know him. He's not like you saw tonight. He can be kind and considerate."

"I like him," I said.

She put her head back onto my shoulder. "No you don't," she said. "I can tell. And it bothers me a lot."

We sat for a while without saying anything.

"Do you ever feel afraid?" Amber asked me.

"Afraid of what?"

"Afraid of what might happen. Or afraid of what you might do."

"No," I said, even though I was afraid that my mother was not coming back, and I was afraid that my father would be a failure at his new job, and I was afraid that the Russians would attack, and I was afraid I might be a dull person who no one could love.

Amber moved against my shoulder.

"Well, I do," she said. "Mostly I think about what's going to become of me if Wayne doesn't marry me. Of what's going to become of me and my baby. How we'll manage on our own." She breathed out a long ragged sigh. "Sometimes it overwhelms me, and I end up doing whatever it takes to make it go away."

As she said these last words her voice broke, and she seemed to struggle for breath. And I remembered her and Wayne together in the tall grass along the river, and I wondered if that's what she meant about doing whatever it took.

"You can talk to me about it," I said, because in that moment I felt I was a stronger person than she was—perhaps because I was afraid of so many things but had learned to deal with them—and could help her bear up against the things that frightened her.

"Thanks," she said. She sniffled a few times. "Maybe I'll take you up on that someday." She turned and put her arms around me, and I pulled against her, pressing my face into the smooth curve of her neck.

We sat like that for a moment, neither of us moving. And it felt exciting to be holding Amber, to feel the weight of her body in my arms, the comfortable bulk of a woman's body pressed up against my own. But it felt strange, too, and vaguely wrong, and I think she noticed it, too, because I suddenly felt her stiffen slightly.

"I suppose I should go in," she whispered.

"I think I'll stay out here for a while longer." I spoke the words into the warm curve of her neck.

"Okay."

She squeezed my hand and then let go. I turned and watched her walk up toward the house. She passed in front of a window, and I saw her thin girlish figure silhouetted by the yellow light. I raised my hand to wave, even though I knew she could not see me. Then she went inside.

I turned and looked back out onto the water. It was a clear moonless night. The lake was a black emptiness stretching out before my eyes. Here and there along the far shore I could see the lights from houses. People were in those places, I thought, although I didn't know who they were or what they were doing. Some of them were probably afraid, as Amber had said she was, and they felt alone and on the brink of being overwhelmed. And then I wondered if they had someone to confide in, someone to help them bear up, as I had tried to do for Amber.

In a moment I would go into the cabin. I would tell my father that I'd stayed late at school and had lost track of time and that someone else's father or mother had driven me home and dropped me off alongside the highway. I would not tell him about going to Granite Falls with Amber and Wayne or about the fight at the Texaco gas station or about holding the blood-soaked money on the drive back to McBride. And I would not tell him how I had sat with Amber and held her in my arms while she had told me she was afraid. And I would not tell him how I was afraid of many things myself but had not said it.

Just then another light came on across the lake, and a bright white reflection shot across the windless surface of the water, as if some giant hand had suddenly struck the lake in two.

I stood and headed up the slope toward the cabin.

Chapter Nine

WHEN I CAME INTO THE CABIN after being down by the lake, my father and Harriet Walker were in the kitchen making dinner. Harriet Walker was standing by the stove stirring something in a steaming pot. She wore my mother's apron, blue with a large sunflower design. Underneath she had on a green sweater and a gray woolen skirt. Her dark hair was drawn back in a bun so you could see her ears and neck. She stirred the steaming pot with one hand and held a drink with ice cubes in the other.

"Look who's agreed to come back to help us again, Danny," my father said. He was sitting at the kitchen table wearing his starched white shirt, the tie loosened. He stood up and went over and put a hand on Harriet Walker's shoulder. Then he picked a drink up off the counter.

"You both looked so pathetic when I was leaving this morning that I thought I'd sign on for a few more days," Harriet Walker said. She came over and kissed my cheek, holding her drink away. "Besides, I started to think that you might have a relapse and I wanted to be around to pull you through, if that happened. All my cures come with a guarantee, you know. Maybe I forgot to tell you that." She put her hand on my forehead and held it there for a moment, her eyes narrowed in concentration. "Although you seem to be all right now," she said. "Still in the normal range, I'd say."

"I feel good," I said.

"Well, that's the most important thing," she said, and she spoke in a way that made me think she was a little drunk. "In that case I can play doctor with your father tonight, instead of with you." She laughed and looked over at my father.

"Don't be giving the boy any ideas, Harry," my father said, looking embarrassed. "In this family everything's on the up and up."

"I'm only teasing," she said. She pouted in an exaggerated way.

I went into my bedroom and put my books on the bureau. When I passed back through the living room I saw a brown suitcase standing just outside the door to my father's bedroom.

"Did you have a good day at school?" Harriet Walker asked me when I came back into the kitchen. "Are you a smarter boy than when you left this morning?"

"I think so," I said. "Mr. Horak talked to me about becoming a scientist. He thinks I'd be good at that."

"That sounds promising," Harriet Walker said. She took a sip of her drink. "Maybe you can build a rocket to go up and save that poor little Communist dog they sent up the other day."

"What dog is that, Harry?" my father said. He was putting some bread onto a plate.

"Where have you been?" she asked. "You need to come in out of the woods more often, Jim." She went over and pinched his chin between two fingers and smiled up into his face. "The Communists sent a poor little dog into outer space last week. Pretty soon he's going to run out of air and die."

"That's a shame," my father said. "That borders on cruelty to animals." I was surprised to hear him say that, because he liked to hunt and had killed many animals without feeling sorry for them, as far as I knew.

"He'll run out of air in a couple of days, and then it'll be all over for him," Harriet Walker said. "Poor little doggy. Just a couple of gasps and he'll be gone." She stared blankly across the room as if she was picturing the little dog strapped into his space capsule. For a minute I thought she was going to cry. Then she took a long slow sip of her drink, still staring.

"Come on," my father said. He started to pour the stew from the steaming pot into a serving bowl. "This conversation is getting too morbid for this old soldier."

"I'm sorry," Harriet Walker said. She looked at me and forced a big smile onto her face. Then she sort of twirled around and held her arms out, like an actress coming on stage at the end of a play. And I knew she wanted to be gay for my father, to show him that side of her, so he would like her and be glad she was around.

We sat down and started to eat the stew. My father didn't ask me why I was late coming home, which surprised me. But then I remembered that *he* was late most nights—arriving at the cabin long after me—and probably didn't know what time I normally got there. And several other things surprised me, too: that Harriet Walker had come back to stay with us, that my father had put his hand on her shoulder in that familiar way, that they both seemed a little drunk, and that she'd made a joke about playing doctor. Then I wondered if my father had changed his mind about having my mother come back and was thinking about marrying Harriet Walker or if he just wanted to have a woman in the house for the pleasure of it, to hear a woman's voice and laughter and see her do the things a woman does, like twirl around and get sad about a helpless dog in outer space.

During dinner my father talked about the foreman's job he'd had at the General Motors factory in Grand Rapids and the men he'd supervised and how he'd learned to lead them and gain their respect. I thought he was trying to show Harriet Walker that he'd not always been a salesman, even though that's what he was now and what he'd chosen to be. During his time at General Motors he had taken courses at the Dale Carnegie Institute and he had read Norman

Vincent Peale and learned the importance of having a positive outlook. He was trying to apply those lessons in his new salesman's job, he said, just like he'd done at General Motors, and even though he'd not done particularly well so far, he knew that eventually things would come together and he would find success and a prosperous life.

"The good news is that there's only one way for you to go from here, Jim," said Harriet Walker, "and that's up." She laughed and looked around the kitchen with its knotty pine walls, the porcelain sink with rusty pipes showing underneath, the ancient Amana refrigerator dripping water onto the floor.

"There you go," my father said. "Now you're thinking positive." He raised his glass and swallowed the rest of his drink.

"By the way, Jim, were you in the military?" Harriet Walker asked. "That's something I've been meaning to ask you."

"I *was* in the military, Harriet," my father said. His voice took on a serious tone. "I was drafted in '43 and sent to the Pacific Theater with the supply corps. We kept the trucks and tanks running during the Marshall Islands campaign."

"Did you see any action?" Harriet Walker asked. "I mean direct engagement with the enemy."

"Well, no," my father said. "But I saw the consequences, Harriet. I saw men who were wounded, shot through the gut, or with an arm or a leg missing. Or just gone crazy from the stress of battle. There was a lot of that in the Marshall Islands."

Harriet Walker looked at my father. For a moment I thought she was going to say something else, but then she just smiled and went back to eating the stew. And what I thought she was going to say was something about her boyfriend, Eddie Gilbert, and how he had gotten killed at the Battle of the Bulge.

"MacArthur was a great leader," my father said all of a sudden, like it was an idea that had just come to him. "He understood how to motivate men. How to talk to them in their own terms. A lot of selling is like that."

Harriet Walker looked at my father as if his comment made no sense. Then she looked over at me and smiled. "Let's talk about something else," she said. "Let's not be Gloomy Guses." She took a sip of her drink.

"You were the one who brought up the war," my father said.

Harriet Walker stuck her tongue out at my father. Then she turned to me. "Tell me about your mother, Danny—Joanne, that's her name, isn't it?"

"Yes," I said. I set down my fork and thought for a moment. "She likes poetry," I said. "She went to the university in Ann Arbor for a couple of years and studied it there." I looked at Harriet Walker. "She likes history, too."

"She must be smart," Harriet Walker said.

"I guess she is," I said.

"That's where I met her," my father said. "In Ann Arbor."

"I didn't know you were a college man, Jim," Harriet Walker said. She looked at him with an interested expression.

"I wasn't," my father said. "I wasn't lucky enough to be one. General Motors sent me to Ann Arbor to buy broaches from the Buhr Machine Tool Company on Greene Street. I met Joanne at a coffee shop in the Union when I went up to campus to see what college life was all about."

"Oh," Harriet Walker said. She stared at my father. Then she turned back to me. "Anyway, Danny," she said, "tell me some more about your mother. Is she tall like you?"

"She's tall for a woman," I said. "She's tall and thin and has long brown hair. Sometimes she wears it in a bun like yours." I thought for another moment. "She has a good sense of humor," I said. "When she's in the right mood she can be funny."

"I bet I'd like her," Harriet Walker said. "She and I could be girlfriends."

"That's true," my father said. "I can picture it."

"Does she like to live out here in the woods?" she asked. "Or is she a city girl at heart?"

"She doesn't like it in the country," I said. "That's why she's gone away for a while." I looked over at my father. He seemed to be on the verge of saying something. "She grew up in Chicago," I added, because I thought that would explain things better.

"Maybe I'll meet her someday," Harriet said. "Maybe we can go on a shopping spree together."

"I'll arrange it," my father said. "I'll arrange it when she comes back."

After dinner my father and Harriet Walker went out for a walk along the lake while I cleared the table and washed the dishes. As I stood at the sink with the pots and pans, I wondered where Harriet Walker would spend the night, whether she would sleep on the sofa in her slip, as she had done before, or whether she would sleep in my father's bed, which is what I thought would happen.

After I finished washing the dishes I went into the living room and lit the kerosene stove, because there was a chill in the air and I was afraid my fever might come back. I went into my bedroom and found my winter jacket in the back of my closet. It was a yellow canvas jacket with a heavy wool lining that my father had given me. He said that hunters used them because the canvas protected you from brush and branches, and the deep inside pocket was good for carrying game like pheasants and ducks and rabbits. I put the canvas jacket over my shoulders like a cape. Then I drew up a chair and sat warming my hands in front of the stove.

I tried to think of something interesting to occupy my mind, but nothing felt quite right. I didn't want to think about algebra or West Point or the paper I had to write on free will. And then I began to feel strange. Lonely, I guess, in a way that was new to me. Not from *being* alone exactly, which I was used to by now, but from *feeling* alone, cut off from people who could love me. Unconnected.

For a while I tried to feel less lonely by thinking about Cheryl Hibson, the girl I had known in Grand Rapids. I remembered one winter night, when I had skated with her on the frozen pond in Garfield Park, how her face had looked under the glare of the electric lights, the sound of her voice and laughter, the feel of her gloved hand as we circled the ice, the movements of her body conveyed so perfectly through the touch of our hands. I guess I was beginning to understand that girls were interesting to think about not just because they were different but because they were different while being nearly the same, with hips and breasts and high-pitched voices and a slightly altered way of looking at the world. Small differences, really, compared to everything a person is, but small differences you wanted to think about and that could entrance you.

I got up and went over to Harriet Walker's suitcase. I knelt down and laid it flat on the floor. I moved the tiny latches so the locks snapped open. Inside I found a leather vanity case, a blue silk nightdress, a pair of slippers with fluffy pom-poms, and a pair of underpants. I held up the underpants and saw how they were different from a man's underpants, just different in the way you would expect, made of nicer fabric and with flowered embroidery along the top. Next I opened the vanity case and found a lipstick, a compact, a brush, and some Kleenex. Along one side of the vanity case was a zippered compartment; inside I found a small silver-plated revolver.

I took the revolver out of the vanity case and checked it over. It was hardly any larger than my hand, just a small gun with a plastic handle that a woman would carry to protect herself. The barrel and the cylinder that held the bullets shined like a mirror.

I straightened out my arm and placed my finger on the trigger and pointed the revolver at different objects in the room—the kerosene stove, my father's armchair, a framed picture of the Parthenon—lining up the front sight and making little popping sounds with my mouth. Then I swung around and aimed at the door my father and Harriet Walker had gone through when they'd left for their walk.

I lined up the gun sight and held it steady on the center of the door and slowly eased off the safety. For a moment I imagined someone trying to break into the cabin, an escaped prisoner or a storm trooper with the German army, and I wondered if I would have the courage to shoot them—to shoot a human being if I had no other choice—and I decided that I would. I had fired guns on hunting trips with my father, and I knew how animals acted when they got hit by a gunshot, the sudden relaxation and awkward falling and stumbling that could look almost comical. A human being would act exactly the same way, I decided, not the twisting and thrashing you saw on TV westerns but just a sudden relaxation and dropping to the ground, a sort of collapsing, like a puppet whose strings have been cut.

Just then the telephone rang in the back of the cabin. I quickly closed the suitcase and set it back up against the wall, then went back to the phone. But I didn't pick it up; instead I stood and listened to it ringing, the shrill metallic sound loud in the small space of the cabin, as if whoever was calling had some important information to announce. It rang seven times without stopping. Finally I gave up and answered it.

"Hello, sweetheart," my mother said at the other end. "Is your father there?"

"No," I said, "he's gone out for a while. He's gone out for a walk along the lake."

"Oh, shoot," she said. "I wanted to talk to him."

"I can give him a message," I said.

"That's all right," she said. "I'll just talk to you for a while, sweetie. You're my best boy, anyway."

"All right," I said. Then I said, "How is Chicago?"

"Oh, it's fine," she said.

"Are you still going to the parties on Wednesday nights?"

"Yes," she said. "I go to them sometimes. And I go to the museum, too. They have a wonderful art museum in Chicago, Danny, filled with works by all the European masters. And the Impressionists, too. They're the ones who broke away and discovered a new way of looking at things. It's marvelous, really."

"That's interesting," I said, and I thought to myself that it *was* interesting because I'd heard about the works of European masters— Rembrandt and Leonardo da Vinci and so forth—but I thought you only saw those works in magazines and books. And I also thought it was interesting that artists could find a new way of looking at the world after so many years and that other people would enjoy it.

"How is your father doing, Danny?" my mother asked. "Is he selling truckloads of power tools?"

"I think he's doing fine," I said. "He's going to some different towns."

"Well, that's good," she said. "That shows initiative. He is a hard worker. I'll give him that."

Then I asked: "What if Dad can't build the house this spring, Mom?"

My mother was silent for a long time, even though I believed she knew the answer to my question. At least a minute passed without any words being spoken. I could hear her breath coming and going in the receiver, a gentle rush of air flowing down the wires.

"We'll cross that bridge when we come to it, Danny," she said finally. "Right now your father is confident about his prospects. He's convinced he can square the circle."

"What does that mean?"

"It's when you try to do the impossible, or at least the very difficult. Live in the north woods and make a lot of money. That's a project most people wouldn't touch. But your father seems to think he can do it. He has the optimism of a boy. I'm sure you've seen your share of it."

My mother's voice changed when she made these last remarks, and I suddenly remembered that she was mad at my father, mad that he was trying to do something impossible or difficult when we depended on him. Depended on him for money, I mean. And I remembered the reason she was in Oak Park wasn't just because she liked living in the city, but because my father had broken a sort of promise, and she wanted him to know it.

Suddenly I became aware of a heaviness in my hand, and I realized I was still holding Harriet Walker's revolver. And for some reason it frightened me, frightened me very much, to be holding something that could deliver death in just an instant—an instant of anger or carelessness or fear or stupidity—and I wanted to get rid of it.

"I should go now, Mom," I said. My voice was shaking, and I was suddenly very nervous. I put the revolver into the inside pocket of my canvas jacket. "I've got homework to do tonight."

"All right, sweetheart. Give your dad a big kiss for me."

"I will. Good-bye."

"Good-bye, sweetheart. I love you."

When Harriet Walker and my father came back into the house they were laughing. My father was imitating a man who had a peculiar way of talking. "Yup, yup, yup," he said, in a funny voice. "Yup, yup, yup."

"Stop that, Jim," Harriet Walker said. "That's cruel."

I had finished my algebra homework and was lying on my bed in my pajamas reading a book about curious and unusual things in the world of mathematics. I was reading the part about how the Romans were held back in their civilization because they didn't have a good system for working with numbers, only Roman numerals that couldn't be multiplied and divided.

Harriet Walker came into my bedroom holding a tiny bouquet of dried leaves and grasses. I lay the open book across my chest.

"Here's something pretty." She held the bouquet out to me. "Pretty things are good for people recovering from being sick. It makes them realize that life is still worth living. All the nursing guides will tell you that."

I took the bouquet and smelled it. It had the fresh smell of being outdoors. "Thanks," I said.

My father came into the bedroom and put his hand on Harriet Walker's shoulder. She reached up and put her hand on top of his, and their fingers sort of laced themselves together, just like I'd seen Amber and Wayne do that afternoon. With three people in my bedroom it seemed very crowded.

"We're going to watch some TV," my father said. "*I've Got a Secret* comes on in a few minutes. Harriet's a big fan of Garry Moore. I think she has a crush on him." Harriet Walker turned her head and slapped my father's hand in a playful way. "You're welcome to join us if you're done with your homework," my father added.

"No thanks," I said. "I think I'm going to bed. I feel kind of tired."

"He's probably still recovering, Jim," Harriet Walker said. "His system is still fighting bugs."

She came over and leaned down and kissed me on the forehead. "Good night, sweet prince," she said, and she smiled with her face up close to mine. "May a thousand angels fly you to your rest."

"Thank you," I said.

"Give him one for me, too, Harriet," my father said from the doorway. "He's too old to get kisses from his father, so I'll have to do it by proxy."

Harriet Walker kissed me again, and this time she made a big smacking sound. Her mouth was cool from being outside.

"Good night," she said again.

Then they both went out of my bedroom and closed the door.

I woke up after being asleep for only a short time. I knew it had only been a short time because I could hear my father and Harriet Walker watching TV in the next room. I think they were watching a movie because I heard a man and a woman talk about killing someone and then I heard orchestra music rise up like they use in movies to draw attention to the important moments.

"Watch this," I heard Harriet Walker say. "Something's going to happen here."

"I'm watching," I heard my father say. "I'm watching."

When I woke up the next time it was the middle of the night because everything was dark and there were no sounds of any kind, no sounds of people talking or of the TV playing or of anything. I thought about getting up and going out into the living room, but I didn't know what I would find there and so I stayed in my bed, looking at the silent shadows of tree branches sliding back and forth across the ceiling.

I heard an owl hoot, then the howl of a coyote, way off in the distance. Then I heard voices outside my window.

I rolled over and lifted the edge of the window shade. My father and Harriet Walker were standing just a few feet away from the cabin. I could barely make them out in the darkness, but I could tell it was them. They were standing side by side, holding hands. Harriet Walker's suitcase was on the ground.

I watched them through the window. They were standing in the darkness. My father said something in a low voice that I couldn't understand, and Harriet Walker said something back. Then she moved closer and leaned her head against his shoulder.

Out in the woods I saw a flicker of light. After a moment I could tell it was the headlights of a car coming through the woods along the two-track road. It came slowly, the headlights bouncing crazily and casting beams of light out onto the tree trunks, throwing shadows that swept the air like giant blades.

My father and Harriet Walker took a few steps away from the cabin. The car came up and stopped. Inside a light came on for a moment, and I saw that the driver was a woman wearing a head scarf and a bulky coat.

"Well, here she is," Harriet Walker said. This time she spoke in a slightly louder voice. "Good night, then, Jim."

"Good night, Harry," my father said. "I can't thank you enough for all your help."

"Don't mention it," Harriet Walker said. "I guess I'm just an angel of mercy."

"I care for you a lot," my father said. "I think that's clear."

"Sure," she said. "I know that."

She leaned forward and kissed my father on the mouth, holding one hand flat against his chest. Then she walked over to the car and got inside. I had a glimpse of her face beneath the dome light, her dark hair loose and falling around her shoulders, her skin pale and without makeup. Then the door closed and the light went out and the car backed around and headed out in the direction it had come, the red taillights becoming fainter, slowly disappearing through the tangle of tree trunks.

I lay in my bed, listening. After a moment I heard the door to the cabin open and close. Then water ran for a minute in the kitchen sink, and I heard the clink of a glass being set down. Then the door of my room opened, and I saw my father standing in the doorway, just the black outline of his body against a dim gray background.

"What's happening?" I said into the darkness. "Why did Harriet leave?"

My father came over and sat on the edge of my bed; the mattress sagged under his weight so that I rolled against him. He sat with his hands together and his elbows on his knees, looking out into my room.

"We decided it was best for her to leave," he said. "Her girlfriend came and picked her up."

"Why didn't she stay?"

"She stayed for a while," he said. "But then we decided it wasn't a good idea."

"Did she sleep in your bed?" I asked, because I believed that was what he'd wanted her to do. "Did you have sex with her?"

My father turned his head sharply and looked at me with a surprised expression. I'm sure it was the first time he'd ever heard me speak that way and I knew it would upset him. He did not talk that way himself, not that I had ever heard.

"Is that what you thought was going to happen?" he said. He smiled in a pained way. "I guess it makes sense. You're not stupid."

"I thought you would sleep with her," I said. "Because that's what men and women do. I know that."

"Well, that's what I thought, too, Danny. And maybe it would have been all right."

"Why didn't you?"

He made a kind of grunting noise. Maybe it was a laugh. Or an expression of pain. I couldn't really tell.

"There's a little problem about being married to your mother."

"But she's not here."

"No, but we're still married. We've taken vows."

I didn't say anything.

"And there was another problem," he continued, after a pause. "I couldn't forget about you being asleep over here. The sweet prince sleeping with a thousand angels."

"That's all right," I said, although I didn't know why I said that or what it meant.

"No," he said, and there was a slight edge in his voice this time. "It's not all right. Maybe it'll become all right, but it's not all right now."

We were silent for a few moments then, as if we didn't know the words to use for the complicated subjects that should come next. I could tell he was troubled about having sent Harriet Walker away and that a part of him wished she was still there, waiting in his bed for him to return, ready to have sex if that's what he wanted her to do or to hold his hand and let him talk about the things that worried or upset him or just do nothing at all, simply be close to another human being while he was asleep and helpless. And it frightened me to know that he was confused about Harriet Walker—uncertain about what the right thing was to do—because I depended on him to know things.

He crossed his legs and folded his arms as if he was planning to stay in my room for a long time. And then I had a surprising thought: that in the absence of Harriet Walker he wanted to be close to *me* —that in some strange way I was a substitute, a place he could direct his strongest feelings—to be on hand to protect me from danger, if it ever came to that, because *that* was a commitment he could devote himself to wholeheartedly. At least for a while. A single night.

My father stared out into my darkened room. I could see the white reflections of his watchful eyes. I knew he would be in my room for a long time. And I felt better about it. Better than I had felt just the moment before.

After a while I rolled over and went back to sleep.

Chapter Ten

IN THE WEEKS THAT FOLLOWED the trip to Granite Falls, I saw quite a bit of Amber and Wayne. It got to be a routine. They would pick me up at school after Wayne got off work at Patterson's Lumber, and we would drive out to some lonely spot in the countryside, an abandoned farmhouse or a scenic overlook along the banks of the Muskegon River or a woodlot at the end of a logging trail. Usually we would sit in Wayne's Plymouth with the windows down and listen to rock-and-roll music from WTCU in Traverse City and smoke cigarettes and talk about whatever came to mind: like whether Ford or Chevy pickups were the best or how to cook fish over an open campfire or if a radioactive cloud would wipe out all life on earth or whether there would be a few survivors. Most of the time Wayne did the talking. He would act as if he were an authority on any subject, giving his opinions in a confident voice that made you feel you had to go along—or else risk having a big argument. Amber would sit silently and draw figures in her sketchbook, glancing up from time to time and smiling but otherwise not really paying much attention.

Usually we'd simply talk for an hour or two and then drive back into town. But on some days, after a half hour or so, Amber and Wayne would suddenly leave the car and go off by themselves for a while. It was as if some secret signal had passed between them. Then I would sit in the Plymouth with my feet propped up on the dashboard, a book opened across my lap, knowing that they were lying together in a grassy meadow or under the sheltering branches of a large tree, proclaiming their love and doing the things they'd done in the park at Granite Falls.

I never understood exactly why they wanted to have me along on these excursions, or were willing to, although on Amber's part I'd decided it was because I made a kind of balance to Wayne, or at least a balance to the things in Wayne she did not like and hoped to change. Sometimes as a joke she would call me "Good Wayne" and ask Wayne to pay attention to some idea I had told her about or a word I had used. And sometimes, during one of Wayne's endless harangues, she would interrupt to ask *my* opinion about some altogether different matter, as if it was something that had been troubling her and she needed an immediate answer to what NATO was for or whether southern schools should have to take in Negroes or how a jet airplane worked. She would listen very seriously to my reply, her gaze fixed intently on my face, her head nodding slowly as she registered each piece of information. She believed, I think, that I was different from the people she had grown up around and that my interest in school and my background as a city boy gave me some special insight, as if I knew about a place she could escape to, and I might someday, in some unguarded moment, give away the secret of making that trip.

As for me, the reason I liked spending those afternoons with Amber and Wayne was much simpler: I had nothing else to do. I had not made friends among my classmates, and I had not found a girlfriend of my own. And I suppose I enjoyed being with two people who were slightly older than me, that connection to the authority that comes with a few extra years of age, Wayne's easy profanity, and his offhand references to minor sorts of criminality, all of which was completely different from the way I'd been raised. I suppose that in some odd way I even liked the times when

Amber and Wayne went off together, that connection to lust and sex, a sort of secondhand exposure to the things that lay in store for me someday.

One afternoon when Amber and Wayne picked me up, there was a girl in the car, a girl with long dark hair done up in a complicated wavy style, pale green eyes, and a pockmarked face covered with heavy makeup. She was skinny and flat-chested and she looked a little older than me, maybe fifteen or sixteen. As I got into the backseat she smiled and whispered, "Hi." She was wearing a starched white dress that reminded me of a nurse's uniform. Over that she wore a blue satin jacket with *Charlene* stitched in red scripted letters on the front pocket.

"This is Charlene," Amber said, turning around. "She's a good friend of mine." Amber smiled at me in a tentative way, and I remembered what Wayne had said that day in the park about finding a girl for me.

"Hi," I said to Charlene. She smiled and pushed over so that she was sitting close to my side. Her thin leg pressed up against my own.

Wayne drove through town and out along the river, following the same route we had taken on the day we'd gone to Granite Falls. I asked Charlene what grade she was in, and she said she wasn't in any grade but had dropped out of school and was working as a beautician at a shop in McBride. "I'm learning hairstyling through a correspondence course," she said.

"How do you study hairstyling through the mail?" I asked.

"That's what everyone wants to know," she said. "It's because a lot of it is reading. Health and sanitation rules. And the science of hair and how it grows." She looked over at me and smiled. "And there's written tests, too."

"You're lucky to know what you want to do with your life."

"Yes," she said. "I am."

We were silent for a while, and then I became aware of the gentle pressure of Charlene's thigh riding against my own. It was just a slight sensation, but somehow it felt magnified, as if all the nerves of my body were concentrated there.

I turned and stared out the window, trying not to think about Charlene's leg. Outside, a flock of crows was gathered in a field of harvested corn, thousands of them it seemed, just standing among the stubbly rows of silage. Then all at once, as if on a signal, they lifted up and moved off toward the tree line, a massive black cloud shaping and reshaping itself as it moved through the currents of air.

"They give you a wooden head with a wig on it," Charlene said, watching the crows. "Then you do a hairstyle and mail it to them in a special box that keeps it from getting mussed up. Then they send you back another head to work on." She turned and looked at me. "That's how you get the experience with hair."

"That's interesting," I said.

"For the last part I go to Detroit for three months and work in a shop on Woodward Avenue. Then I graduate." She looked straight ahead with a serene expression on her face, as if she could see her life unfolding in a nice way out through the windshield.

"Charlene's always had an artistic streak," Amber said, turning around. "Though she was never too good at regular school. I think you'd agree with that, wouldn't you, Charlene?"

"I always ended up in the slow group," Charlene said. "Then they did some tests and found out I had a problem." She looked over at me, and I saw that her eyes were very green, greener than any I'd ever seen before. "I see words funny," she continued, still looking into my face. "Turned around and backwards. So I couldn't learn how to read. By the time they found out what was wrong, it was too late for me to catch up."

"That's too bad," I said.

She took my hand and squeezed it, then held it on her lap between both of hers. "It's all right that I can't read too well. There's still a lot of things I can do."

"Maybe you'll have your own beauty shop someday, Charlene," Amber said. "I'd come."

"I'd like that," Charlene said. "I know some styles that could take advantage of your features."

Up in front, Wayne reached across Amber and punched opened the glove box. He took out a small flask of whiskey and unscrewed it with his teeth; then he spit the metal cap onto the floor.

"Here's some fun juice," he said, holding up the flask so we could see the label, which had a picture of a turkey on it. He tipped the bottle up and took a long swallow, his throat working as the liquid went down. Then he held the bottle out for Amber.

"I guess I won't," Amber said. She made a face. "I never learned to like it."

"That's okay," Wayne said. "It's more for the rest of us." He reached his arm back over the seat to where Charlene and I were.

I had never tasted whiskey before but I thought I should do it now, with Wayne and Amber and Charlene there, so I tipped the bottle up and let a good amount run into my mouth. It burned and had an oily taste and seemed more like medicine than something you drank for fun. I held it in my mouth and let it go down my throat a little at a time.

"Not bad, huh, Danny?" Wayne said, looking at me in the rearview mirror.

"It's okay," I said. "It's good." I held the bottle up and pretended to take another swallow, then handed it over to Charlene, who took a long swallow before handing it back up to Wayne.

"Charlene's no coward," Wayne said. "Unlike some people I could mention."

"Shut up, Wayne," Amber said. She sounded mad. "I guess I know more about whiskey than most people do."

"Her stepdaddy's a drunk," Wayne said, looking at me in the rearview mirror. "That's what she's trying to say."

"Just keep your mouth shut, Wayne," Amber said. "That's nobody's business."

"He gets drunk and smacks around that fat woman he's married to."

"Just shut up," Amber said again.

"Sometimes he smacks Amber, too."

Amber looked back over her shoulder and smiled at me in an embarrassed way.

"That's all right. I've seen my own dad drunk lots of times," I said, which wasn't exactly true.

"There you are," Wayne said. "You're two of a kind."

We were driving past the apple orchards where we'd seen the Mexican pickers. The trees were bare of apples now and leafless, too, stark and lonely-looking skeletons lined up against the deep blue autumn sky. Wayne slowed and turned off the road onto a tractor path that led back through the orchard. He drove a long way between the rows of apple trees to where the orchard stopped and the woods began. The car bounced crazily on the rough terrain. Amber and Charlene laughed and yelled at Wayne to slow down.

"You'll wreck the car," Amber said. Both her hands were braced up on the dashboard.

Wayne laughed and gunned the engine to pick up more speed. Then he hit the brakes hard, and we came to a skidding stop.

"What are we doing here?" I asked.

"There's some apples left on the trees," Wayne said. "The pickers never get them all. We're going to fill up a couple of bushel baskets, and Amber's going to make some pies."

"I never said I'd make two bushels worth," Amber said. "Just a couple of pies is all."

Wayne opened the trunk where he had some bushel baskets. He handed one to me and kept one for himself. "You and Charlene go that way," he said. He pointed off to the west where the sun was going down. "Amber and me'll go this other way." He put a hand on my shoulder and looked into my face with a solemn expression. "And don't you kids do anything you'd be ashamed to tell your mommies about." Then he gave me a big wink and slapped me on the back.

"That Wayne's crazy," Charlene said after we'd started walking in the direction Wayne had pointed.

"Yeah," I said.

"But he's funny, too."

"Funny like a crutch," I said.

"Like a what?"

"A crutch."

Charlene looked at me with her face scrunched into a question. "I don't get it," she said.

"It's like saying he's not funny, only in a backward way."

Charlene furrowed her brow and stared down at the ground. "Oh," she said after a moment. She laughed in a sort of forced way.

We found some apples and started to fill up the bushel basket. Some of the apples were on the ground and some were still hanging up in the trees. Twice I climbed up to get an apple from a high branch. Charlene stood down below and looked up at me through the branches, smiling and looking pretty in her starched white dress and blue satin jacket. Once she threw a rotten apple at me, and I had to dodge it while balancing on a branch, which must have looked funny because it made her laugh. Then I threw an apple back down at her, not to hit her but just a lazy throw that made her skip off to one side.

"You think we've got enough?" Charlene said, after a while. We were holding the bushel basket between us and walking down a row of trees. The bushel basket was almost full.

"I guess so," I said. "Maybe we should head back?"

"Let's rest a minute," Charlene said.

We went over and sat down under one of the apple trees. The sun was low in the sky and golden light slanted through the orchard, glancing off the ground and lighting up the underside of the trees. Everything seemed bright yellow.

"Amber says you're smart," Charlene said. She dug in the ground with a little stick. "Tell me something smart."

I looked at her, thinking she was teasing, but when I saw her face I knew she was serious. *Smart* to her was probably just a quality like any other—like living in a certain place or having a drunk for a father or going to beautician's school—just a plain fact of life that could be talked about like any other.

"I like mathematics the most," I said. "But it's hard to explain anything without having a pencil and paper."

"So tell me something else," Charlene said. She made a furrow in the dirt with her stick. Then she threw the stick away and scooted over closer to where I was sitting.

"I pay attention to the space program," I said. She smiled into my face in a kind of rapturous way. "I know how rockets work and the different kinds there are."

"Okay," Charlene said. She put her hand up onto my shoulder and stared into my face like she'd noticed something there that needed to be examined.

I tried to think of what to say next, feeling Charlene's gaze on my face. At first I thought I'd tell her about the dog the Russians had sent up in the satellite, but then I remembered how he'd died from lack of oxygen, and I didn't want to have to tell her that. Then I tried to think of something else, but it was hard to think clearly with Charlene looking at me that way, her green eyes so intense and filled with curiosity.

"You have pretty eyes, Charlene," I said all of a sudden. It was just an impression that came out ahead of any thinking.

"Thank you," she said, still looking into my face. Then she said, "You can kiss me if you want to."

I looked at Charlene, at her green staring eyes and her red slightly parted lips and her skin dusted with pale powdery makeup that seemed to make her face glow in the setting sun. Shadows of the bare tree branches moved over the ground and across her face. It was as if we were both caught together in a giant fishnet.

I had never kissed a girl before but I wanted to kiss Charlene. So

I leaned forward and Charlene leaned forward and we closed our eyes and our mouths came together. And it felt strange, different from how I expected, Charlene's lips soft and smooth and alive and slightly sticky from the lipstick and moving and then opening and then opening mine.

I pulled away. "What are you doing?" I asked.

Charlene laughed. "That's a way to kiss I learned about. Haven't you heard about it? It's nice."

She closed her eyes and we started to kiss again, kissing for a long time now, our mouths opening and closing and then opening again, each holding the other's shoulders and feeling the other's breath, the smell of whiskey strong and the smell of Charlene's perfume strong and rising up and the smooth powdery feeling of Charlene's makeup when my mouth glided onto her skin and the exciting stickiness when my mouth came back and found her lips.

Charlene pulled back. She stared up into my face, her green eyes solemn. Her breath was coming fast and so was mine. "You can touch me if you want to," she whispered in a quick voice. "It's all right. Other boys do it. I like it."

I leaned forward and pressed my face into Charlene's neck. My hand moved lower on the blue satin jacket until I found the edge and my hand went under to the place where I knew Charlene's breast was. And I could feel the swell of it, a small firmness beneath the hard-starched fabric, almost nothing but a smoothness and a loveliness and a mystery. And I wanted more than anything in the world to bear against it, to feel the sweet yield of Charlene's warm flesh against my hand, just like I'd seen Wayne do with Amber.

But something stopped me. I just froze, my hand resting lightly on Charlene's white dress. And I think part of it was me, some limit to what I wanted to do on that particular afternoon in early November or dared to do or could do. And part of it was the picture of Wayne and Amber that came into my head, the two of them together in the long grass along the river, lost in their feelings and saying they were in love. And part of it was Charlene, her eagerness for something she understood and had done before but I had not.

I moved my hand back up onto Charlene's shoulder. I felt her softness beneath the hard-starched fabric of her dress. I kept my face pressed into her neck.

After a moment Charlene stirred; it was as if a feeling had suddenly left her and been replaced by another. Her breathing slowed. Then she swallowed, and I felt the muscles of her throat move against my cheek.

"I'm sorry," I said. I squeezed my eyes shut.

"That's all right," Charlene whispered. Her hand came up to the back of my neck. She stroked it lightly. "It was nice."

"I like you, Charlene," I said. "You're wonderful."

"Shhh," she said. "Just be quiet now. That's all you need to do."

I held Charlene, my face pressed into the smooth curve of her neck. I felt the faint touch of her fingers on the back of my head, just the barest sensation. I squeezed my eyes shut to keep any tears from coming.

When we got back to the car, Wayne and Amber were already there, leaning against the front fender with their arms around each other's shoulders. Wayne was holding the flask of whiskey. It looked almost empty.

"That was too long for just picking apples," Wayne said. "I smell a rat called feeling-up-Charlene." He sounded drunk.

"Shut up, Wayne," I said. "It's not any of your business."

"Whoa," Wayne said. "I guess that settles it." He looked at Amber and grinned. "Denial is nine parts guilty conscience."

"Leave them alone," Amber said. She looked over at me and then she looked away.

"I'm just saying he felt her up," Wayne said. "Not fucked her." He turned and looked again at Amber. "Which is exactly what you wanted to happen, if you remember."

Amber gave Wayne an angry look. Then she looked over at me and Charlene.

"He's just an idiot sometimes," Amber said with a forced smile. "Don't pay any attention to him."

"What did you say?" Wayne said, and he said it in a hard voice.

He threw the empty bottle onto the ground, and it shattered against a rock, scattering bits of sparkling glass. Then he came around and stood in front of Amber and placed both hands on the fender so that she was trapped in between.

"I said you were an idiot," Amber repeated. She looked at him with a defiant expression.

Wayne glared at Amber, his face up close to hers, as if he was trying to figure out what to do next. And I thought that one of the choices was to strike Amber and the other was to say something that would make her feel afraid.

"You better watch your mouth," Wayne said, "if you want that baby of yours to have a daddy some day."

Amber looked at Wayne, trying to stand up to his angry stare. Her eyes were narrowed and there was a hardness in her expression that I'd never seen before. And I knew in that moment that she didn't love Wayne and didn't want to marry him. And I knew something else, too: that she wished she could tell him that but couldn't.

Suddenly Amber's expression changed. It just collapsed in an instant, like a child who's been scolded for being naughty. Her glance darted back and forth between Wayne and the ground.

"You know I didn't mean it, honey," Amber said. She sounded frightened now. "I was just teasing you."

"That's better," Wayne said. He smiled a mean smile at her.

"You *are* an idiot," I said.

Wayne turned slowly in my direction. "What did you say?"

"I said you're an idiot. And a thief, too."

Wayne stared at me with a puzzled expression, as if he couldn't remember who I was or what I was doing there. And I knew he was trying to figure out what to do next, just like he'd done a moment ago with Amber, and the choices this time were to rush forward and hit me like he'd hit the man in Granite Falls or to laugh and make it seem like I wasn't worth bothering about.

He walked over and stood in front of me, his thumbs hooked inside his belt. I could smell the whiskey on his breath. Charlene backed away.

"Stop it, Wayne," Amber said. "He didn't mean anything by it."

"Well, maybe he should apologize then," Wayne said. He moved his face up close to mine. "If he didn't mean it, he should say he's sorry."

"Maybe you should apologize to Amber first," I said.

Wayne was taller than I was, and he had a man's hard muscles in his arms and shoulders. He could beat me in a fight—I knew that—but I thought if I moved quickly I could land a couple of punches that would make him sorry for what he'd said to Amber, even if I ended up getting hurt myself.

I stood as tall as I could stand, my arms at my side. I wrapped my fingers into fists.

"He never felt me up," Charlene said, all of a sudden. "We just kissed."

Wayne turned and looked over at Charlene. He blinked a couple of times, as if his concentration had been broken. Off in the distance I heard the thud of a shotgun blast, followed by the sound of a dog barking. Then Wayne laughed.

"Okay," he said. He smiled and put his arm around my shoulder. I smelled the stink of whiskey and I smelled his sweat, too, a dank barnyard smell. "I take back all the mean talk," he said. "You're a regular gentleman, Danny. A little Lord Fauntleroy. And I should be more like you are, just like Amber is always telling me." He squeezed my shoulder. Then he kissed me on the cheek.

I shrugged and pulled away. "Goddamn it," I said, wiping my cheek with my hand. Wayne laughed some more. Charlene laughed, too.

"Let's get out of here," Wayne said. "None of this is fun anymore."

"You can say that again," Amber said, although she sounded relieved, glad that a fight had not happened between Wayne and me.

We started walking toward Wayne's car.

"It's true," Charlene said, after we'd gone a few steps. "We only kissed."

We drove back to McBride in the gathering darkness. As we came into town the streetlights were just coming on along Main Street. Only a few people were out on the sidewalks. Most of the stores had already closed. There were just a few dim lights and shadows showing through the store windows.

Wayne dropped Charlene off in front of a small frame house on the edge of downtown. I thought she would kiss me before getting out of the car, but she just opened the door and stepped out onto the pavement. "See you later," she said, leaning back into the car. She smiled at me. "I had fun."

"Me, too," I said. I reached out to touch her but she was already gone.

Wayne headed out of town on the road that went toward the lake. Amber sat beside him, her hand resting on the back of his neck. Whatever had been wrong between them was evidently over now and forgotten.

A lot of things were going through my mind, and I thought they were things that anyone would wonder about. Not unusual in any way. I wondered why Amber had wanted me to get together with Charlene. And I wondered why Amber acted differently when she was around Wayne than when she was with me alone. And I wondered if I'd be brave enough to fight Wayne someday if it ever came to that.

"Take it easy, tiger," Wayne said after I'd got out of the car on the highway at the end of my road. "No hard feelings, right?"

"No," I said. I was standing just outside the open rear door.

He leaned back over the front seat and looked out at me. "Let's get together tomorrow," he said. "We can have some of that pie Amber's going to make."

I looked at Amber. She was staring out through the windshield as if she had her mind on something else.

"Okay," I said. I slammed the door and walked out into the darkness toward the cabin.

Chapter Eleven

THE NEXT DAY I STOOD BY the flagpole after school waiting for Amber and Wayne, just like I'd done every afternoon for the last couple of weeks. But they didn't come and finally, after about half an hour, I gave up and walked over to the field where the football team was practicing. I stood and watched through the chain-link fence as the players did their blocking and tackling drills, the coach standing off to the side and blowing his whistle and yelling instructions, the boys breathing hard and grunting when they collided in their pads and helmets. After a while the team divided into two squads and ran plays against each other. I spotted the boy who played the end position, a lanky red-haired boy I had seen around school, and I followed him with my eyes, paying close attention to how he blocked and ran the pass routes. I tried to imagine myself doing those things next year when I would try out for the team, and it didn't seem so hard, watching from the sidelines like that.

After a while I started to feel kind of lonely, sort of cut off from things and people. Part of it was because Wayne and Amber had forgotten about me, I think, and part was because I was watching the football players from the sidelines. I walked three blocks over to Main Street where I knew there'd be some people. I started at the north end of town and walked all the way through to the other end, stopping a few times to look in store windows and once to examine the posters for the movie *Giant*, which was playing at the movie theater: one showed Elizabeth Taylor staring dreamily into Rock Hudson's eyes, and another showed James Dean looking smug and cocky in a cowboy hat. Just about then I started thinking about Charlene. I don't know why but I just did. I thought about walking with her through the apple orchard and joking around with her and kissing her and how I'd almost touched her breast. It was stupid that I hadn't touched her breast, I decided, especially after she'd said it would be all right, and I couldn't understand why I hadn't done it. And then something seemed to change, because the more I thought about Charlene the more I couldn't *stop* thinking about her, and the more I couldn't stop thinking about her the more I wanted to see her, and to see her right away.

Julia's Shear Delight was the only hair salon in town, as far as I knew, so that's where I went to find Charlene. It was a single-story cement-block building standing between a dry cleaner and a bowling alley. The outside was plain, but inside it was crowded and bright and cheerful and sweet smelling. Five chairs were lined up along one side where the hairdressers worked.

I spotted Charlene way off in the back, working on a gray-haired woman with curlers in her hair and a blue towel draped over her shoulders. At first she didn't see me, but after a minute she glanced up, and I caught her eye and half waved, and she looked surprised and half waved back. She held up one finger and then, after a couple more minutes, she walked the gray-haired woman over to a hair dryer and came up front.

"What're you doing here?" she said with a smile. "Don't you know this place is off-limits to men?" She took my hand and led me out the front door.

"I just thought I'd come by and say 'hi,'" I said.

"Well, aren't you sweet," Charlene said, and she squeezed my hand. Then she reached into the pocket of her smock and took out a pair of sunglasses and unfolded them and put them on.

"I'm a movie star," Charlene said. She put one hand on the back of her head and pretended she was posing for a camera.

"You could be one," I said. "You're pretty enough for it."

"I'm the one that man turned into a princess. Grace Kelly."

She turned and posed in another direction.

"I was thinking that maybe we could do something after you get off work," I said.

"Oh," Charlene said. She stopped posing and looked at me. I saw my reflection in the lenses of her sunglasses, two small misshapen copies of myself.

"Like do what?" she said. She started walking slowly along the sidewalk.

"I don't know," I said, following after her. "Maybe we could go bowling."

"I'm not too good at sports," she said. "It's because of that same problem I told you about with reading."

"Okay," I said. "We can do something else then. Whatever you want."

"I don't know. . . ." She glanced back over her shoulder and flashed me a sort of nervous smile. Then she was quiet for a moment. Then she said, "I'm not so sure we're a good match. You're nice . . . but you're sort of different. Kind of brainy. I think maybe you're too brainy for me."

"I'm not that way all the time," I said. I forced a smile, even though she wasn't looking at me.

"I know Amber likes you," Charlene said, speaking as if she hadn't even heard what I had said. "But *she's* kind of different, too, if you want to know the truth. I like her a lot but she's different. She's *gotten* different."

"What are you talking about?"

"Well . . ." Charlene stopped walking and turned around and faced me. "She used to be fun—always ready to do something crazy. In fact she was pretty wild. But then a couple of years ago her daddy died and it seemed to change her. I can't exactly explain, but she got a lot more serious. And then a few months after that, her momma married that guy Ray and that seemed to change Amber even more. Or maybe it changed her momma. Because after she married Ray it was like she could only pay attention to him. Amber got pushed out."

Charlene folded her arms across her chest. She looked at me.

"How did her dad die?" I asked.

Charlene shrugged. "It was cancer, I think. One of those." She grimaced, like the subject made her queasy. Then she turned and started to examine a crack in the window of the bowling alley. "Her stepdaddy's mean," she said. She began tracing the crack with her fingertip. "And he drinks too much, too, just like Wayne said. But her momma didn't have much choice. She needed someone to take care of her and Amber. She took what she could get."

I stood watching Charlene trace the window crack with her fingertip, not knowing what I should say next. I wanted to steer the conversation back to her so I could make her change her mind about going out with me. And then I thought that maybe I should just go ahead and kiss her. I'd seen movies where men had kissed women who weren't interested in them, but then the women had changed their minds and started to kiss the men back. And I wondered if I would have the nerve to try that, just put my arms around Charlene and kiss her, and if she would eventually like it.

"Your new hairstyle looks great," I said.

She smiled happily. "It's called a chignon. It's good if your facial features aren't too large." She touched the side of her head in a dainty way. "It wouldn't work if you had big ears or a long nose."

"It looks great on you," I said. I stepped closer and touched the thick coil of braided hair at the back of her head. I was close enough now so that I could kiss her if I wanted to try.

"Be careful!" Charlene said. She ducked out from under my hand and stepped away. "You'll make it come loose."

Charlene smoothed back her hair on both sides with the palms of her hands. She frowned, as if she was afraid her hairdo had been ruined. I still wanted to kiss her, but now—with her ducking away like that—I didn't think it would happen.

"Don't look so sad," Charlene said, when she was finished smoothing her hair. "I bet there's plenty of girls who'd love to go out with you." She reached up and touched the corner of my mouth like she was trying to make me smile. "I'll think of one and tell you. Some girl who'd like to know about satellites and mathematics." She laughed, as if the statement was ridiculous. Then she stepped forward and kissed me lightly on the cheek.

"Now I've got to go," she said. "Mrs. Sheriden's under the dryer."

She smiled one last time and turned and walked back toward the hair salon. I watched her walking away, the feel of her lips still burning on my cheek. Then she went through the door of the hair salon, and the ghostly feeling went away.

After I left Charlene I walked through town again. I stopped in Glenn's Sporting Goods and looked at some fishing lures; then I went to the Dairy Bar and drank a Coke while I watched an older boy play pinball.

I was feeling a little angry because Charlene had turned me down—sad and angry both, I guess—and I began to think again if *any* girl would ever like me. Though deep down I realized that what Charlene had said was true: we didn't really belong together; we had nothing in common, no interests that overlapped, nothing we could make a conversation about. But then I thought of Amber and Wayne, and of Amber's mom and Ray, and of my own mother and father, and I realized that all of them had differences, too—things that didn't overlap—and yet they'd all still managed to get together. And then I wondered if *anyone* ever found exactly the right person to fall in love with or if you just found someone who was close to what you wanted and let it go at that.

At five o'clock I left the Dairy Bar and started walking in the direction of Highway 56, thinking I'd hitch a ride back out to the lake, which was something I'd done before. If I got a ride quickly I'd be home ahead of my father and could have dinner ready when he got there.

I had gone as far as the edge of town when I heard a car coming up behind me. When I turned around and stuck out my thumb I saw Amber smiling at me through the windshield of the Chevy pickup.

"Want a ride, handsome?" she said, leaning out the side window.

"Sure," I said.

"You and Wayne let me down," I said after I'd gotten into the pickup.

"What are you talking about?" She was looking back over her shoulder, waiting for an opening in the traffic. When one came she eased out the clutch and we started forward.

"You didn't pick me up like you said you would."

"Oh," she said. Then, after a pause: "Well, things have changed."

"What do you mean?"

"I've got a job now."

We were coming up behind a slow truck carrying cattle. Amber braked and downshifted into second gear, then accelerated and pulled out into the passing lane. I looked over as we passed the truck. Cows stared out through the slotted sides, their big brown eyes looking sort of sad and panicked, as if they knew what lay in store for them.

"I waitress at the Shamrock restaurant from noon to seven starting tomorrow," Amber continued, "so we won't be running all over hell and creation like we've been doing." She glanced over at me, then back ahead. "I decided I should start earning some money." Her gaze flicked over at me again. "I've waitressed before. I guess that's a talent you didn't know I had."

"Is it all right to waitress when you're pregnant?"

"Sure," she said. "At least for a few more months. Until I get too big to drag myself around. Or until people can't stand to look at me anymore."

"What does Wayne say about it?"

"I haven't told him yet." She stared ahead, her chin tipped up a little. "I guess I don't really care," she added after a pause. "He'll just have to like it."

I stopped asking questions then because I felt Amber had said as much as she wanted to say about her new job. But I was surprised she didn't care what Wayne would think, because I was pretty sure he wouldn't like it, and I'd seen how he could be when he was angry.

"Here," Amber said. She reached across and took a stack of index cards from under the visor. "Quiz me on my French words."

And that's what I did for the rest of the ride: I went through the words that Amber was studying on that day. *Tenir* and *circonstance* and *manquer* and *drôle* were some of them, and also the conjugation of the verbs *taire*, which means "to be quiet," and *abriter*, which means "to have a place to stay." It surprised me that she still wanted to learn French after dropping all her classes, because French didn't seem like something she would need to be a waitress at the Shamrock restaurant—or anyplace else in McBride.

We got to the lake, and Amber drove up to the back of her house. A light was on in the kitchen window. I saw the curtain drawn back and Amber's mother's face appear behind the glass; then it disappeared.

"Did you like Charlene?" Amber asked.

"She's nice," I said.

"Then you ought to see her again. She'd probably let you."

"Maybe I will," I said vaguely.

I didn't want to tell Amber that I'd just been to see Charlene— probably because I'd have to tell her that she turned me down. But part of me *did* want to tell her what Charlene and I had done in the apple orchard, to explain how it had felt to kiss her and to hold her in my arms, because in some strange way I felt that Amber would like to know about it. *She* had been the one who'd brought the two of us together, after all—Charlene and me—and I believed now that she'd done it as a sort of substitute for something she couldn't do for me herself. But I didn't know the words to express those feelings, and I guess I didn't want to admit that Amber was out of reach for me and needed to have a substitute. So I said something else.

"Amber."

"What?"

"How did you and Wayne get together in the first place?"

"What are you talking about?"

"How did you meet and decide you were in love? That's something I've wondered."

Amber put her hands up onto the steering wheel and looked ahead, like she was still driving the car.

"It wasn't anything amazing," she said. "We just started going out together one day. I don't even remember why. I guess everyone else was getting together, and so we thought we should, too. And then one night . . ." She stopped talking for a moment as if she was trying to think of the right words. "And then one night we went to a party, and Wayne got drunk and . . . well, I let him have what he wanted."

"But it was just that once."

She turned and looked at me with an expression that was hard to read—disappointment, maybe.

"It was then," she said, after a long pause. "But . . . you know . . . there were some times after."

"Wayne's a fool," I said, because I wanted it to be only about him now.

Amber kept looking at me with that disappointed expression. She looked at me for a long time. And I couldn't tell if it was herself she was disappointed in or if it was me—some lack of insight or failure to comprehend the situation—or if it was the world in general.

She placed her hands onto her lap and laced her fingers together across her stomach. "Nothing's perfect," she said, and she spoke in a small voice, almost a whisper. "That's a notion you've got to accept early or your life will turn into real tragedy." She kept staring down at her stomach, but I could see that her eyes were shining and I knew it was from tears. "That's my word to the wise for today, Danny. You can have it for free. That's my gift to you."

For a long time nothing happened. We just sat together in the pickup. Then Amber pulled the door handle and got out and went into the house.

Chapter Twelve

WHEN MY FATHER GOT HOME that night he announced that he wanted to eat at a restaurant in town rather than spend time fixing something at the cabin. He looked tired, drawn, and slightly worried, like the day had not been a good one for him. In the car driving to McBride, he talked about a deer-hunting camp he'd gone to years ago with Harry Sherwood in the years before my father was married and how he'd found an oak tree that had been shaped by Indians into a sort of cross and how he'd stood at its base and had good luck shooting deer. Harry Sherwood had been like a second father to him, he said, after his own father had died. He had taught him about hunting and fishing and how to get along in the woods, and he hoped that he and I could have those experiences, too, and that I would learn to love the outdoors and want to spend time in it.

"That's part of the reason I wanted to move up here," he said to me. "It's a life that's not available to very many boys. Not anymore. Everything's turning into cities and highways. There's no room left where a man can be alone."

"I like it here," I said, because I knew that's what he wanted to hear. He was trying to make a good life for us—I was convinced of that—but I think he didn't know how to do it anymore, or else things had changed in a way he hadn't yet come to grips with. He had forgotten how life is about trading—that's something my mother had said about him once—how you bargain with the parts of your life until you reach a good balance, something that works and feels comfortable, and don't worry about the rest.

When we got to McBride we drove down Mechanics Street, past the train depot and the Catholic church and into a neighborhood I had never been in before. The streets were lined with small wood-framed houses; most had lights on and through the windows I could see people going about their nighttime business: sitting at a table having dinner or reading a newspaper or relaxing in an armchair in the flickering glow of a TV screen. Just the normal things families do at night.

We turned a corner and went down a street and stopped in front of a small restaurant with a blue neon sign that said The Logging Camp. Through the large front window I saw a group of deer hunters seated around a table. They wore heavy woolen jackets with hunting licenses in plastic holders pinned to the middle of their backs. At another table a man and a woman were holding hands. On the walls hung tools for taking timber out of a forest: axes and cant hooks and climbing spikes and crosscut saws.

"So tell me what you studied today at school," my father said. We had taken seats up at the counter, away from the other customers. On the back wall a long mirror reflected the scene behind us. A pass-through window went back into the kitchen, with a ledge for setting plates of food and a wire for holding orders clipped up with clothespins. A blackboard gave the daily specials: today it was meat loaf with green beans and baked potato or pork loin with applesauce and salad.

"In math we learned about the polynomial equation," I said. "That's a shortcut way to solve polynomials."

"Tell me about it," my father said. He was reading the menu.

"It's just a formula that you memorize," I said.

"Does it always work?"

"As far as I know."

The waitress came and took our order. She was a short heavy

woman with the shadow of a mustache on her upper lip, and she walked in a slow, flat-footed way. Her pink uniform had a tiny white collar and a plastic name tag that said *Debbie*.

"What else?" my father said after she'd left.

"In history Mr. Miller talked about the Dred Scott decision."

"That's the one about the runaway slave, isn't it?"

"He wasn't a runaway," I said. "His owner took him into a free state and then died. Dred Scott thought he should be free because of that. But they said he couldn't come into the court to argue about it because he was a Negro."

"That seems harsh," my father said. He inserted the menu into the clip on the side of the wire basket that held the salt and pepper shakers. "I'd say we've made some progress since those days."

"I guess that's true," I said, because it seemed like a reasonable statement.

The waitress came back and set a mug of coffee on the counter for my father and a glass of milk for me. My father looked down at the steam rising from the liquid.

"Anything else?" he asked me.

"What?"

"Was there anything else interesting you learned today?" He took a trial sip of the coffee, slurping in a little air so it would not burn him.

"In English we read a poem by Robert Frost called 'The Death of the Hired Man.'"

"Well, you have me at a disadvantage there, son. That's something I don't know anything about."

I couldn't tell from his comment if he meant the poem itself or poetry in general. Either one could be true.

"It tells about an old man who comes back to a farm where he used to work. And then he dies."

"So it's about death," my father said. He took another sip of his coffee, looking over the rim back into the kitchen.

"It's more about what home is," I said. "What home means to different people."

"I don't follow you there, Danny."

Just then the waitress came and took our plates from the pass-through window, where they had been sitting, and set them in front of us. I had ordered a hot roast beef sandwich, and my father had ordered the pork loin with applesauce and salad. I thought about how I was going to answer him.

"It's like everybody needs a home of some kind to go to," I said after the waitress had gone away. I sat with my hands in my lap looking down at my food. "Even a lonely old man should have someplace to go where they have to take him in."

At the deer hunters' table everyone started to laugh. Then someone said, "I swear it's true. Ask Ed if you don't believe me. He'll vouch for me."

My father turned around to look at the hunters. One of them caught his eye and grinned. Then he raised a hand over another man's head and jabbed his forefinger in the air, as if he wanted my father to understand that the other man had caused all the ruckus. My father smiled and nodded his head.

"Those are true words," he said when he'd turned back. "I guess we're all hired men in one way or another."

"I guess so," I said.

We sat in silence and ate our dinners. I thought about "The Death of the Hired Man." But then all of a sudden I began to think about what had happened the day before in the apple orchard with Charlene. It was a memory that rushed into my head without any warning, out of nowhere really: how eager she had been, the way her breath had come so fast. And then I remembered something a boy had said at school about how girls liked to have sex just as much as boys did, and how they'd beg you for it at certain times. It had been a shocking thing to hear, different from anything I had ever expected, and it had bothered me until I decided it wasn't true. And I thought now—sitting there in The Logging Camp beside my father, eating a hot roast beef sandwich—that I still did not want to believe it. At least not about any of the girls I knew.

Next I thought about the house my father planned to build for us and I wondered whether it would be ready in the spring. We were sort of in between homes, I realized, and so maybe the truth of Robert Frost's poem was different for us, different from what it would be for most people and different from what it would become for us later, after we were back together again and settled. Then I thought about my mother and I tried to imagine how things would be different if she was there with us, seated on a stool between my father and me, smiling and looking pretty and making clever remarks. She had a way of picking up a gloomy situation and turning it around—that's something I remembered very well—a talent for finding the odd things that could make you laugh and engage your interest. Although I remembered, too, that she had another side, a side that could plunge her into long periods of silence—her "black spells" my father called them—and she would sometimes break out in bitter tears for no apparent reason or take to her bed with those headaches.

"Why don't you go down to Chicago and get Mom?" I said to my father all of a sudden. My voice sounded loud, coming after the long silence. "Make her come back."

"What are you talking about?" My father blinked, as if I'd interrupted his own private thoughts and he was coming back from them.

"You should go to Chicago and tell Mom she has to come home. Or whatever you call it where we are now."

I was thinking of Amber and Wayne now, how Amber had backed down when Wayne had gotten mad at her, and I thought that my father could do the same thing with my mother.

"That's not the way it works, Danny. She's free to make up her own mind about where she wants to be."

In the mirror behind the counter I saw the man and woman get up to leave. The hunters at the other table turned to watch them. The man held the woman's blue coat. She pinned the sleeves of her dress with her fingers and slid her arms into the coat. Then she turned and smiled at the man and touched his cheek.

I shifted my gaze over to my father's reflection. He was watching the man and woman, too. Then he moved his gaze over to mine, and we looked at each other through the mirror.

"Do you think she's ever coming back?" I said.

My father stared at me a moment. Then he set down his fork and stared off to the side.

"I don't know," he said. "She's said some different things lately, son, when we talk on the telephone."

"What things?"

My father pushed his plate away. Then he sat forward and leaned his elbows on the empty counter. "It doesn't matter," he said. "She's mixed-up. It's the kind of things people say when they're mixed-up."

I didn't say anything.

"I love her," he said after a while. He stared ahead at the pass-through window. But not as if he was looking at anything in particular. It was just an empty stare. A stare at nothing.

"And she loves me, too," he continued. "I'm convinced of that. And as long as that's true I know she'll be coming back."

Suddenly he turned in my direction. "Do you agree with that?" he asked.

I had never heard my father speak about love in such a frank way, and it shocked me as much as it had shocked me to hear the boy at school say that girls wanted to have sex. And what I decided in that moment was that my father was wrong: he did not understand the things that were happening to him, how he had made choices that had pushed my mother away. His life was broken, just like a machine that hasn't been properly cared for, and he didn't know how to put the pieces back together. And it occurred to me that it—his lack of knowing—was because he had not had a father himself and had not been told certain important things that fathers tell their sons. And then I wondered if I would lack the same important knowledge, because he did not have it to give to me.

"I don't think that's right," I said, answering his question with my own idea. "I think you have to go down there and bring her back."

My father looked at me. For a long time he just looked at me. Then he got up and went over to the jukebox that sat against one wall. He stared down at the list of songs, then dropped a quarter into the slot and pushed one of the plastic buttons. Inside the machine, a light came on and the mechanism started to move.

"This is a song your mother likes," my father said when he got back to the counter. He smiled at me as if he thought this was something I would like to know. "We'll play it in her honor."

He sat on the stool with his arms folded and a calm expression on his face and we listened to the song, which was "Tennessee Waltz" by Patti Page, while I finished eating my dinner. And all I could think about was that I wished he had not played the song that my mother liked, because it didn't seem right to play it when she wasn't there to enjoy it, and it didn't seem right to play it in a place like The Logging Camp, which was dark and dingy and not a place my mother would have chosen for herself.

That night I lay on my bed reading my history book, while my father talked to my mother on the telephone in the back of the cabin. He spoke in a slow, steady voice, as if he were explaining complicated things that needed to be expressed in careful language. He spoke for a long time and I waited, half reading and half listening to his occasional, disconnected words, thinking that he would eventually call me and let me talk to her. But he hung up without calling me.

I stopped reading and lay the book open across my chest. From the kitchen I heard the refrigerator door open and close, then light switches being snapped off in other parts of the cabin. My father called out "Good night, son," and I called out "Good night" back to him.

I lay on my bed a while longer, thinking about what I would've said to my mother if I could have talked to her. I decided I would've told her about "The Death of the Hired Man" because she liked poetry and would probably have an interesting opinion about it, and I decided I would've told her about eating the hot roast beef sandwich at The Logging Camp and how it was not as good as her own cooking. But all of this was just my own thinking and didn't mean anything, because the phone had already been hung up and I was not going to talk to her that night. And when I realized that fact I began to think about something else, Charlene, and what had happened in the apple orchard yesterday, and how Wayne and I had almost had a fight. Those were things I'd actually done, new things that I would have to do again—have sex with a girl, argue with a man—basic things that were bound to be repeated. And so it made sense that I should think about them so that I could do them better the next time.

And then I thought of something else, and this was the last thing I thought about before I went to sleep. I thought I would tell my father that I wanted to go to Chicago for Thanksgiving and visit my mother. And I thought that when I visited her I would persuade her to come back and live with us, because that was something we both wanted—my father and I—and something I believed I could do.

After a while I pulled the chain on the bedside lamp and drew the covers over me and went to sleep.

Chapter Thirteen

WHEN I TOLD AMBER I was going to Chicago to visit my mother for Thanksgiving she told me I should be sure to go to the Art Institute.

"I've read about it," she said. "They've got paintings by all the great artists. Picasso's one. And Cézanne and Degas and Monet, too. And I think there's some van Gogh. He's the one who cut off his ear."

"Why'd he cut off his ear?"

"He did it for a woman. To show how much he loved her."

"He must have been crazy."

"Artists are. A lot of them."

"You're not."

She laughed. "I'm not an artist yet. Maybe it's still going to happen to me." And then she crossed her eyes and stuck her tongue out to imitate a person who's lost his mind. But then I suddenly remembered what had happened in the taxidermy shed—how she'd broken down in sobs and asked me to take care of her—and I thought that maybe that was a little like being crazy.

"Anyway, get me some postcards," she said. "They have postcards that show the famous paintings. Get me some postcards of the ones you like best. I'll pay you for them—don't worry."

I was sitting in a booth at the Shamrock restaurant. Ever since Amber had taken her waitressing job I'd been going there after school to do my homework. The Shamrock was a good place for homework because the booths were like desks where you could spread out your work, and I liked being someplace where there were people around, even if I didn't know who they were and didn't have anything to say to them. And I liked talking to Amber, too, when there was a lull between her customers.

"Be sure to tell your momma that you miss her," Amber said. She was standing next to the booth, her hip cocked against the edge, looking out at the gravel parking lot where some new customers had just pulled in. "And be sure to take her a gift, a bottle of perfume or a pretty scarf or a music box. Women like to get gifts from the men they love."

"*Tu es bonne conseillère*," I said, which was a phrase I'd put together from Amber's French words. *You give good advice.*

Amber's eyes widened. She laughed out loud. "*Et toi, tu es bon fils*," she said. *You are a good son.*

Some customers turned around and looked at us.

On the day before Thanksgiving I took the bus to Chicago. It was a long ride because we stopped in many towns along the way: Cadillac and Reed City and Cedar Springs and others whose names I have forgotten. In the late afternoon we passed through Grand Rapids and I saw the city I'd lived in until the previous summer. The sky was overcast, the sun a faint white blur not strong enough to make shadows, so that everything—the office buildings and factories and church steeples—looked flat, like scenes painted on a canvas. The wide river flowing through the center of town moved sluggishly between its concrete banks, seeming tired and used up, not like the trout streams I'd become used to seeing in the north, which had swirls and ripples and cascades and seemed alive. We drove down Monroe Street past the Pantlind Hotel and Steketee's Department Store, where as a child I'd gone each year at Christmas to see the mechanical figures in the display windows. As we were leaving town, we passed the General Motors factory on Wyoming Street, where my father had worked; it was a huge windowless building spreading out over many acres, surrounded by an asphalt parking lot filled with cars. I turned and watched out the back window as it receded in the distance, its twin smokestacks belching brownish plumes into the cold November sky.

I thought about how much my life had changed since we'd left Grand Rapids. I lived in the woods outside a town that nobody had ever heard about, a place I hadn't known existed one year ago, and my mother lived away from us in Chicago. I had met a pregnant girl who was not married, and I had seen a man strike another man and take his money, and I had heard my father say he wanted to sleep with a woman who was not my mother. All of these were different things from what I would have expected one year ago, amazing things, really. And then I decided that's what life must be like—a constant stream of things you didn't expect, things that took you by surprise and blotted out your old life piece by piece, replacing it with another life that was completely different—and I just needed to get used to it.

But then, I thought about things in a different way and I decided this—this helplessness—was not a true idea. Or perhaps I merely *wanted* it to be untrue. Because I was going to Chicago to try to change things. To try to change things with my mother. To make her come back home.

The bus pulled into the Harrison Street depot at nine o'clock. Through the window I saw my mother standing at the edge of the parking lot, hugging herself against the cold wind, wearing a blue cloth coat and black leather gloves and high-heeled shoes. An electric street lamp shone down from overhead, casting her shadow out into the parking lot and making her seem like a character on a stage. Seeing her like that, all alone and cold and pretty at the edge of the parking lot, the electric lamp shining down, affected me more than I'd expected, and as soon as I got off the bus I ran over and hugged her and told her that I loved her and had missed her. I had not planned to greet her in this emotional way, but that was how it happened.

"Have you eaten?" she asked after we'd gotten into her car, which was the red Pontiac Star Chief she had driven in Grand Rapids.

"Yes," I said. "Dad packed me some sandwiches, and I bought a candy bar in Reed City."

She smiled in the darkness of the car, a sweet lingering smile that I'd forgotten but recognized immediately. She was wearing rouge and lipstick, and her hair was arranged in a different style, short and upswept along the sides, so that she looked almost girlish. "We'll just go directly home then," she said.

We drove away from the bus depot and turned down a side street and then onto a bigger street filled with traffic and lights.

"What's your father doing this weekend?" she asked me.

"He's going deer hunting tomorrow," I said. "With a friend who lives near Kalkaska. I think he's staying there to have Thanksgiving dinner."

"Are you living on the wild game he shoots these days? Is that the diet he's giving you?"

"He doesn't hunt too much," I said. "Most nights he doesn't get home from work until after dark."

"Is that so?" my mother said. "Don't tell me his great experiment isn't working out as well as he expected."

My mother turned onto a ramp leading to a big highway that ran next to Lake Michigan. I could tell we were headed north because the water was on our right.

"Aren't we going to Oak Park?"

"No," my mother said. "Your grandparents left for Florida two weeks ago. Besides, I'm not living with them anymore. I've taken an apartment in the city. It's a small place near the office where I work. That's where we'll be staying."

"I didn't know that," I said. "About your new job and the apartment."

"Didn't you?" she said, although she didn't sound surprised. "I keep the books for a law firm on Wacker Drive. The billings and the financial statements. I told your father about it. I guess he forgot to tell you."

I just looked at her.

"I did that kind of work when your father was in the army. I guess you didn't know your mother had that amazing talent."

"No," I said, and I recognized that Amber had used that same word—talent—to describe her waitressing job, and I wondered what it meant or if it meant anything at all. "I didn't know you could do that kind of work."

She turned to me and smiled, then turned back. "I'll be working there for a while," she said. "A few months anyway."

With her eyes fixed on the road ahead she reached across and found my hand. She squeezed it hard. Then she turned and looked at me.

"It's wonderful to see you, Danny boy," she said.

Her eyes caught the light of a passing car and sparkled for a moment. I felt the smooth coolness of her gloved hand.

"It's wonderful to see you, too, Mom," I said.

The next day was Thanksgiving. After breakfast in my mother's small apartment, which was on the upper floor of an old three-story building near La Salle Street, we took a streetcar downtown and went for a long walk by the river. None of the stores were open because it was a holiday, and there were not too many people on the streets, just a few who looked like they didn't have anyplace in particular to go. As we walked along my mother pointed out the famous Chicago landmarks–the Chicago Stock Exchange and the Wrigley Building and the Tribune Tower and the Fifth Street bridge—and then she showed me the building where she worked, although we didn't go inside. After that we went to the Field Museum and strolled among the exhibits of stuffed animals and the dioramas of ancient cultures and civilizations. We had lunch in the cafeteria there.

During all the time these things were happening, I kept wondering when I should talk to my mother about coming back to live with us. Riding down on the bus, I had already decided what I was going to say to her. I was going to tell her that the cabin felt odd without her there to liven things up, and I was going to tell her about the night my father and I had had dinner at The Logging Camp and how he had said he loved her and had played "Tennessee Waltz" in her honor. I was also going to tell her some of the good things I'd learned about living in the country: like how the lake looked in the early morning with the mist rising off it like smoke; and how the wind died in the evening and the lake became perfectly flat and mirrorlike and the shadows of pine trees crept slowly toward the water's edge like stalking animals; and how you could go out to the marsh at dusk to watch the sandhill cranes returning to their nests, see them flying back high in groups of two or three or four and then dropping out of the sky so fast it almost took your breath away and then circling down and down in long slow endless-seeming glides.

Those were some of the things I was going to say to my mother to try to persuade her to come back to live with us. They were not the normal things a boy would say to his mother, but they were the kind of things I believed she would like to hear.

At six o'clock we took a taxi to the Drake Hotel on Walton Place to have Thanksgiving dinner. When we arrived a man was waiting for us. My mother pointed him out as we stood in the entrance to the dining room. He was seated at a linen-covered table, holding a glass of wine that a waiter had just poured for him. He was a small man with a mustache and wire-rimmed glasses and he had on a suit and a tie. As we walked up he saw us and smiled and stood up and took my mother's hand. Then he leaned forward and kissed her on the cheek.

"This is Robert Henry," my mother said. She was still holding his hand. "Bob, this is my son, Danny DeWitt."

Mr. Henry put his hand out and I shook it. He had a handsome face with thin lips and dark hair combed straight back. He looked like one of the people my mother had told me about: someone who is comfortable with money and satisfied with the way his life is going.

"Robert's joining us for dinner," my mother said. "He's all alone in the city tonight, just like us poor little lambs, so we thought it'd be nice to get together. Robert's an attorney at the firm where I keep the books."

"That's right," Mr. Henry said. "Joanne and I both toil in the cause of American justice."

"Robert's a specialist in corporate law," my mother said. She sat down and smoothed her hands over her skirt. "That means he tells rich people how they can become richer." She turned in Mr. Henry's direction and grinned. "I think that's about right, isn't it Robert?"

"That's putting the worst construction on it, Joanne," Mr. Henry said with a laugh. He turned to me. "I understand you live in northern Michigan, Danny." He put his elbow onto the table and leaned in my direction.

"Yes, sir."

"That's wonderful country. I've been known to spend some time up there myself, though you'll never get me to shoot a deer or catch a fish. I've been a guest at the Crabtree Reserve on the Black River. That's Andy Waxman's place. He owns the power company in Alpena."

"I haven't met him," I said. "We don't know too many people up there yet."

"Well, it's all wonderful country," Mr. Henry said. He reached out and touched the side of his wineglass, where beads of sweat had started to form. His fingers were long and thin, and the nails were shaped and smooth. "What does your father do up there?" he asked.

"He's a salesman. He sells power tools."

"I see." Mr. Henry said. He pursed his lips and nodded his head slowly, as if he were agreeing to something I had just said. Then he smiled at my mother, just a quick smile that came and went on his lips almost before you knew it was there.

"Danny's father is trying an experiment," my mother said. "He wants to relive the last century. Once wasn't enough, I guess."

Mr. Henry looked at my mother as if he didn't know what she was talking about. Then he smiled and turned back to me. "Are you a football fan?" he asked.

"Yes, sir. I'm a Lions fan."

"It's a good year to be one, from what I hear."

"Yes, sir. So far they've done pretty good."

The waiter came back and poured water into our glasses. Then another waiter came and took our orders. After that there was a silence that stretched out for a while. My mother picked up a saucer and turned it over to see where it was made. Mr. Henry unfolded his napkin onto his lap, then put his hands together on the tabletop as if he were going to say a prayer. Finally he turned to my mother and said, "Does Danny have your aptitude with numbers, Joanne?"

"You can talk to me," I said, because it felt strange to have Mr. Henry talk to my mother like I wasn't there.

"What's that?" he said. He turned in my direction. His eyes blinked a few times.

"I can talk for myself."

Mr. Henry looked at me, then he looked at my mother, then he looked back at me. "Well, of course you can. I didn't mean to imply that you couldn't. I hope that's not the inference you drew."

"I'm good with numbers," I said. "It's my favorite subject at school. That's the answer to your question."

There was an awkward silence. Mr. Henry folded his hands again. "Well, your mother has a wonderful talent, Danny. She's been a great help in straightening out the financial situation at Bates-Gillmore."

"I know that," I said. "She told me already."

During dinner, my mother and Mr. Henry talked about some movies they had both seen—*3:10 to Yuma* was one; *And God Created Woman* was another—and what the themes of the movies were and how the director had used the camera to create a certain impression. Then Mr. Henry talked to me about his law firm. It was an old firm, he said, a very old and established Chicago firm, but they had recently done some things in corporate taxation that would put them in the forefront of the profession—that's how he described it—things that would bear fruit for many years to come. If I thought I might be interested in the law he would be glad to give me some pointers, he said, and steer me in the direction of the better schools. He knew some people at Northwestern and would be glad to put in a word for me when the time came.

"You have to think about your future," he said. "It comes at you fast."

"Danny thinks he wants to be a scientist," my mother said.

"Well, that's a fine profession, too," Mr. Henry said, "though there's not much money in it, I'm afraid."

I turned and looked at my mother. "I don't feel too good," I said. "I think I ate something that didn't agree with me. Maybe I should go back to the apartment."

"Oh, Danny, no."

I pushed back my chair and stood up. "I think I should go back to the apartment. Otherwise I could get sick and spoil your dinner."

My mother started to say something but Mr. Henry had already stood up. "You better let the boy go, Joanne. He won't have any fun if he's not feeling well." He took out his wallet and passed me a five-dollar bill. "Here, Danny," he said, "get yourself a taxi."

"Oh, no, Robert," my mother said. "That's too much."

"Have the doorman call a Yellow Cab," he said, paying no attention to my mother. He reached into his pocket and took out a quarter. "Give him this for his efforts."

My mother walked me out to the lobby. We stood next to a marble column that rose up to a tall ceiling with plaster angels. She bent down and felt my forehead. Then she put her hand against my cheek and looked into my face. "Are you really sick, Danny," she asked, "or do you just want to get away from Mr. Henry?"

"I don't like him very much," I said.

"He's different than the men you're familiar with," she said. She looked back into the dining room where Mr. Henry was sitting alone at the table, sipping a glass of wine. "But he's a very good attorney. He's a man of considerable accomplishments. You could learn some things from him, I'm sure."

"Is he your boyfriend?" I asked.

She laughed out loud, but not as if what I'd said was funny. "Oh, my goodness, no," she said. Then she looked back in the direction of the dining room, and I thought she was trying to decide about something.

She leaned in close to me. "He's queer, Danny," she said, speaking as if she were imparting some wonderful secret. "You know what that means, don't you?"

"Of course," I said, though to be truthful I wasn't exactly sure.

"It means he likes men and not women. In a sexual way, I mean. He's a homosexual; that's the proper term."

I had heard kids at school use those words before—queer and homo—but I didn't know it meant a man who liked other men. I'd thought it was someone who wanted to live alone, like a hermit or a recluse, because those seemed to be the kinds of people they used the words on.

"So there's not much chance Robert Henry will become my boyfriend, Danny," my mother continued. "Just about zero, I'd say." She smiled as if the thought amused her in some private way. "Besides," she added, putting her hand on my cheek again, "I'm married to your father. That's an important fact."

"Is it?" I said.

"Well, of course." She tilted her head and looked at me strangely.

"Then why aren't you living with us?"

"Oh, Danny," she said. She took a big breath and blew out a stream of air so that her cheeks puffed out slightly. I felt her breath move against my face. "Let's not get into this now, okay?" Her face seemed suddenly tired.

"Okay," I said. "I'll see you later, then."

"I'll be along in a little while."

She kissed her fingertips and touched them to my cheek. Then she pressed her apartment key into my hand, and I turned and went out of the hotel and into the dark streets of Chicago. But I didn't take a taxi as Mr. Henry had suggested. Instead, I walked back to my mother's apartment. Walking gave me a chance to think about some things I wanted to think about—like how a man became a homosexual and how it was that men had sex with other men. I wondered if it was possible for a person to *be* a homosexual without knowing it and how you *would* know it, especially if you had never had sex with anyone, neither a woman nor a man, as I had not yet done. But then I remembered how I'd felt when I'd seen Amber that first night with the wind folding the white dress up against her body and when I'd sat with my hand on Harriet Walker's shoulder while she had fallen back asleep and the afternoon in the apple orchard when I'd kissed Charlene and almost touched her breast. And I decided that I was probably not a homosexual and I could relax about it.

As I came down the hallway to my mother's apartment I heard the telephone ringing inside. Instead of opening the door I stood in the hallway with the key in my hand, waiting for the ringing to stop. I thought it was probably my father calling to wish us a happy Thanksgiving; but I didn't know how to explain to him the things I knew I would have to—that my mother was at a restaurant with a man, but that it was all right because he was a homosexual and could never be her boyfriend.

I wanted to talk to my father about his deer-hunting trip and about the Detroit Lions football game with the Green Bay Packers, which had been played that day. But it wasn't worth taking a chance on the other. So I just stood there in the hallway and listened to the telephone ringing. After a while it stopped and I opened the door and went inside.

The next day my mother took me to the Art Institute, where I had said I wanted to go, and we walked through the galleries of paintings. At first she didn't say anything, but then she began to talk about the different paintings we were seeing, why they were important and what their special features were and how the artist had used color and shape and composition to achieve something or other. And I was surprised by this, because I'd never heard my mother talk so much about art before, just as I'd never realized she knew bookkeeping or would go out to dinner with a man who was not my father. And it frightened me, in a way, to have this new side of her revealed, like a secret she'd been keeping from me all these years. But then I remembered that she'd been to the university in Ann Arbor and had studied history there and I thought now that she must have also studied art but had just never mentioned it. Art didn't figure in our lives in Grand Rapids so it wouldn't have made much difference to anything we did or talked about.

"Are you finding this the least bit interesting, sweetheart?" my mother asked me. We were standing in the marble gallery that opened up to the wide staircases.

"I like some of them," I said. "I like the Impressionists."

"So do I," she said. "They're the ones that speak to me most." She smiled, and I could tell she was excited about the paintings. There was a breathlessness in the way she spoke, and color was in her cheeks. I had never seen her look so happy.

That night—which was my last night in Chicago—we had dinner at a Rexall drugstore. We sat in a booth and ordered ham sandwiches and chocolate malted milks. My mother talked about her job and how she liked being responsible for keeping track of the books in the law firm. "They take in thousands of dollars every day, Danny, and every penny has to be accounted for. If there's a mistake it'd be my head." She drew a finger across her throat and made a soft gagging sound.

After that we were silent for a while, each of us eating and thinking. Then I said, "Dad and I had dinner a few days ago in a place that looked something like this. It was a restaurant in McBride called The Logging Camp."

"Oh," my mother said.

"He played 'Tennessee Waltz' on a jukebox because he said it was your favorite song."

"Did he?" she said. "That's sweet."

"He said he wanted to play it in your honor. Then he said he loved you and he knew that you loved him."

My mother looked across the table as if I'd said something to hurt her. She stared at me for a long time with that expression on her face. But then the expression changed, and I had the feeling she'd made up her mind about something.

"What if I told you I wasn't coming back to McBride, Danny?" she said, speaking in a quiet voice. She started to stab at the malted milk with her straw.

"What do you mean?"

"What if I told you I wanted to stay in Chicago?"

"I wouldn't like it," I said, "because I'd hardly ever see you."

"You could come live with me," she said, "if that was your choice." She stopped stabbing the malted milk and held the straw off to one side. Brown drops fell from the tip and made a small puddle on the Formica. "You could live in Chicago instead of McBride."

I didn't say anything for a long time—at least two or three minutes—and my mother didn't say anything either. She stared across the table at me, her hand holding the straw in the air, as if she'd forgotten she had it. Finally I said, "You should just come back and live with us," and I used a louder voice than was normal for me, a voice like Wayne had used that time in the apple orchard to make

Amber apologize for calling him an idiot.

"Is that so?" my mother said.

"Yes," I said, "that's where you belong." Then I said, "There was a woman who stayed with us when I was sick. She took care of me until I got better and then she stayed for two more days."

My mother didn't say anything.

"And she put her arm around me one night on the sofa because she was sad about her boyfriend being killed in the war and she wanted to be near somebody."

"Be quiet, Danny," my mother said. "I don't want to hear this."

"And I liked her." My mother was looking off to one side of the room, as if trying to pretend I wasn't there. I cast around in my mind for the next words to say. "And Dad liked her, too," I finished.

My mother reached across and slapped my face.

Everything got quiet. The man behind the counter turned and looked at us. Some other customers looked, too. My cheek burned where my mother's hand had struck me.

"Don't try to bully me," she said, leaning in close. "I have a life, too." Her eyes were blinking; tears were in them. "And there are things I'd like to do, and maybe they can't happen in the place your father's chosen to live right now." She reached across and grasped my arm as if she was going to shake me. "And maybe I wouldn't mind being in the company of a man once in a while." She spit the words out, as if they were weapons that could hurt me. "And if I want to do it, I guess I will."

The next day I got up before the alarm clock went off and began packing my duffel bag. I heard my mother in the kitchen, the sound of her heels striking the linoleum floor, cupboard doors opening and closing, the gentle clink of dishes. When I came out she was standing by the sink with a cup of coffee in her hand, staring out the window at the city skyline. She wore a gray skirt with a white pullover sweater and black high-heeled shoes.

"There's some bread and jam in the refrigerator," she said, still staring out. "You can make toast if you'd like."

"Okay," I said. I set my duffel bag down against the wall and went over and opened the refrigerator.

"Are you feeling better this morning?" she asked. She turned and watched me putting bread into the toaster. "Or are you still inclined to lecture your mother?"

"I don't want to lecture you," I said.

"Are you sure?" she said. "Maybe you'd like to tell me how I should dress." She held her arms apart as if she was presenting herself for my inspection. "Or the friends I should have. Perhaps Robert Henry isn't suitable."

I didn't say anything. After a minute the toast popped up. I put it on a plate and carried it over to the kitchen table, along with the jar of jam. I could feel my mother follow me with her gaze. After a minute she came over and stood beside me. She put her hand on my head and ran her fingers through my hair.

"I suppose this isn't the best time to say it, Danny," she said, "but if you'd like to come and live with me here you're welcome to do it." She sat down facing me across the table, still holding her cup of coffee. "I can't tell whether you like living up there with your father or not. I wouldn't have thought you'd like it, but maybe you do. Or maybe you've changed. Maybe you've become an adventurer like your father. You're a mystery to me on that score."

"I like living there okay," I said.

"Well, that's good. I'm glad to hear it. I'm happy for you. Truly."

"Are you going to divorce Dad?" I said after a minute.

"No," she said, and she said it quickly, as if she'd been expecting the question. "Because I love him. He's right about that. I suppose that's hard for you to understand right now, but it's true."

I looked up at her. She was staring off to the side. A series of lines stretched across her forehead.

"He's the only man I've ever really loved," she said, and her voice sounded calm and reasonable. "I met him when I was very young,

Danny. I was a student and he'd come to Ann Arbor to buy tools for General Motors. He seemed very mature and sophisticated compared to the college boys I knew, very serious about life." She laughed briefly, as if she was embarrassed to speak this way to her son. "This ... ." She raised her hand to indicate the apartment and everything surrounding it, and I was reminded of the gesture my father had made in The Logging Camp, which was the same gesture but about a different place. "... this doesn't have anything to do with your father. It's about something else entirely."

She stood up and walked over to the sink and began rinsing out the coffee cup.

I kept eating my toast.

On the drive to the bus depot we talked about architecture, and my mother pointed out some other famous buildings. Then she asked what I was reading in school, and I told her about "The Death of the Hired Man." She recited some of the lines that she remembered, something about the moon dragging the sky and something about home being a place you didn't have to deserve. When we were standing next to the bus, waiting for them to call the passengers, she put a sack of sandwiches into my hand and hugged me. She held me for a long time, my cheek pressed into the collar of her blue coat.

"Oh, Danny," she said. "You probably should forget some of the things I said to you last night."

"It's all right," I said. Then I said, "I know it was true."

"It was true, but it's not what people say to each other. People who love each other don't say those things. You don't say everything that's on your mind. That's a prescription for disaster."

"It's all right," I said again.

Over her shoulder I saw the bus driver standing with one foot up in the doorway, staring at us and smiling.

"Oh, Danny, Danny," my mother said. She was crying, but I was not.

I think she believed she might never see me again or never see me in the way she had seen me before, which was maybe the same thing.

On the bus ride back to McBride I watched the shallow hills of southern Michigan roll past the window, the leafless trees looking exposed and frail under the wide lead-colored sky, the farm fields empty of crops, the earth upturned in furrowed rows and blackened by the mist hanging in the air.

I thought about the day my mother had left for Chicago, in late September when the days were still bright and color was just coming onto the trees. She had acted then as if it were a kind of joke or a scene from a TV comedy—a woman leaving the wilderness to seek a bit of comfort in the city. "I need to see something other than trees," she had said, laughing, and, "It'd be nice to shop somewhere other than the five-and-dime, if that's still allowed," and, "Maybe someone is still making movies somewhere," because the movies that came to the tiny theater in McBride were several years old. I thought now that she must have been fooling herself then, or fooling us, or didn't understand what was happening. And then I wondered if leaving had opened her eyes to something that had been there all along, some quality about her life she couldn't see until she was away from it and looking back or didn't want to see when she was in it, because seeing it would leave her feeling helpless. I knew now that her going away was more than just wanting to live in a certain place and do a certain thing. She had started a new life, maybe by accident and maybe for other reasons than she'd had in the beginning. But it was a life she didn't want to leave. Not yet anyway—and maybe not ever.

And I believed this, too: I believed that she loved me and that she loved my father, just as she'd said that morning in her apartment. But I believed it was a love that had to make room for other things that were important to her, the best love she could give, maybe, but not complete, not total. And then I remembered what Amber had said about being halfway in love with me, and I wondered if that was all you ever got and that expecting more was asking for too much and you should learn to be content with it.

The bus worked its way up through Benton Harbor and Paw Paw and Kalamazoo and then into Grand Rapids. Through the grimy window I saw the city landscape I'd seen three days ago. It all seemed remote and disconnected now, like a place I'd learned about from reading a book or overhearing someone's conversation, not a place I'd lived a life in.

I slept for a while. When I awoke we were somewhere out in the country, passing down a two-lane road with farm fields along both sides. I stood up and got my duffel bag down from the overhead rack, and I opened it and took out a small cardboard box. Inside, wrapped in tissue paper, was a gift I'd planned to give to my mother but had forgotten about, a serving dish for butter made from clear sparkling glass. I looked at the dish, which had the image of a rose etched into the cover, and I wondered what I should do with it now. When I'd bought it from the Kresge clerk it had seemed like the perfect gift for my mother, something delicate and fine, but now I wasn't so sure. There was a side to my mother that I had never seen before, a hardness—a ruthlessness even. And so choosing a gift for her was more complicated than I had thought. *She* was more complicated than I had thought, like a precious stone that looks different depending on how you hold it toward the light.

After a minute I wrapped the butter dish in the tissue paper and put it back into the cardboard box. I wrapped a shirt around the cardboard box and wedged it into the corner of my duffel bag where I knew it would stay safe.

Chapter Fourteen

THERE WAS NOT TOO MUCH TALK between my father and me about the trip I'd made to Chicago. Driving home from the bus depot in Cadillac, he asked in an offhand way about my mother—how she had looked and whether she seemed happy and what her apartment was like. But he did not press for details about the life she was living there, and he did not ask if I had talked to her about coming home and what the result had been. Possibly he'd already spoken to her by phone about these things and knew as much as he needed or wanted to know, or possibly he sensed something from my behavior, some evasive or awkward quality, which put him on guard. Or perhaps he simply believed his life had reached a point where he could not count on what was coming next—as he'd always done before—and wanted to keep it that way, just wanted his life to flow along in its natural channel without too much thought or attention or concern—at least until something happened to change it, to force it out of that channel and into another.

In the following weeks I noticed he was drinking more—drinking in the cabin and in other places, too—although he was not getting drunk as far as I could tell. At least I never saw him acting drunk in the way I'd seen him that night in October. And he was seeing Harriet Walker again and talking more openly about the things they did together: a meal at a restaurant or a television show they'd watched in her apartment in town or some clever remark she'd made.

On a few occasions he did not come home until one or two o'clock in the morning. From my bed I would hear his car drive up and coast to a stop outside the cabin wall, the car door open and close softly against its frame, his footsteps on the gravel and then on the plank flooring of the cabin. Once I smelled Harriet Walker's perfume on his clothing, and once I heard him call out her name in the middle of the night—suddenly and with a kind of desperation—when he was asleep.

None of this surprised or frightened me. After my trip to Chicago, I had decided that people did things for themselves first and that whatever they did for others came afterward, from whatever love or compassion or courage was left over. My father wanted the companionship of a woman; it was a natural thing for a man to want—as natural as the baby that was growing inside of Amber or the radio waves that came through the air from WTCU in Traverse City. Just the way people behaved with one another, nothing more or less than that.

But there was one person who contradicted this bleak version of the world and that was Amber. She was the one person I knew who was putting up with all sorts of troubles for the sake of someone else—her unborn baby. When I told her about my trip to Chicago—the dinner with Robert Henry, the great happiness my mother felt from living in the city, the conversation in the drugstore on the night before I left—she reacted in a surprising way.

"I think she's frightened," she told me. We were walking together in the woods next to the cabin. Amber had a thoughtful expression on her face, as if it was important that she give me the best information she possibly could. "That's what it sounds like to me," she continued. "I think she's frightened that her life is getting away from her, the life she wanted and expected before she married your father, and she's trying to hold on to some pieces of it. When life's not what you expect, it can scare you."

Amber stopped walking and looked down at the ground, and I thought she was thinking about herself now and how *her* life was not what she'd expected. And then I realized how much she was like my mother in this way, because the waitress job was *her* attempt to take control of her life—to make it go in the direction she wanted.

She had been using a sort of wooden staff to keep her balance on the uneven ground, a long straight stick she'd found lying under a hemlock tree. Suddenly she grasped it at the center, leaned back, took a few sideways steps, and threw it in the direction of the lake. The stick sailed out over the water in a long graceful arc, then landed in the shallow water with barely a splash, sticking into the lake bottom.

For a moment Amber stood looking out, amazed by what she had done. The stick angled up from the water like a flagstaff planted by some New World explorer.

"Anyway she's probably not coming back," I said. "That's the bottom line, isn't it?"

"I don't know," Amber said. "I wouldn't be so sure about that." She turned around and looked at me, then shrugged. "You can never tell what's going to happen, Danny. So you better prepare yourself for everything. That's my theory, anyway."

I was spending time with Amber at the Shamrock restaurant after school and sometimes—on the afternoons when she got off work early—she and Wayne and I would drive out into the country, like we'd done before. But it was different between them now and somehow I could tell. Amber still acted as if Wayne was her boyfriend, saying the things you'd expect her to say and putting up with his occasional abuse and going off with him whenever he wanted her to. But she was only going through the motions. I could tell she did not love him and did not want to marry him. Seeing him was a way to keep her parents from troubling her about the baby. At least that's what I believed.

And there was another thing that made me feel that way: she was still studying French vocabulary and making her sketches and talking about Montreal. If anything, she was doing these things with more focus and determination. She carried the index cards in the pocket of her waitress's dress, and I would see her studying them as she stood at the counter waiting for an order to come up or as she sat across from me in a booth, a frown of concentration clouding her features. After work, on the drive back out to the lake, she would ask me to quiz her, and if I mispronounced a word or was slow to give a definition she would sometimes flare up in anger, as if she couldn't stand to lose a single minute. Afterward, though—after one of her outbursts—she would apologize and beg me to forgive her, and sometimes she would cry despairingly and say she couldn't stand it if I wasn't her friend.

She was beginning to show a little more of being pregnant, although not too much because it was still early. Her belly looked slightly more swollen, and it stretched out the front of her dress a little tighter. Once she said she'd soon have to start wearing different clothes, and she didn't know what she would do then because her parents had said they wouldn't buy them, and she couldn't afford to buy them for herself.

"Maybe I'll just stitch together a few potato sacks," she said. "That'd be a pretty sight, wouldn't it?" She put both hands on her stomach with the fingers spread, as if she were measuring the amount of cloth it would take to cover it.

"How does it feel being pregnant?" I asked. It was an afternoon when she had gotten off work early; we were out on the lake in the rowboat, going down to a cove where I'd seen a blue heron's nest I wanted to show her. I was rowing, and Amber was sitting in the stern, facing forward, wearing her pink waitress dress. The sun was shining. You could tell it was one of the last nice days before winter.

"It feels all right," Amber said. "At first I was sick all the time. In the mornings, anyway. But now it's all right."

"Can you feel the baby?"

"No, not yet. It's just a lump now. Eventually it'll start to move, but not for a while."

I pulled on one oar so we'd come up close along the shore and see some turtles sunning themselves on logs or lily pads, which always made Amber happy. We were passing in front of the small abandoned resort hotel that sat on a shallow rise above the water. Rotting picnic tables were propped against tree trunks and the windows were covered with sheets of plywood.

"I'm gaining weight though," Amber said. "I'm getting bigger all over. The doctor says that's to be expected." She hitched her shoulders forward, as if she were trying to make room inside her dress for her bigger body. Then she leaned back against the transom and began to trail one hand in the water. "My breasts are bigger, too," she said after a minute in a kind of dreamy voice. "That's because they're filling up with milk."

We were coming up to a little island of reeds. I pulled hard on the oars to shoot us through. The reeds scraped against the sides of the boat. They made a scratching sound and slowed us down.

"Can I see them?" I said to Amber.

I pulled hard on the oars and moved us a little further into the reeds.

Amber didn't say anything, which surprised me, because I thought she would laugh and make it seem like a joke. She held one hand up so the tips of the reeds brushed against her palm. Water ran down her arm and dripped from her elbow.

"It'd be interesting to see what they look like that way," I said.

She looked back at me with an odd smile. She said, "Like a scientist examining a specimen, huh?"

"Yes," I said. "Something like that."

"Have you ever seen a girl's breasts, Danny?"

I pulled on the oars. The boat moved a little further through the reeds. Then it stopped completely, and I stopped rowing.

"No," I said, looking straight at Amber. And I was embarrassed to admit this, because I thought most boys my age had already seen a girl's breasts, and some had probably seen them many times.

Amber held her hand up, feeling the tips of the reeds. Then she looked back into my face, staring for a long time in that quiet way she had. Her gaze was sort of turned inward, her eyes tired and wise.

"Are you really sure you want to?" she said.

"Yes," I said, because I wanted to and I believed that it would be all right.

"Oh, Danny," she said, and she let out a long sigh. She looked at the reed tips. Then she looked back at me. "I'll do it if you really want me to. But only if it's really important to you."

"It is," I said.

Amber took a deep breath and exhaled it with a little whistling sound. Then she sat up and started to unbutton the front of her dress.

"I feel strange," she said. "This isn't usually the way it happens."

I watched her hands working the buttons.

"Usually some boy is fumbling with my dress, and I'm telling him to stop." She laughed in a sort of odd way. "Not that it ever makes any difference."

"I could do the buttons," I said.

She looked at me with a stern expression. "No," she said. "This is different. You know it is."

"Yes," I said. And I understood she meant that she was doing it because it was important to me and not because I was her boyfriend.

She finished with the last button. Then she stopped and looked at me, holding her dress together with one hand. She smiled in a funny way. "You're not going to go crazy with lust, are you?"

"No," I said, and I was surprised she would say such a thing, even as a joke.

We were stopped completely in the reeds now. They surrounded the boat on all sides, making it seem like we were together in a small room. Some of the reeds leaned over the sides of the boat and touched us.

Amber slid one arm out of her dress, holding the front together with her other hand. Then she did the same thing on the other side. Then she made a funny face, kind of like a grimace, and let the dress fall down around her waist. With a quick movement she reached behind and undid the back on her brassiere, looking off to the side with a frown. Then she slipped the satiny straps off her shoulders, one at a time.

She blew air out through her mouth. "Okay," she said. "You get one minute to make your examination, doctor. That's all." She took her hand away and let the brassiere fall onto her lap.

At first I closed my eyes, but after a moment I opened them. Amber was looking up in the sky as if something overhead had caught her attention: a flock of migrating cranes, perhaps, or the trail of a jet airplane. Her shoulders were bare and pale, and they had bumps and ridges where the bones pushed out beneath the skin, and her breasts were white and round and slightly saggy and soft looking and lovely. The nipples were dark brown and they spread out more than I expected, more than I had seen on the women in photographs. Tiny blue veins traced beneath the skin in places.

"Not so great, huh?" Amber said, still looking up into the sky. She made a face.

"They're nice," I said. "They're pretty."

Amber laughed, a single fast expulsion of air that sounded like "huh."

I felt my breath coming faster, like I couldn't get enough air into my lungs. A hardness was starting, which I hadn't expected and I didn't want to happen. "I see what you mean about them being big," I said. My voice felt tight in my throat.

"Yeah. Well that's usually something to be desired. Boys like it. But it's different when it comes from being pregnant."

I pulled my gaze away from Amber's breasts and looked at her face. She was staring down the shore now, looking in at the old hotel, and I suddenly realized she didn't want to see me watching her, and I felt ashamed of that.

"Okay," I said. I tried to keep my voice steady. "Thanks."

Amber looked at me. It was the first time she'd looked at me since she'd let her dress fall open. For a split second it seemed like something passed between us, some little particle of recognition or understanding. Then it stopped.

"You're sure?" she said. "Because there's not likely to be a repeat performance."

I tried to laugh but it came out sounding choked and strange. I hoped Amber didn't notice.

"I'm sure," I said.

Amber picked up her brassiere. She worked the satin straps over her shoulders one at a time like she was putting on a shirt. Then she leaned forward so that her breasts sagged away from her body and went into their places in the brassiere.

"They're nice to look at," I said, watching. My voice was still tight. It sounded like someone else's voice.

Amber glanced at me, trying to get the brassiere closed in back. "Well, someday when you have your own girlfriend you'll like them even better." She frowned, her arms up behind her back working the brassiere. "But at least now you'll know something. You won't be completely stupid. That's the only reason I did it."

"I understand," I said. "It was nice of you." Then, "How does it go together in back?"

"There's a tiny hook," she said. She bit her lip in concentration. "Two of them, actually. Here." She turned around on her seat. I sat forward and examined where the hooks were. The shiny fabric looked odd against Amber's pale white skin, her back long and straight and lovely and me wanting to touch it but not daring to.

"You can work them," she said. And I worked the hooks a couple of times to see how they went together and came apart, and then Amber finished putting her dress back on.

Later, after we'd seen the heron's nest, we drifted offshore in front of the abandoned hotel. A wispy breeze pushed us slowly up the shore. I had my fly rod out and was casting around the edges of some lily pads. The sun was still out, though it was low in the sky.

"Someday you can teach me how to fly-fish," Amber said. "I've fished with worms and crickets but never with flies." She was leaning back with her arms on the transom. Her face was turned up toward the setting sun and her eyes were closed. "That can be your payback for showing you my breasts."

"It's easy," I said. "I could teach you in just a couple of minutes."

I brought the rod back, and the line came up off the water. I worked the rod back and forth, the line curving out in giant circles over our heads.

"It's all a matter of timing," I said. I brought the rod tip forward, and the line shot out straight along the water, settling silently, the tapered leader drifting down last, the fly a white speck at the end.

"It seems so peaceful," Amber said. "But powerful, too. Like you're in control of all the space above the boat."

"That's a funny way to think of it," I said.

We drifted for a while in silence.

"Do you think it was wrong of me to open my dress?" Amber said. "I've been sitting here thinking about it and I think it was a mistake."

"It was all right," I said. I glanced back at her. "It made me feel funny for a minute, but I'm all right now."

"Funny?"

"Sort of hot. And tight in my throat."

Amber stared at me, her eyes narrowed slightly. I could see she thought it had been wrong to show me her breasts and I wanted to say something to make it seem all right. Like a thing she had done for my sake only, which is what I believed, and not for any other reason.

"Now I'll know what to expect when I have my own girlfriend," I said with a small laugh. "I'll be prepared."

Amber laughed. "I hope so," she said. "Prepare yourself for disaster, because that's usually how it ends up."

A gust of wind caught the boat and swung it in toward shore. I bent down and pulled on the oars to move us out again, holding the fly rod with my free hand. First I pulled on one oar and then I pulled on the other.

"My parents say if I don't get married pretty soon I'll have to do something about the baby," Amber said.

"You mean give it up for adoption?"

I brought the line up and cast it out in a different direction.

"Either that or get rid of it."

"Get rid of it?"

"Take it out before it grows any bigger."

"I didn't know they could do that."

"They can, but you're not supposed to. You go to this special doctor in Saginaw. My stepdaddy learned about him somewhere."

"Tell them to go to hell," I said.

"I don't want to do it," she said. "But they'll make me if I don't get married soon."

We were silent for a while, just drifting and fishing.

"Wayne and I are going to drive to Cadillac next week to get married," Amber said. She said it as if it was just a normal thing to say.

"What are you talking about?"

"We're going next Friday and get it done at the courthouse. Wayne said he'd do it."

"Are you in love with him?" I asked, even though I already knew the answer.

Amber didn't say anything. After a moment I glanced back at her. She was trailing her hand in the water and watching the ripples it made.

"I guess I haven't thought about love too much," she said. "That's sort of a luxury I can't afford right now." Then, after another moment, she said, "Being pregnant can make you feel lonely, Danny. I think it's because it's kind of a private thing. It happens inside of you. If you don't have someone to share it with it's hard."

I cast the fly out along the lily pads, concentrating on trying to bring a fish up. There are special ways to make a fly attractive to a fish. To give the impression that it's a living thing. I tried to think about that and not about Amber and Wayne.

After a while I looked back at Amber. She had turned away, as if she were looking at something on the shore. Then I saw that she was crying.

I brought the line up off the water and cast out in a different direction. I worked it back and forth over our heads.

"I wish I was older," I said, watching the line run out. "Then I'd marry you myself." It was a stupid thing to say, but I felt like saying it.

"Wouldn't that be nice?" Amber said, and she spoke in a husky voice. "That would solve everything. Then we could go fishing every afternoon."

"And I could look at your breasts anytime I wanted to."

Amber laughed. She touched a finger to the bottom of her eye to wipe the tears away.

I watched the fly, a tiny speck riding on the ripples of the water.

"Maybe we could do it," I said. And even though it was a joke, I wanted Amber to take it seriously, at least for a moment, and to talk about it as if it were a thing that could actually happen. "I could quit school and get a job," I said. "Pumping gas or something like that. We could live in the old hotel." I pointed the rod tip at the broken-down building onshore.

Amber's hand came up to shield her eyes. She looked in the direction I was pointing.

"Do you think there's anything left inside?"

"What do you mean?"

"Like curtains and furniture. Things that people could use."

I brought the fly rod back. The line came up off the water with a slight whistling sound. I worked the line overhead, moving it around so I could cast off to a different part of the lily pad bed. Then a gust of wind came up and the boat swung under my feet and I had to take a lurching step to keep from falling. The fly rod jerked in my hand and I felt a tug as if the line had snagged on something. Then I heard Amber scream.

I turned around. Amber was holding a hand up to her ear. She had a strange expression on her face, as if something terrible had happened but she didn't know what it was. Then I saw blood running through her fingers and down onto her arm.

I moved to the stern of the boat and took Amber's hand and pulled it away. There was blood all over her ear. The fly hook was caught near the top, just under where her ear curled over. The barbed end was sticking through.

"What is it?" Amber said. She made a little whimpering sound. "What happened?"

"The fly got hooked in your ear. A gust of wind took it."

I got a rag from the bottom of the boat and dabbed some of the blood away.

"The hook went all the way through," I said. "If I pull it back out it'll rip your ear."

"Oh, God," Amber said. She started to whimper again.

I looked around to see if there were any other boats around, but we were the only ones out on the water. The sun was just barely above the treetops. In a few minutes it would start to get dark.

"I can get it out," I said. "But I can't do it in the boat. We'll have to go in and do it on shore."

"Just hurry," she said. "It hurts bad."

I rowed into shore; at the last minute I pulled hard on the oars so the bow ran up on the sand. Then I helped Amber out, holding her hand as she stepped across the seats and over the bow. She was trembling. Blood was running down the side of her face and onto the shoulder of her pink dress.

"Wait a minute," I said.

I went over and got down one of the picnic tables from where it was propped up against a tree. I told Amber to lie down on it. Then I took off my jacket and made a sort of pillow for her head.

"Have you ever done this before?" She looked up into my face. Her eyes were big.

"Sure," I said. "It's not hard."

Amber looked at me as if she knew I was lying. Tears were running down her cheeks and mixing with the blood on her neck, thinning it and making it look pink. Her eyes were wide and staring.

I went back to the boat and got my tackle box out from under the bow seat. I found the pliers I used for crimping on lead sinkers and I cleaned them in the water. Then I went back to the picnic table and stood at the end looking down into Amber's face.

"You've got to turn your head and hold it still, Amber," I said.

"I don't know if I can hold still when it starts to hurt."

"You can. I'll help you."

I turned Amber's head to one side. Then I leaned my forearm against the side of her head and pressed forward with my weight.

"Are you all right?" I asked.

"Yes." Beneath my arm I could see her staring out at the lake. I brought my hand up with the pliers but there was so much blood I couldn't see where the barb was. Blood covered Amber's ear; it had run down the side of her face and soaked into her hair and onto my jacket. Then I saw the barb, a jagged bit of steel sticking out just below the top of her ear. I put the cutting part of the pliers into position; then I brought the pliers together hard.

Amber screamed.

"The barb's off," I yelled.

"Goddamn you," Amber said, sobbing. "You didn't warn me."

"I'm sorry. I thought it would be better that way."

"You bastard," she said. She was crying and trying to move her head. More blood was coming out of the wound.

"I've got to pull the rest of the hook out now."

"No," she said. "I don't want you to do it."

"It'll get infected if it stays in."

Amber glared at me with something that felt like hate. Then she started to breathe in slow deep breaths, like she was trying to calm herself down. I held her hand and stroked it with my thumb.

"Think about your baby," I said. "That'll take your mind off the hurt."

After a minute she seemed a little better. She looked up at me. The hatred was gone from her face, but nothing else had replaced it. Her expression was completely blank, as if a part of her had moved to a place that couldn't be reached. But she wasn't crying anymore.

"Do it then," she said. "Get it over with. But warn me this time."

"I will." Amber turned her head without me telling her to do it. I leaned forward and pressed down with my forearm, like I'd done before.

"I'm going to do it now."

"Wait a minute."

"Don't be frightened. I won't let anything happen to you." Then I said, "Because I love you too much."

Amber's eyes flashed open, and I knew my words had taken her by surprise. But then she closed her eyes again and took in a deep breath and let it out slowly. Then she took in another breath and held it.

"All right," she said in a small voice. "I'm ready."

I pulled on the steel shank but the hook didn't move. Then I pulled harder and something let go and it started to come out.

"I've got it," I yelled. I held the pliers up with the bloody piece of steel so Amber could see it. "It's out."

"Oh," Amber said. And then she started to cry: hard, quick, choking sobs like she knew it was all over and she didn't have to worry about being hurt again. Tears were on my face, too.

Amber lay on the picnic table while I went down to the shore and found some mud to put on the wound to make the bleeding stop. Then I wet the rag and used it to clean the blood from Amber's face and neck. She lay calmly on the picnic table and let me clean her off. All of the panicky feeling was gone now, both from Amber and from me.

"You took good care of me," she said later. We were rowing back in the darkness. I had the oars, and Amber was in the stern. I could hear her but I could not see her; she was just a dark shape against the gray expanse of water.

"I was the one who hooked you, remember?" I said. "It was my fault."

"It was an accident. The important thing is that you took care of me." Her hand touched the place on her ear that was covered with mud. "You didn't abandon me. That's more than most people would do. At least in my experience."

I stopped rowing and let the boat drift forward. I looked in at the shore. A black band of trees separated the grayness of sky and water. Further along I saw the concrete foundation of an old sawmill. It looked ghostly in the moonlight, like the ruins of some ancient civilization.

I started rowing again, leaning forward and dipping the oars and pulling hard. The regular motion felt nice after all the confusion with the hook.

Amber laughed softly. "You said you loved me."

"I don't remember that," I lied.

"Well, I do. And it was a nice thing to hear. Nice at that particular moment when I was so frightened."

"You let me see your breasts. Maybe that's what I was thinking about."

"I don't think so. Though you liked that well enough, too, I bet."

We came around the curve of the shore below Amber's house. I turned to get my bearings. Someone was walking back and forth along the shore with a flashlight in their hand. As we came closer the person aimed the flashlight and caught us in its beam.

"I love you, too, Danny," Amber said in a quiet voice. She held her hand up to shield her face from the glaring light.

I stopped rowing. The boat drifted forward. We were about a hundred feet offshore.

"I guess I want you to know that," Amber said. "I don't know why but it feels important." She leaned forward and put her hand on my knee, like she wanted to be touching me at that particular moment. "It's not regular love," she said. "Not the kind they always sing about on the radio. But I think it's still love. Maybe it's better love. Who knows?"

Just then I heard Amber's mother's voice call out from shore. "Is that you, Amber?"

Amber made a face, like there was more she wanted to say to me but she realized she couldn't.

"Yes, Momma," Amber called back. "It's me and Danny."

"Get in here right now."

I wanted to say something to Amber but with her mother standing there it was impossible. I brought the boat into shore. Amber's mother took the bowline and wrapped it around a tree branch. "Get out," she said.

"We had an accident, Momma," Amber said, stepping over the side.

"I hooked her with a fly hook," I said. "The wind moved the boat, and I lost my balance."

Amber's mother turned the flashlight onto Amber's face, which still had smears of blood on it. Then she moved it down onto the bloodstained dress.

"Fooling around in a boat at all hours," she said. "And you think you're ready to take care of a baby."

"I'm sorry, Momma. But it was an accident."

"Get up to the house," she said. "I'll let Ray handle this."

"It was an accident, Mrs. Dwyer," I said. "I just wanted to show Amber a heron's nest."

"Shut up and get yourself home where you belong. And don't come around here anymore. You're just another boy looking to have fun at my daughter's expense. Only she's too stupid to know it."

"That's not true, Momma," Amber said. "We're just friends."

Mrs. Dwyer turned to face Amber. "I guess that's why your dress is buttoned up all cockeyed." She shined the flashlight onto the front of Amber's dress where she had missed a buttonhole. "You're carrying one boy's baby and showing yourself to another. What kind of girl are you?"

"Oh, Momma," Amber said. "You don't understand."

Amber's mother slapped her. It sounded loud in the stillness of the lakeshore—like the snapping of a branch—and it made me jump.

Amber put her hand up to her cheek. A trickle of blood started to run from her ear. It traced a dark line over her hand and down along the curve of her cheek. Drops fell onto her dress.

"You're no better than a whore," her mother said. "That's what the Bible calls women like you."

Amber stared at her mother as if she couldn't believe what she had said. Then she turned and ran up toward the house.

Mrs. Dwyer watched Amber going away. I wanted to say something but I didn't know what. All my thoughts were jumbled together. Things had changed so fast, I couldn't make sense of anything. Then Amber's mother turned in my direction and shined the flashlight into my face. Behind the blinding white glare I could just make out her face, swollen with rage.

I turned away and took a few steps in the direction of our cabin. But then I stopped. "You need to put some antiseptic on the cut in Amber's ear," I said.

"I guess I can take care of my own daughter."

"I guess you better," I said.

"What did you say?"

"I said you better take care of Amber."

Mrs. Dwyer came over where I was standing. She stepped up close, holding the flashlight beam right into my face. She stood like that for a long time, and I stood looking back. I could hear the gentle lap of waves along the shore.

"I ought to call the sheriff," she said.

"Go ahead and do it. I'll tell him you want to get rid of Amber's baby."

Mrs. Dwyer held the flashlight on my face. Then she turned and started walking up toward the house. The flashlight beam swung wildly with each step she took.

Chapter Fifteen

WHEN I GOT BACK TO THE CABIN my father already had dinner on the table. He asked where I had been and I told him I'd been out fly-fishing and lost track of time. That seemed to satisfy him.

We sat down at the kitchen table and started to eat. He talked about where he'd been that day—Roscommon and Mackinaw City—and a big sale he'd made to a farm implement store, which pleased him very much and made him think that things might be turning around for him. Then the telephone rang in the back of the cabin, and he went to answer it. I heard him say hello, and then he listened for a long time without saying anything. Then he said a few quiet words and hung up.

"That was a Mrs. Dwyer from across the lake," he said when he came back to the table. "She was quite upset. I'm not sure I understood everything she was trying to tell me. Something about you and her daughter, Amber. Do you have any idea what she was talking about?"

"Amber's a girl I know," I said. "She was out fly-fishing with me."

"Tonight you mean?"

"Yes."

"And there was an accident, I guess. Is that right?"

"I hooked her with a fishing fly when the wind blew the boat. In the top part of her ear. But I got the hook out and stopped the bleeding."

"I see. Well, that was good." He was quiet for a while, watching me. "Is that all?"

"Yes, sir."

"Wasn't there something about her dress being mixed up? A missing button or something like that?"

I set my fork down onto the table. I touched the edge of my plate with my finger.

"She opened up her dress," I said. "For just a minute."

Out of the corner of my eye I saw my father shift in his chair. Then he pushed back from the table and crossed his arms.

"It was all right," I said. "She's pregnant. I wanted to see what a girl's breasts look like when she's pregnant. That's all."

The radio on the counter was playing softly. I hadn't noticed it before but now I did. It was a song with violins and horns, like you'd hear in a concert hall.

"You haven't been fooling around with this girl in any other way, have you?" my father said. His voice came to me through the music. "In a sexual way, I mean. Other than what you just said."

"No, sir. I haven't been fooling around with her. And it wasn't for sex. It was just because she's pregnant."

My father stood up and walked over to the cupboard where he kept a bottle of whiskey. I thought he was going to pour a drink. But then he just stood looking down at the floor, as if he'd forgotten what he'd gone over there to do. He came back and sat down again.

"Look, Danny, I can't say I understand exactly what's going on here. But you'd better not see this Amber girl again. That's what her mother said, too. She was quite clear on that point anyway."

I looked down at my plate where the grease from the hamburger had started to harden into a whitish glaze. Then I looked across to where my father's hands were curled on the tabletop. They were soft hands now—a salesman's hands—not rough and cracked like they'd been when he'd worked as a tool-and-die mechanic. And I thought it was odd that his hands had become soft after he'd come to live in the north woods of Michigan, which seemed the opposite of what you would expect. And then I realized that fact didn't matter to anything that was happening now.

"I love her," I said. The words just came out of my mouth.

My father snorted in a derisive way. "That's crazy."

"And she said she loves me, too."

"You don't know what you're talking about, Danny. Besides, her mother said she's going to marry the boy who impregnated her."

I raised my gaze. My father stared back at me with a calm expression, as if everything was under control. "To his liking" was a phrase he might use to describe how the conversation was going. And for some reason I felt a fierce anger rise up in me. It came from nowhere and seemed to flood me. And in that moment I wanted to hurt my father in some awful way, strike out against his softness and his calm steady gaze.

"*You* have a girlfriend," I said, still staring at him. "That Harriet Walker."

My father raised his arm, and for a second I thought he was going to strike me. But instead he slammed his hand down hard against the tabletop. Coffee sloshed out of his mug; a brownish stream traced a wavering path over to the edge of the table and began to drip slowly onto the floor.

"What goes on between Miss Walker and me is none of your business, Danny." His voice was clotted with anger.

"And that's not the only thing," I said. "Mom feels the same way."

"What?" He held my gaze.

I didn't say anything. I sat very still. In the background I heard the radio playing—horns and violins.

My father leaned forward. He gripped my forearm as if he was afraid I might get up and leave the room. "Did something happen in Chicago, Danny? Did your mother tell you something?"

I sat with my hands clenched into fists and my father's hand clutching my arm. I thought about what my mother had said about wanting to spend time with a man and I knew that the next words out of my mouth would be important ones—words that could set things into motion that couldn't be stopped. And I tried to know the words before I spoke them, so I could make them be the ones I wanted them to be. But everything had speeded up and all my thoughts were mixed together so I couldn't hold on to a single good thought and trace it to a conclusion in the way I'd always done before.

And then in the middle of all of this speeded-up thinking, I remembered what my mother had told me when she'd driven me to the bus depot that last morning in Chicago—about not saying everything that's on your mind because it can bring disaster. And that advice seemed like something I could depend on, because it had been said in a moment that felt like truth.

I looked at my father. His face was close to mine. The muscles in his jaw were tight.

"She said there were some things she wanted to do and she needed to be in Chicago to do them," I said. "That's why she couldn't be up here."

My father's grip relaxed. "Is that all?"

"Yes."

My father stared at me for a moment, like he wasn't sure if he believed me. He got up and walked over to the cupboard. This time he took down the bottle of whiskey and poured himself a drink. He poured it into a glass without ice or water. His hand was shaking. Then he came back and stood behind my chair.

"She told me that, too," he said. "Not in so many words, but it amounted to the same thing. That's her big experiment."

On the radio, the music rose into a big surge and then subsided.

"That's what she said about you, too," I said.

"What's that?"

I turned around to look at him. The glass was partway to his lips.

"She said you were trying an experiment. That's why you wanted to come up here to live."

He lowered the glass without drinking from it. Then he came

around and sat across from me. For a while he just stared at the radio with a quizzical expression on his face, as if he were trying to figure out the notes of some strange new song that had just started to play. Then he felt me watching, and his gaze swung in my direction. And for the first time that night his expression didn't have anything in it, not anger or fear or regret or disappointment. It was just the face of a man looking at his son across the kitchen table, nothing more. And I was glad for that.

Chapter Sixteen

WHEN I CAME HOME FROM SCHOOL the next afternoon I found Amber sitting on the concrete stoop at the back of our cabin. She wore a faded yellow housedress that was much too large for her. Over that she had on the heavy mackinaw jacket I'd seen her wearing that afternoon with Wayne. Her face was drawn and tired looking. There was a bruise on one cheek.

"Do you like my new dress?" she asked in a mocking voice. She stood up and held out her arms and did a graceful little pirouette.

"Sure," I said. "You look fine."

"It's a hand-me-down from my momma."

She sat back down on the stoop, leaning forward with her elbows on her knees. I walked up and touched her chin. "What happened to your cheek?" I asked.

"Nothing."

"Did someone hit you? Did your stepdad hit you?"

"I had an accident," she said. She pulled her chin away. "I've been having accidents lately. A boy even hooked me with a fishhook." She turned her head and held back her hair on one side. Just below the upper part of her ear was the wound from the fishhook, a jagged tear about a half inch long, tinged with dried blood.

"I'm sorry about that," I said.

She shrugged. "It doesn't matter."

I sat down next to her on the stoop. For some reason I reached out and took her hand. She let me hold it.

"Do you think you can drive the pickup?" she asked after a moment had passed.

"Of course. I told you I know how to drive."

"Can you come with me tomorrow to Saginaw?"

"What for?"

"I'm going to that special doctor I told you about." She slipped her hand out of mine and placed it on her lap, folding it together with the other one. "They said I'll need someone to drive me home."

I didn't say anything. Then I said, "Won't your folks drive you?"

"Jesus Christ," she said. Her hands clenched together so that the knuckles turned white.

"I'm sorry," I said. "I'll do it. But I was just wondering."

"I don't want them involved in this. Don't you understand that? This is my own decision, and I don't want them involved." She was silent for a moment. "Besides . . ."

"Besides what?"

"Look, I just want you to come along when I get it done. Is that asking for too much?" There was a shrillness in her voice now that frightened me. It reminded me of the way she'd been that afternoon in the taxidermy shed.

"Does Wayne know about it?" I asked.

"No. It wouldn't matter if he did."

"So you're not going to marry him."

"No."

"Have you told him that?"

"No."

We sat for a while in silence.

"I thought you wanted to keep the baby," I said.

"It's not a baby," she said. "It's just a clump of cells."

"Whatever it is, I thought you wanted to keep it."

"I've changed my mind. It's too much trouble." Her hands were still clenched together.

We sat for a long time, both of us staring out into the forest that surrounded the cabin. I wanted to ask her more questions but I felt I shouldn't. It was really none of my business, when you got right down to it. Beyond the strict mechanics of helping her to do it, it was none of my business. I could have an opinion but in the final analysis it was up to her.

"What time?" I asked.

"Eight o'clock. I'll come over and pick you up."

"When will we be back?"

"I don't know how long it will take. I don't think it will take very long."

"Okay," I said. "That's fine. It doesn't matter."

She stood up and started to walk away. The yellow housedress flapped around her knees below the black-and-red checked jacket.

"Amber." She stopped and turned around.

"*A demain,*" I said and smiled.

She stared at me as if I were completely crazy. Then she turned and walked away.

The next morning I waited for Amber outside the cabin. At exactly eight o'clock she drove up in the pickup. She was wearing the yellow housedress again; only this time she had on a heavy red sweater instead of the mackinaw jacket. She looked at me for a moment after I got into the pickup. Her face was wide open. Blank of any expression. The whole situation reminded me of times when I'd set off in the early morning with my father on fishing and hunting trips, when you are too tired to feel much of anything and just go through the motions.

Amber drove out the two-track drive to the county road and headed away from town. We drove for about a half hour and then she turned onto a larger road that was paved, which ran south. We were out of the Manistee Forest now and into a broad flat landscape of meadows and open farmland. It was all new territory to me.

"I told my momma I had to work a different shift," Amber said. It was the first thing either of us had said since setting out.

I looked at her with a puzzled expression because I didn't understand what she meant.

"That's why they let me take the pickup," she said, glancing over. "That's what I'm trying to say."

"Do you want me to ask you some French words?" I said.

"No," she said. "Never mind about that. That's all over." She reached across and punched open the glove box and drew out a Shell Oil Company road map. "But you should study this so you'll know how to get us back home. I don't know how much help I'll be to you on the return trip."

I unfolded the road map and began to study it. It took a minute to find Saginaw but then I found it and saw the highways that would lead us back to McBride. I calculated the distances between the major turning points, adding up the mileage numbers in my head. It felt nice to be able to think about what we were doing in terms of directions and distances and highway numbers and not in terms of Amber.

After a while I folded the map and put it back into the glove box.

"Tell me what's going to happen," I asked.

"What do you mean?"

"How you'll be on the trip back. Is there anything I have to do besides drive the pickup?"

"It's just a simple procedure," she said. "They lay you on a table and do a little scraping, that's all. They do a little scraping on the inside."

"Is there blood?" I asked, because I had seen the sheets and towels in the small storage space behind the seats.

She glanced over at me. "There might be some," she said. "But it shouldn't be bad. It'll be like having a period. That's what they told me."

I didn't say anything, although hearing Amber talk about it made me feel a little sick.

After a minute she said, "I'm sorry, Danny. This probably isn't the way you want to think about girls."

"It's all right," I said.

"Maybe you can consider it like a scientific experiment," she said, and she laughed in an odd high-pitched way. "Like when you saw my breasts."

"Sure," I said. "Maybe."

We drove on through the morning. The sun rose higher into the sky, shortening the shadows and making the landscape seem flatter than before. Nothing about the countryside here was very interesting, just empty furrowed fields and open meadows with small farmhouses and barns set far back from the road. To occupy my mind I thought about electricity, and then I thought about radio waves, how they can cut through almost anything. I didn't want to think about what was going to happen to Amber because it wasn't my choice and it wasn't my business. All I had to do was drive her home when it was over. That's all she had asked me to do. I didn't have to be involved any more than that.

And I understood this, too: that I didn't *want* to be involved any more than that. Because sometimes when you get involved you can't get out of it. You become connected in ways that cause trouble and are hard to untangle—like the complications Amber had with Wayne and my parents had with each other and my father had with Harriet Walker.

But after a while I couldn't stand it anymore and I had to ask her something.

"Amber, why are you doing this?"

"Isn't it obvious?"

"No. Because you always said you wanted to have the baby."

"I thought I wanted to have it. But I've changed my mind. Is that so awful?"

"But Wayne said he'll marry you. You told me that. That takes care of everything, doesn't it?"

"Just shut up," she said. "Please just shut up."

We drove on for several more miles. I thought about saying something more to Amber, not asking her a question but just telling her that I loved her and wanted her to be safe. I had said those things to her when I had taken the fishhook out of her ear, and it had seemed to help. Helped calm her down, I mean, and helped let her see things straight. But I remembered what had happened later— Amber's mother getting mad and then my father saying that my love was crazy—and so I just sat there in silence, feeling awkward and stupid and confused.

We came to a small town with a river and a dam with fingers of white frothy water tumbling down a spillway into a quiet pond, and then we were out of the town and into the countryside again. For a while the highway ran next to a railroad embankment; the steel rails sparkled brilliantly in the sunlight. Up ahead, I saw the rear end of a train, a red caboose, and some passenger cars. We gained on it slowly, closing the distance between us in steady increments. I was just beginning to see the faces of some passengers through the train windows when the tracks veered away and the train disappeared behind a shallow hill.

All of a sudden Amber slowed the pickup and coasted off onto the shoulder of the highway. She reached for the ignition and turned off the engine.

We sat there for several minutes. I didn't know what to say or do. I didn't know what was happening. I thought something was happening but I didn't know what it was. I sat with my hands folded on my lap.

Suddenly Amber began to pound her fists against the top of the steering wheel. She struck it over and over again, hitting so hard that I could feel the blows vibrate through the pickup. She didn't say anything and she didn't show any emotion; she just hit the steering wheel as if she wanted to destroy it.

I reached over and grabbed her wrists. But she jerked away and started to lash out at me, using her fists and the flat of her hands. She was crying and saying things that didn't make any sense, saying she hated me and hated everyone and wished she'd never been born.

"I'm sorry," I said, even though I didn't know what I was being sorry for. I tried to fend off her blows without hurting her. "I'm sorry."

And then she stopped. She just suddenly stopped. But I knew it wasn't because anything had changed, because it hadn't. She'd just run out of energy. The fury was still there but she didn't have the strength to do anything about it.

I held my arms around her, feeling her body heave as she gulped in air. I felt her tears on my cheek. Cars passed from time to time. When they did, the pickup tilted a little on its springs. This was because of the pressure wave that forms in front of a car when it speeds along the highway. That was something I'd read about somewhere.

After a while Amber's breathing became steady, and she pushed me away. She looked at me with a tired smile. She was pale, and her eyes had dark circles under them. It was hard to say that she looked pretty anymore.

"For a while it seemed like it would be something I could love and something that would love me back," she said. "But then the other night I was convinced it wouldn't happen that way. Something would come along and ruin it just like everything else."

I turned away and looked out at the wide shadowless landscape. I didn't want to say anything because I thought I'd already said too much. But I knew Amber was trying to hold herself together and I knew she wanted to hear some words, even if the words didn't make sense. Even if it was just the sound of another human voice. So I said the first thing that came into my mind.

"You can still have that."

What I meant was love, though I didn't want to use that word because in that moment it felt too dangerous.

We sat for a while longer; then Amber reached forward and turned the key in the ignition. She moved in a slow deliberate way, as if she had no choice left in the matter. Then she turned in my direction and stretched out her hand. For a moment I thought she was going to touch my face, but instead she reached behind and grasped the seat back and drew herself around. She looked back over her shoulder at the road behind. Then she let out the clutch, and we began to make a wide U-turn across the highway.

I didn't say anything.

I had asked that one question, and it had changed everything. But it didn't feel like a victory of any kind. It felt like I had started something that I was connected to.

After we had gone a short way, Amber said, "I guess being married to Wayne won't be the worst thing in the world, will it?" She glanced over at me, but I didn't think she was really expecting an answer. In any case, I didn't have one to give.

PART/THREE

Chapter Seventeen

THE NEXT DAY AFTER SCHOOL I did not go to the
Shamrock restaurant to see Amber. Instead I stayed and watched
the football team practicing on the muddy field behind the teachers'
parking lot. I was tired of thinking about Amber and all of her
problems. I loved her in a certain way—I understood that now—but
I'd already done enough to help her. I had agreed to go with her to
Saginaw, and then I'd changed things by asking that one question. It
seemed like that should be enough. Anyway, she was going to marry
Wayne now, so there were really no problems left to worry about.
She would marry Wayne and keep her baby and everything would
be all right. They would make a life together. Maybe not a great life
but probably just as good a life as most people have.

It was cold. The radio said a weather front had moved in from
Ontario, causing the winds to back around in a northerly direction.
Tiny particles of ice swirled in the air like dust and gathered in
whitish patches on the frozen blades of grass. I looked through
the swirling ice onto the football field and tried to find the boy I'd
seen before—the boy who had been playing the end position—
but I couldn't spot him. Then I wondered if he'd been cut from
the team or if he'd given up trying to be a football player because
he was no good at it. When I'd seen him before he had seemed to
play well enough to be on the team, but perhaps I hadn't known
what to look for.

The wind gusted up for a moment, driving the sleet slantwise and making everything seem off balance. I hunched my shoulders and stuck my hands deep into the pockets of my jacket. In the left side pocket I felt something hard. I felt around and realized it was the revolver I'd placed there several weeks ago, on the night my father had brought Harriet Walker back to our cabin.

Still looking out onto the football field, I wrapped my fingers around the knurled plastic handle, feeling it grow warm from the heat of my hand. I reached up with my index finger and felt the safety button and flicked it on and off several times. For a while I pretended I was a secret FBI agent who had been sent to spy on one of the football players; I tried to find the football player who looked most guilty, like he had something to hide from the world, and eventually I spotted a blond-haired boy sitting by himself along the sideline. But then I felt silly and so I stopped pretending and took my hand out of my pocket.

Just then I heard a car drive up behind me. When I turned around Wayne was getting out of his black Plymouth and walking in my direction. The first thing I thought was that he'd heard about what had happened in the rowboat and was coming to beat me up. But then I saw the grin on his face and I relaxed.

"Are you watching the football players or trying to sneak a look at the cheerleaders' panties?" he asked. He looked over to the side of the field where the cheerleaders were clapping and practicing their flips. Some of them wore woolen gloves that made their claps sound hollow.

"Maybe both," I said.

"Well, there's hope for you after all," he said, laughing. "Maybe Charlene was the right medicine for you."

We stood watching through the chain-link fence. The coach had the players line up and run a play. One of the players ran down the sideline and caught the ball in a diving catch, stretched out so that he looked for an instant like he was flying.

"Not bad," Wayne said.

The football player ran back to his teammates, holding the ball over his head like a trophy.

"Amber told me you're getting married next week," I said. I kept looking through the chain-link fence.

"That's right," Wayne said in a matter-of-fact voice. "I decided to make an honest woman out of her."

Neither of us said anything for a while. The team ran a couple of plays. Down along the sidelines the cheerleaders asked people to spell McBride.

I turned and looked at Wayne. His gaze out on the practice field held a kind of curiosity, and I knew that his attention was already back on the football team. Marrying Amber had occupied his thoughts for just a moment.

"Amber doesn't want to get married," I told him.

His head swung in my direction. "What are you talking about?" he said. He sounded puzzled.

"Her parents won't let her keep the baby if she isn't married. That's the only reason she's doing it."

"That's a lie." Wayne grabbed the front of my jacket and pushed me back against the chain-link fence. It rattled down along the fence posts.

"She doesn't love you," I said, looking right into his face. "She told me that. And she doesn't like living in McBride. She wants to go to Montreal. That's why she's studying French."

"That's a lie," Wayne repeated. And then he hit me.

I had never been struck with a fist before and I didn't see it or feel it happen. Suddenly I was lying on the wet ground with my jaw hurting and blood filling my mouth. Wayne was standing over me, but I couldn't see him clearly; it was as if I were looking at him through campfire smoke or a window smeared with dirt.

"Goddamn you," Wayne yelled. His face was swollen with rage, but his eyes were filled with a strange kind of pleading, as if by getting me to take back my words it would make things be all right again. And for the first time I realized that in his own way he really did love Amber. Loved her very much. And that thought upset me even more.

Wayne swung his leg and kicked me in the side, and I felt a slight bump, no more than you would feel if someone had nudged you in a crowded room. But that was followed a second later by a terrible pain that ripped into my body in a sudden rush.

"Get up and fight," I heard a voice yell from far away. "He's not so tough." And then Wayne and I were in the center of a crowd of kids. Some were cheerleaders because I remember pleated skirts and sweaters with large red Ms, and some were football players, still in their pads and plastic helmets, and some were kids who had not gone home from school yet. *Stragglers* my father would call them.

I got to my knees and pushed myself up because I wanted to fight back in front of the other kids, even though I was afraid and felt the terrible pain in my side. For a second I wondered if something might be wrong with me, like a broken rib or a ruptured spleen. But then I lost that thought and rushed in Wayne's direction. And my only thought was to hurt him.

Wayne jumped aside and hit me in the back of the head, and I went down again.

I lay on the ground, gasping for air and feeling the pain in my side and a new pain in the back of my head. I still wanted to hurt Wayne but I knew he was bigger and stronger than me. Then I remembered Harriet Walker's revolver, still in the pocket of my jacket, and for a moment I thought about taking it out and using it to frighten Wayne, or even to shoot him, because I believed that might be allowed since he had struck me first. But then I put that thought away, because it seemed completely crazy.

"Amber doesn't love you," I said for the second time, my face just above the mud. "She needs a husband so she can keep her baby. That's the only reason she puts up with you."

Out of the corner of my eye I saw Wayne walk up behind me. I knew he was going to kick me again so I rolled over and curled into a ball. And then I felt his kick, and this time it hurt immediately, not with the little delay I'd noticed before. And I remember thinking that in a bizarre way this might be a good sign, because it meant I was getting used to pain and could handle it better.

I must have blacked out for a few seconds because the next thing I remembered was the football coach kneeling over me, a large beefy man with a brush cut and a silver whistle hanging from a string around his neck. People stood behind him, looking over his shoulder. Wayne was gone.

"Are you all right, lad?" the football coach said. He was slapping my face with little taps.

"Yes, sir," I said, even though I still felt the pains in my mouth and my side and the back of my head. I propped myself up on one elbow.

"That was quite a beating you took," the football coach said. "Do you and that boy have a grudge going between you?"

I rubbed my jaw. When I took my hand away there was blood on it. I tasted blood in my mouth and turned my head and spit onto the ground. It made a little puddle next to my shoulder, a brilliant red blob against the drab brown earth. I stared at it dumbly, astonished at the contrast of colors, as if it were the most fascinating thing I had ever seen. But then I remembered the coach was waiting for my answer.

"I'm all right," I said. I tried to stand up, but the coach held his hand against my chest. Then it occurred to me that I had probably made a bad impression by not fighting better, and I might have spoiled my chance to make the team next year. "I'm going to kick the shit out of him when I see him again," I said, which seemed like the right thing to say with the coach around.

"Take it easy, lad," the coach said. "Why don't you go into school and report this to Mr. Hargrove? Let him take care of it."

I looked at the coach. He was smiling at me in a reassuring way, trying to get things back on track, which was his job. Behind him some football players were talking to some cheerleaders. Other kids were looking at me and grinning.

"What happened to the boy who plays the end position?" I asked. And even as I said it I realized it didn't make any sense. It was something I'd had on my mind when Wayne had arrived but not anything that was important now, after Wayne had beaten me up.

"What's that?" the coach said. "What did you say?" He turned to look back at the other players. "What did the lad say?"

"He asked about the end position," one of the players said, and a few of them laughed. "He's talking about Gordon Biers?"

"You'd better go in and see Mr. Hargrove, lad," the coach said. "I think you might be a little mixed up." He put a hand on my shoulder, as if he was trying to steady me, and I was grateful for that, because it seemed like something a person would do to someone he cared about.

"All right," I said. "That's a good idea. I'm probably just mixed up. I'll do that."

I walked away from the coach and from the kids who had gathered to see the fight, but I didn't go into the school and I didn't go to Mr. Hargrove's office. Instead I went around to the other side of the school where there was an empty baseball diamond. I sat on the visiting team's bench and waited for my thoughts to clear. A baseball diamond is a good place to sit in November, I decided, because there is no one there to bother you. It's not baseball season, and so the field is empty. Even when it's cold and sleeting it's not so bad, because you are alone to think about the things you want to think about. And one of the things I wanted to think about was Amber and what I'd done by telling Wayne she did not want to marry him. And the other thing I wanted to think about was Wayne and how I was going to fight him the next time I saw him.

But underneath the thinking I was feeling miserable, and none of my thoughts were going anywhere, not leading to any conclusions. To make myself feel better, I forced myself to think of some mathematical fact, some puzzle or calculation I could occupy my mind with, so I wouldn't have to think about the other things that were bothering me. First I thought of pi, and I tried to run the digits out as far as I could remember, but I only got three or four places before everything broke down. Next I tried to calculate the cube root of seventeen, but that broke down, too. Finally, in a kind of panic, I thought about Amber again. I remembered how I'd told her that I loved her and how she'd said she loved me, too, but in a special way that wasn't normal love. And then I wondered if the love we had could be a better sort of love than normal love, because it didn't have anything else attached to it, not sex or jealousy or the fear of being left behind. None of the things that can get in the way and spoil it.

My mind was going very fast now, my thoughts like waves breaking on a rocky seashore, one right after the other, so that none of my thoughts were being resolved or settled or concluded; there were only the feelings that the thoughts brought with them, the fear or sadness or shame or disappointment, and nothing after that. And suddenly I felt overwhelmed by all the feelings and I began to cry, not in a dramatic or noisy way but only quietly, the tears welling up and running down my cheeks and falling onto my jacket one by one.

After a while I left the baseball diamond and headed downtown. I wasn't exactly sure where I was going, though I knew I needed to tell Amber what I'd said to Wayne. But then I saw Charlene. She was coming out of the hairdresser's shop, wearing a heavy green woolen sweater over her white starched hairdresser's dress. She looked kind of like a picture in a movie, a pretty girl standing in a swirling mist of ice.

I stood for a moment wondering what to do. I knew I should go to the Shamrock restaurant, because it was important to tell Amber what I had done so she could deal with Wayne. But I felt lonely and confused and afraid, and I wanted those feelings to go away. More than helping Amber, I wanted those feelings to go away.

I called out Charlene's name. She stopped and looked around with a puzzled expression. Then she spotted me standing on the far side of the street, beyond the parked cars and through the passing traffic, and a smile came onto her face just in the instant that she saw me, and it was nice to see that smile, the nicest thing that had happened to me all day it seemed, the most beautiful smile in the world. And suddenly I felt the feeling coming back that I'd felt that afternoon in the apple orchard when I'd held her in my arms. It seemed to rise up out of nowhere and overwhelm the other feelings that were in me, all the other feelings that were swirling around and that I couldn't make sense of.

I dodged a passing car and went over.

"What happened to you?" Charlene said. She reached up and touched my cheek, where I could feel a bruise starting to come.

"I had a fight with Wayne."

Charlene's fingertips moved up along my cheek and across my forehead and down along the other cheek. She brushed back my hair on one side. "You boys," she said. She shook her head in a disapproving schoolmarmish way.

"Never mind about that," I said. "I'm all right." And then I asked her about the correspondence course in Detroit, because I knew it was important to her and she would like to talk about it. And we talked about that for a while, standing in the swirling sleet. And then we talked about some other things that were important to her—anything else she wanted to talk about, really, just anything at all. Next I said she had nice hair—because hair was important to her and I knew she would like that, too—and then I reached out and touched a strand of it, delicately, like it was a thing that might be damaged if I handled it too roughly. And then I said she looked beautiful—because I knew she would like that, too—and I took her hand and drew her back into a sort of alleyway, a sheltered recess between two brick buildings, and we started to kiss like we'd done that afternoon in the orchard, only this time I went ahead and touched her small hard breasts, my hand between the stiff starched cloth and Charlene's warm giving skin, first slowly and then fumbling and hurriedly and urgently, and then moving to the place down lower and then pressing back against her on the hard brick wall and all the while saying she was wonderful and that I didn't ever want to leave her.

"Oh, Danny," she whispered, turning my name into a sound I had never heard before.

"Oh, yes," I said. "I love you."

But not meaning it. Not meaning a single word. Just saying it because it blotted out all the rest.

Chapter Eighteen

WHEN I GOT BACK TO THE LAKE after hitchhiking out from town, my father was already home. I found him out behind the cabin by the woodpile chopping wood. He was still dressed in the clothes he had worn to work, brown woolen trousers and a white starched shirt. I stood next to a tree and watched him in the twilight.

After a while he stopped. He was breathing hard.

"Look here," he said. Bits of bark and mud had flown up and stuck to his white shirt. He tried to brush them off, but they left dark smudges. "I think I've ruined a perfectly good shirt, Danny. Your father's a fool."

"It'll probably clean up," I said.

"Let's hope so." He looked at me. "What happened to you?"

"I stayed after school and played football with some kids. I got tackled a couple of times."

"I guess you did," he said, smiling. He stepped over and touched my chin and lifted my face toward the light coming from the lake. "That's quite a shiner. But honorably earned on the field of battle."

"Yes, sir," I said. "I think so."

We went into the cabin, and he fixed dinner while I washed up and changed into clean clothes. I couldn't stop thinking about what I'd done to Charlene. I felt guilty about pretending to be in love with her, and I wondered how I could make up for it. I had lied to people before, but I had never lied for the reason of taking something away from them, the way I'd sort of taken Charlene's body away from her for a while. But then I remembered I had a more important problem to deal with, and that was how I'd messed things up for Amber. She needed to marry Wayne so she could keep her baby, and now I'd messed that up. Wayne would break things off, and she'd be on her own again, alone like she had been when I'd first met her.

During dinner my father ate in silence, as if he was absorbed in his own private thoughts. I kept waiting for him to begin his interrogation, to ask me what I'd learned that day at school. But instead he suddenly began to talk about something else—the five-mile-long suspension bridge being built across the Straights of Mackinac. It was going to change things in northern Michigan, he said, open up the region for tourism and development and ruin a part of the world that should stay wild and unspoiled. Then, after we'd finished eating and had pushed our plates aside and he had lit up a cigarette, he got out a pencil and a pad of paper and showed me how to calculate stresses in the steel beams that held a bridge together, using vectors and trigonometry to determine how the forces are distributed. And it was odd, I thought, that he would be against the construction of the bridge and yet teach me how to calculate the stresses in the steel, as if his thinking was divided between wanting to understand the thing and being opposed to it. And it seemed to me to be the thinking of a man who was lost, at least in that moment, and didn't know which way he wanted his life to go.

After he finished showing me the calculations, he suddenly changed the subject, as if it were a conversation we were continuing from an earlier time: "You're going to have to deal with women, Danny," he said, "and it's important that you have standards so you'll know what choices to make." For a moment I thought he was speaking about Charlene and what had happened in the alley, but then I realized he didn't know about that. And so it had to be something else. Just women in general.

He took a puff of the cigarette and stared at me through the curling strands of smoke.

"But you should know," he continued, "that if a person fails once in a while it doesn't mean the end of everything. You'll have other chances to be a good person."

"I understand," I said, and I believed I did, because I'd seen people be good and bad at different times—the same people, I mean—although I thought it was unusual that he would speak about women after he'd talked about the suspension bridge and the stresses in the steel. And I decided, finally, that the subject of women was uncomfortable for him, and approaching it as he'd done—making it seem like just another subject that had come up in the course of our evening together—was a way to make it seem less strange.

"I'm going to stop seeing Harriet Walker," he said next, and suddenly I realized he had been talking about himself, and the failure he had spoken of was his own.

He held the cigarette between his lips, one eye squinting against the smoke sliding up his face. "That's probably something that needs to be done," he added after a moment.

I didn't say anything. I didn't look at him.

"You'll have to decide if that's all right with you," he continued, "whether it's enough to set things right between us." He took his cigarette and crushed it into the ashtray, then brushed his fingertips together, as if he were getting rid of some particles of tobacco. "I'd like you to stay living here," he said. "It means a lot to me to have you close by. And I think it's good for you, too, though you may not always think so. Living in the country is an experience not too many boys have these days. It'll make you a special person, I believe, although I can't promise it'll make you a better person. Only that you'll be different." He pressed his lips together, and his gaze flicked off to one side, then came back. "But if you decide to go and live with your mother in Chicago, I'll understand. I've spoken to her, and she'd be happy to have you there."

"She told me that, too."

"Did she? Well, you know it to be a fact then."

"Are you in love with Miss Walker?" I asked after a little time had passed.

"No," my father said, and I think the suddenness of his response surprised him and made him ill at ease. In any case he turned his head away, staring off to the side of the room where a calendar hung from a nail. The calendar was from a hardware store in Newaygo and had a picture of a fisherman about to land a large rainbow trout. The man was crouched low above the stream, his landing net stretched forward, an excited expression on his face.

"Or maybe I do," my father continued, still staring at the calendar. "Maybe I love her in a different way than the way I love your mother." He put his hands flat on the tabletop, as if he were trying to draw some wisdom through its surface. "I guess you can love more than one woman, Danny. I've never thought about it, but I guess it's true. Maybe love is easy. It's what you do about it that's hard."

A moment passed, and then I felt it was my turn to talk and that I should say something to respond to what my father had just announced, which was that he wanted our life to move forward as it had before, which seemed like a good decision. "I knew you were seeing her," I said vaguely, for no reason I understood. "That's all."

"Yes," he said. "Well, I suppose it's best that we talk about it in the open."

We were silent for a long time. After a moment I looked over at the calendar again. Earlier in the fall my father and I had had a kind of stupid joke about it: each night at dinner he'd observe in mock amazement that the man had *still* not caught the fish, as if the scene should actually be unfolding, and not be forever frozen in that wonderful expectant moment, and I would say he needed to play the fish more, to tire him out before he tried to land him.

"I hope this hasn't ruined something, Danny," my father said. His voice was almost a whisper.

"No, sir," I said. "It hasn't." And then I said something that surprised me. "You can keep seeing her if you want to. I understand how it is between men and women." Because I was thinking about Charlene now.

My father looked at me with a surprised expression. Then he grinned. "That's very open-minded of you," he said. "But I'm not sure you understand everything that needs to be understood. Not yet."

"Okay," I said. "I believe you."

And in an odd way his words made me feel better, relieved that there were things still unknown to me—because I thought those might be the things that would explain the many confusions still remaining in my mind.

My father sat and smoked his cigarette. I waited to see if he had anything else to say. The radio was tuned to a station in Cadillac, and a song was playing about the moon and pizza pie and how that feels like a certain type of love. I listened to the words and tried to grasp the song's meaning, but it made no sense. And finally I decided that it was just a song that used the word love as a kind of ornament, in order to get people's attention and not to explain anything that was important or true about it, as my father had just tried to do for me.

The song ended, and I looked over at my father. He was still smoking quietly across the table. And suddenly I understood that we had made a sort of bargain—something given and something gotten back—and I went over and stood before him and shook his hand, because I thought that's what people did at such a moment.

Chapter Nineteen

THE NEXT MORNING I AWOKE early. My room was still in darkness. I had been dreaming about Charlene, her smile, and the smell of her hair and the way her skin had felt beneath my hand. For a while I tried to keep the dream going, tried to hold on to the pleasant feeling and step back into it. But then the dream slipped away, like a landscape disappearing into a fog, and the feeling disappeared, and I let my thoughts go to other places.

I lay and watched my room lighten with the rising of the sun. Slowly pieces of furniture came into view: a battered oak bureau, a ladder-back chair with my clothes hanging off the back, a goosenecked reading lamp.

I began to think about Amber again, and about her and Wayne, and about what I'd done by telling Wayne that Amber did not love him. It seemed now, after talking to my father, that I'd been wrong to get involved. There are different kinds of love—that's what he had told me—and maybe the feeling Amber had for Wayne was just another kind. Or maybe it could *become* love later, even if it wasn't love in the beginning. Love wasn't the pure constant thing I'd always thought it was; it was more complicated than that, something that could be created and something that could be lost. Something that could change.

After a while I heard my father moving around in his bedroom. Then I heard him out in the kitchen making breakfast, the sound of eggs frying, the *glub-glub-glub* of coffee percolating on the stove, the clink of silverware. The normal sounds of morning.

But I did not get up, and he did not come into my room to wake me, and in that way it was not a normal morning.

After a while I fell back asleep.

When I awoke for the second time it was two o'clock. I had slept through the entire morning and into the afternoon. Wind was blowing. I could hear it moving through the bare tree branches. Cold air leaked in around the window frame, brushing against my cheek. I tried to prop myself on one elbow so I could raise the window shade, but as soon as I rolled over I felt a stab of pain in my side where Wayne had kicked me. I lay back down without looking out.

My father had said I needed to decide on my standards, and I wanted to do that now so I could move ahead with my life and make the right choices. But I didn't know where my standards should come from or how I would know which ones were right. It seemed the way I'd thought about life was all wrong now; I'd always believed that life was simple and you didn't have to wonder too much about where you stood or what you should do next or who you should love. All you had to do was put the facts together and find the truth of a situation, just like in mathematics. But it was different than that, not much better than when you are a child and don't have anything to guide you, no facts or experiences and no formula to put the facts into, even if you had them. And then I imagined how it would be if I went off and lived by myself, and for a while I let my mind drift along in this direction. I thought about the summer cottages around the lake—the ones that stood empty after Labor Day—and the abandoned farmhouses you saw out along the country roads, and I imagined myself breaking into one and taking it over and making a life in it, hunting for food and cutting wood in the forest to burn and keep warm, and not having to see anyone I didn't want to see or not having to see anyone at all, if that was my choice. And then I thought about Amber and I wondered if she would like to come and join me, because her life seemed in-between, too, and needed a new direction.

I'd told Wayne that Amber did not want to marry him, and now she was going to be on her own again. It was as if everything I'd done had brought her back to where she'd started—the place she'd been when I'd first met her—alone and frightened in the taxidermy shed, asking me to take care of her.

And then, without even thinking about it, I knew what I had to do next.

I walked down to the end of the two-track road and hitched a ride into town. It was turning into a miserable day. The sleet from the previous day had changed to snow, and white patches were starting to accumulate on the ground. When I got to the lumberyard I followed the sound of whirring saws until I found the shed where they cut lumber. Wayne was alone, standing behind a table saw pushing sheets of plywood through the spinning blade with a notched stick. He wore goggles and a blue stocking cap. After a minute he noticed me standing off to the side. He finished making the cut and turned off the saw. The whine of the spinning blade started to run down.

"What do you want?" Wayne asked me. He pushed the goggles up onto his head. His clothes and arms were covered with sawdust.

"I want to talk to you about Amber."

"You already did," he said. "You told me everything I need to know."

"That's what I mean," I said. "What I told you wasn't true. I only said it because I was jealous of you."

Wayne looked at me. "You're crazy," he said.

"I was jealous of you," I said, "because I'm kind of in love with Amber myself."

Wayne laughed out loud. "No kidding," he said. "Why don't you tell me something I don't already know?"

"Look," I said. I took a step closer and put my hand on his arm. The sawdust made it feel like I was touching the pelt of some animal. "I'm sorry for what I said. It was crazy and it wasn't true. Amber loves you and wants to get married."

Wayne looked at me as if I were a madman. Or maybe it was a look of sympathy. I couldn't really tell. "No, she doesn't," he said. "She likes you and all your grand ideas. Mathematics and French and all that other stuff. Now get the hell out of here."

Wayne tried to pull his arm back, but I gripped it tighter. For a moment I thought he was going to hit me, but instead he just smiled.

"Look," he said. "You did me a big favor because I never wanted to marry Amber anyway. I just wanted someone to fool around with."

He pulled his arm away with a vicious jerk, then he stepped over to the saw and pulled the goggles down over his eyes. He acted as if I wasn't there, like he'd already forgotten about me.

I put my hand into the pocket of my jacket and took out the revolver. I pointed it at the middle of Wayne's chest, holding it steady with both arms out straight. Then I yelled for him to stop.

Wayne turned and looked. I could see his eyes through the goggles looking down at the gun. Then his gaze came up to my face and he laughed. "What are you going to do, Danny? Shoot me if I don't agree to marry Amber? That's a brilliant idea." He held his arms apart like he was making himself a target.

I held the gun steady on the center of Wayne's chest. I knew I wouldn't shoot him, but I wanted to show that I was serious, and the gun seemed to be the only way. But all of a sudden something changed inside me. It was as if a small shift had happened, like weights rebalancing on a scale. And suddenly I knew I *could* shoot Wayne. I could shoot him and I could watch him suffer and I could let him bleed to death. And not only because of what he'd done himself but for all the other reasons—the things that *other* people had done—the things that everyone did but that they didn't tell you about, the things you had to figure out for yourself.

"Goddamn you," I yelled. My arms began to shake. I tightened my finger slightly on the trigger.

Wayne flipped the switch on the wall. The saw began its high-pitched scream.

"Goddamn you," I yelled again.

But I knew he couldn't hear me now. It was too late. No one could hear me with all that sound. It filled up the shed, pressing against the walls like a caged animal trying to escape.

Wayne picked up a piece of plywood and hoisted it up onto the table, using his knee to give it an extra boost. When he got the plywood into position he started to push it toward the saw blade with the notched stick.

And then something collapsed inside of me. It was as if the little weights had shifted back. I lowered the gun and turned away, because it was too late to do anything about Wayne. With all the noise it made no sense. Even if I shot him, the noise would still continue. There was nothing I could do about the noise. If I was going to help Amber I had to find some other way.

I walked out of the shed, followed by the whine of the saw. Outside, it was still snowing. The wind was blowing hard. I took a few steps in the deepening snow. Then I started running in the direction of the Shamrock restaurant. When I reached the street I heard the pitch of the saw blade change as it began biting into fresh wood.

Chapter Twenty

AMBER WAS BUSY WITH CUSTOMERS so I sat in a booth by the window and read from a book I'd been carrying in my pocket. From time to time I looked up. Outside, the snow was still coming down. Inside, Amber went back and forth to the booths and tables, taking orders, carrying plates of food, cleaning up. She went about her work in a stiff, mechanical way. Whenever she passed my booth she looked straight ahead, as if she didn't know I was there—or didn't care. I assumed she was upset about the trip to Saginaw—the trip that hadn't happened—and the part I'd played in changing her mind.

After a while there was a lull and she came over and sat down heavily in the booth. She pushed around so her back was against the wall and her legs were out toward the aisle. She took in a big breath and released it. I noticed that the bruise on her cheek had started to fade into a mottled greenish blotch.

"*Comment ça va?*" she said in a flat voice. She stared straight ahead, as if she were talking to herself.

"Good," I said. "I'm doing good."

"You're supposed to say '*ca va.*'"

"Okay. *Ca va.*"

"*Qu'est-ce que tu fais ici?*"

"I don't know what that means."

"It means 'What are you doing here?'" she said, sounding exasperated. "I'm not supposed to be seeing you, remember?"

"I don't care," I said. "We didn't do anything wrong."

"You and I know that, but our opinion doesn't count. It's like I told you already: some people have bigger votes. Anyway . . ." She looked around to see if she was missing any customers. ". . . Wayne's picking me up at six so I guess he can protect me if I need protecting."

I didn't say anything.

"What's that you're reading?" Amber asked. She reached across and turned the book in her direction. Her eyes skimmed down the page.

"It's a book about relativity," I said. "Einstein's theory that told how to make the atomic bomb. It's supposed to explain it in simple language."

"It doesn't look simple to me," she said, pushing the book back.

"It says if you traveled in a rocket at the speed of light you'd never get older."

"That's crazy," she said.

She turned in the booth and looked out into the parking lot. The snow was coming down harder than before. Big heavy flakes swirled past the window. Drifts were starting to form.

"You should see Charlene," Amber said, still looking out. "That makes more sense than coming around to see me all the time. Just call her up and say you want to see her."

I looked at Amber, trying to tell if she was kidding, because for some reason I thought she might know about what had happened the day before in the alley. But she was just staring out at the snow as if everything were fine.

"Maybe I will," I said.

She glanced over at a booth where two men had just sat down. The men looked at her; one of them raised his hand to get her attention.

"She's not exactly your type," Amber said. "I'm aware of that. But everything doesn't have to be perfect."

"Yes." I said, and I wondered if she was thinking about her own life now and Wayne.

"And it doesn't mean it's not important. Or that Charlene isn't important."

"I know that," I said. "I like Charlene."

I felt guilty to be pretending that I hadn't seen Charlene, but I didn't want Amber to know what I had done. And it wasn't what I'd *done*, exactly, but how I'd made it happen—telling Charlene that she was wonderful and saying that I loved her. Those words had come from a strange kind of gratitude, I decided, or because I'd wanted to make what we were doing seem all right or because I'd wanted it to keep happening. But in any case they had been a lie.

Amber stood up, pushing against the table as if she needed that extra boost to get herself upright. Then she looked down at her stomach and placed her hands there.

"Maybe I'm just jealous," she said, and her voice sounded tired, "because I'm past the point of new things happening in the love category. I'm just holding on now."

"Miss!" one of the men called out from across the restaurant. Amber turned and looked at him with a blank expression, then looked back at me. "You can learn from my mistakes, Danny," she said. "I can be a backward example. That's what I'm good for."

She went over to the booth and began to take the men's orders. I watched her standing in the aisle, one hip cocked against the weight of her stomach, a yellow pencil in one hand and a notepad in the other. She stood and smiled and answered the men's questions and wrote down their orders. When she walked back toward the kitchen the men watched her going away, watched down low where her hips and legs were moving inside the pink dress. When the kitchen door swung shut they turned and looked across the booth and smiled at each other in a leering way. And I suddenly realized that they thought Amber was something to make a joke about because she was pregnant, maybe, or because she wore a pink uniform with a tiny collar and a name tag or because she was a young pretty girl whose job it was to take down their orders and bring them food. And then I thought that it—the way the men had acted—was just something that Amber had to deal with all day long. And I guessed that she had probably gotten used to it by now and had found a way to live with it.

One of the men leaned forward and said something to his friend, just two or three words, and then they both looked over at me. And I wondered if they thought *I* was the father of Amber's child—had been the one who'd had sex with her and made her pregnant—and in the next instant I realized I *wanted* them to think that, to believe that she and I could have been close in that way, and I stared back hard until they got tired of looking and turned away.

As it got closer to the end of Amber's shift, she glanced up whenever a car drove into the parking lot. I knew she was expecting Wayne, but I was afraid to tell her he wouldn't be coming.

At six o'clock her shift ended, and of course Wayne had not come, and of course he had still not come by six-thirty, after we had sat in the booth in an awkward silence, watching through the window as the sky grew dark and the streetlights came on and the snow beneath them blew like smoke across the pavement.

Finally Amber stood up.

"We might as well go," she said. She drew her blue coat around her and fastened it with a belt. Then she pulled a red stocking cap over her head.

"How are we going to get home?" I asked.

"I can borrow Andy's car," she said, meaning the Negro cook who lived above the restaurant. "He'll let me."

Amber went back into the kitchen. I heard some voices, hers and Andy's. She came back holding a set of keys.

We left the restaurant and walked north on Main Street. Deep drifts were beginning to form against the sides of buildings. Amber walked behind me so she could put her feet into the footprints I made.

When we got to the car—an old blue Pontiac Star Chief with a battered front fender—I used the book about relativity to scrape snow off the windshield. Then we sat and waited for the engine to warm up and the heater to come on. It was very cold. My feet were cold and wet from the snow, and I knew that Amber's were, too, because she was wearing only sneakers. The book in my hand was wet; the snow had begun to melt and soak into the pages.

"Jesus, Mary, and Joseph," Amber said under her breath. She shivered. Her breath pumped out in little clouds that rose around her face.

"I guess Wayne had to stay late at the lumberyard," I said, even though I knew that wasn't true.

Amber didn't say anything. She shivered again and drew in a sharp breath. "Can a baby be hurt by cold?" she asked.

"I don't know," I said.

"Don't you know anything useful?" she said. Her voice was shaking from the cold. "Or do you just know about parabolas and relativity?"

"I'm sorry," I said.

"Don't be sorry," she said. "Just don't be stupid all the time." She was angry, and I knew it was because Wayne had not shown up to drive her home, and she was cold and frightened.

"I don't think cold can hurt a baby," I said. "Cold is natural."

"Now that's a brilliant statement," Amber said. She glanced over at me. Her face was very angry. A sheen of sweat was on it and dark circles were under her eyes. "There's the voice of experience talking, ladies and gentlemen."

I didn't say anything because I knew Amber was mad and nothing I could say would change it. She reached across and turned a knob. Hot air began blowing out around our legs. Small semicircles began to grow through the frost on the windshield, one in front of me and one in front of Amber.

"That's more like it, ladies and gentlemen," Amber said. She reached down under the seat to warm her hands in the hot air blowing out. Then she shifted the gearshift and let the clutch out, and the car began to roll forward.

We drove slowly through McBride. There were no pedestrians and hardly any cars. We passed the city park, a wide white emptiness with lights shining down on empty swing sets and teeter-totters. Then we passed the VFW Hall with the artillery cannon pointing to the sky. Yellow lights glimmered through the windows. A handful of cars sat in the parking lot covered by thick blankets of snow; they reminded me of a herd of slumbering animals.

"The old soldiers are having a party," Amber said. "If we get stuck we can call out the cavalry."

Out on the highway the drifts were deeper; Amber had to speed up to break through the deeper ones. The car skidded going into some of the turns, a sickening feeling like the earth was rolling out from under us. Amber worked to hold the speed steady and steer the car straight.

"You're doing good," I said.

Amber sat forward with her arms wrapped around the steering wheel, peering out through the little triangle that the defroster had cleared on the windshield. The headlights of an oncoming car—the first one we'd passed since leaving town—lit up her face like a mask; then it got dark again.

"How come you put up with Wayne?" I said, because I knew it was all over between them now, and I wanted her to be ready when she found that out.

"What do you mean?" She answered distractedly; she was concentrating on driving.

"You're a hundred times better than he is."

Another car came up and flashed its headlights through the

windshield. The sheen of sweat on Amber's face glistened in the reflected light.

"You mean the father of my baby?" she said sarcatically. "And the person who stands between me and a life of poverty? Is that who you're talking about?"

"I mean the person who orders you around and drinks too much and beats people up and doesn't bother to pick you up when it's snowing."

"Keep your mouth shut, Danny," she said. "I've made my decision. It's none of your business."

I thought about what I'd said to Wayne—how I'd set things in motion that Amber didn't know about.

"You don't need him," I said. "You're smart enough to take care of yourself."

We drove along in silence, the car skidding in the turns and Amber jiggling the wheel to bring us out of it.

"Fuck you," she said in a cold hard voice.

I didn't say anything, though I was shocked by what she said— shocked very much. Then I wondered if she was turning back into the person she'd been before she got pregnant, the one Charlene had told me about, the one the women in the doctor's waiting room had talked about.

The car skidded to the left and Amber jiggled the wheel to bring it back straight. Then it skidded again and the headlights swung off and I had a glimpse of mailboxes rushing by. After a few seconds Amber got the car back under control.

"Damn," she said. She slowed the car and downshifted. "The snow's getting worse."

"Maybe we should go back to town," I said. I turned around and looked out the rear window. All I could see were snowflakes swirling in the reddish glow of the taillights. Everything else was black.

"We're nearer to the lake than we are to town," Amber said.

"Okay," I said. "Just be careful."

"Have I ever let you down?" Amber said. She looked over and smiled, and it was nice to see the meanness gone, even if it was just for a moment.

"No," I said. "You haven't."

We drove another mile or two without seeing any cars. It seemed we were the only ones out on the road. Then a pair of headlights appeared way off in the distance, two faint white dots. They came steadily closer, becoming brighter, and then there was a moment of startling whiteness as the two cars passed, followed by a blast of air and a sideways heaving. Then everything quieted down again and was like before, the two headlights boring through the snowy blackness.

"Shit, shit, shit," Amber said under her breath.

"You're doing great," I said.

"Can you tell where we are? Can you see where we're supposed to turn?" She leaned forward, trying to spot the turnoff that went through the forest to her house. Her nose almost touched the windshield.

I wiped a clear space in the fog on the side window and peered out. Tree trunks flashed by in the dim reflection of the headlights. I got a split-second glimpse of a mailbox on a tilted post, then a telephone pole, then a No Trespassing sign nailed to a pine tree. Then I saw a clear space and a faint depression in the snow.

"That was it," I said. "We just passed it."

Amber brought the car to a skidding stop. She backed up and turned off onto the two-track road. She kept playing with the clutch to get traction in the fresh snow.

"Slow down," I said.

"If I go any slower we'll get stuck."

We went along the two-track road, and then I felt a bump, like we'd struck something under the snow. The car lurched to the left, as if a giant had grabbed it and thrown it in a different direction, and the headlight beams swung wildly. Amber forced the steering wheel around, hand over hand, and the headlights swung back. I glimpsed the clearing where the road ran through the forest; then the headlights swung further and the car heaved over in the other direction. The next thing I knew we were heading down a small embankment, the car bumping crazily, tree trunks rising up before us.

We hit something, and the car came to a sudden, wrenching stop. It tipped and started to roll over, and Amber fell against me. For a moment we hung suspended, half rolled over, and then the car fell back upright with a sickening shudder. A cloud of snow rose up around us like a bomb had exploded. Amber cried as she was thrown back hard against the door. I was thrown on top of her. Then there was silence.

"Are you all right?" I said after a moment.

"I think so." Her voice was shaking.

I crawled back to the passenger's side and opened the door and stepped out. The snow was almost up to my knees. It pushed up inside my pant legs, cold and wet against my skin. I made my way up to the front of the car and knelt down so I could see what happened. The big chrome bumper was wedged up against a large rock, and the right front tire was twisted under like the axle had snapped. The headlight beams angled down, making a pool of brilliant whiteness on the snow.

I walked back and opened the door, and the dome light came on. Amber was huddled against the driver's door, her legs drawn up and her arms hugging her knees.

"We'll never get out of here without a tow truck," I said. "I'll walk ahead and see how far it is to your house. Then I'll come back with some boots and get you."

"Don't leave me here," Amber said. There was a kind of panic starting in her voice.

"I'll just be gone for a couple of minutes. I'll bring back a heavy coat and some boots."

"Do you promise?"

"Of course."

I looked at Amber. She reminded me of a rag doll that some child had tossed into a corner. She closed her eyes and took in several slow deep breaths, holding each one before letting it out. Then she opened her eyes and looked across at me. I could see that the panic was gone, at least for now; she looked calm and brave.

"I'll be right back," I said again. Then I slammed the door and the dome light went out and she disappeared in the dark interior.

Chapter Twenty-One

I CLIMBED THE EMBANKMENT and started walking in the direction of the lake, following the clearing where the road ran through the forest. Once I got away from the glare of the headlights I could see much better, almost as clearly as if it were daylight. Snow was still falling but not as hard as before. Just a few icy flakes drifted down in the frigid air.

It was hard walking in the deep snow. After each step I had to pause for an instant to gather my strength for the next heave forward. It was an awkward, off-balance way of walking, and I fell down several times.

After I'd gone a short way I had to stop to catch my breath. The cold air rushed in and out of my lungs. Looking back in the direction I'd just come from, I could faintly see the glow of the headlights lighting up the patch of snow.

I looked up. Through the tree branches I saw the clouds beginning to thin and separate, exposing sections of black sky studded with brilliant stars. I tried to spot a familiar constellation—Orion or Cassiopeia or the Bear or the Twins. But none of the stars made any sense to me; they were too chopped up by clouds, too random and confusing to make sense of.

I started walking again. The only sound was the crunching of snow beneath my feet and the rasp of my breathing. As the road got closer to the lake it dipped slightly then sloped back up into a long gentle rise. At the top of the rise the trees fell away and the lake opened up. And then I saw the back of the old abandoned resort hotel, and I knew that we had taken the wrong road.

I walked around the side of the hotel and down to the shore of the lake. The picnic table where Amber had lain two days ago was under the pine tree where we had left it; only now it was covered by a thick blanket of snow. In the shallow water along the shore a black skim of ice had started to form. The lily pads I'd fished in looked different now, the thin green membranes misshapen in the arcticlike air, twisted and curled in ways that made them look grotesque. I moved my gaze along the shore, picking out landmarks—the pilings from an old lumbering pier, a ramshackle boathouse, the pulsing red light of a radio tower—until I saw the light from Amber's house. Then I shifted my gaze further along the shore until I spotted the light from our cabin.

My father would be home by now and wondering where I was. I pictured him walking to the rear window, lifting the curtain and peering out, hoping to catch sight of me trudging up the two-track road or see the headlights of a car—a teacher bringing me home from some after-school activity or a neighbor who had spotted me shuffling along the highway and given me a lift. Soon he'd set out to search for me, I thought, and after that he'd probably call the sheriff's office in McBride although I couldn't imagine exactly what he would tell them. *My son did not come home tonight. He has no place to go. My wife is in Chicago. He's just a boy.* Any of those seemed possible.

I stood on the shore wondering what to do. There didn't seem to be any good choices. We could spend the night in the car and hope that someone would find us in the morning; that was one possibility. We could walk several miles along the road to Amber's house, breaking a trail through the deep snow. Or I could make my way alone along the shore, splashing through the water where the brush and trees grew right down to the bank. Those seemed to be the only choices.

And then I remembered what my father had said about having standards—how you needed them before you could make choices—and I wondered what *my* standards were. I'd been taught about honesty and kindness and generosity, and I'd learned the Ten Commandments, and I'd read about duty, honor, and country. But I'd never actually needed those ideas before, not in any way that really mattered. And I realized then that what a person did and what a person had to do were all mixed up together, and it was impossible to know how you would act in any situation until you actually faced it.

I ran back up the bank, slipping and falling a couple of times in the deep snow. When I reached the top, the front of the hotel rose up above me, a wide dark slab cutting off half of the sky.

I made my way along the front of the hotel, examining the sheets of plywood that were nailed across the windows. I felt around the edges until I found one with a loose corner and I pulled against it, jerking back with my weight until it loosened up a little. Then I found a long stick and used it to pry with. When the last nail came loose, the plywood tipped away and fell heavily onto the ground, sending a cloud of powdery snow up into my face.

With the end of the stick I broke out a pane of glass, then reached inside and undid the lock. I raised the sash and stepped inside.

It was very dark. But after a minute my eyes adjusted and I saw that I was in a large empty room with a stone fireplace and a wide curving staircase. It looked like the kind of room where hotel guests would gather after dinner to relax and tell stories and watch the sunset. On the back wall two mounted deer heads stared out into empty space, big ten-point bucks with flared nostrils and glassy eyeballs. Further along, a collection of canoe paddles was nailed up, twenty or thirty at least. When I went over, I saw they was inscribed with writing, though I couldn't make out what it said.

I climbed the rickety staircase, holding on to the curving wooden banister and testing each step before trusting it with my full weight. At the top a kind of gallery opened up, with another stone fireplace and a hallway leading off into the back of the building. It was brighter up here because the windows had not been boarded up. A pale wintry light filtered through the grimy panes of glass, casting a series of perfect rectangles onto the dusty wooden floor. Further away I could faintly make out a desk and a table and a chair and a wall with a map on it and a bookcase with stacks of loose magazines.

Then I remembered Amber's question from two days ago about whether the hotel was a place you could stay. And I realized it was possible, even though it was old and broken down and dirty. We could stay in the old hotel and be warm and safe. At least for one night.

That was the best of the bad choices we faced.

Chapter Twenty-Two

WHEN I GOT BACK TO THE CAR, Amber was cold and very frightened. All the heat had gone out of the car, and frost had started to form on the windows. She was shivering and her teeth were chattering. I put my hands on her cheeks and held them there until her face warmed up. Then I rubbed her hands until she got some feeling back in them.

"You've got to keep the circulation going," I said. "That's what keeps you warm. When you start to walk you'll feel better because your heart will pump the blood faster."

"Mister Einstein," Amber said, her voice shaking from the cold. She smiled a little through her shivering.

"It's a scientific fact," I said.

"How far do we have to go?" she asked.

"It's not too far," I said. Then I said, "But it's not your house we're going to. It's that old hotel."

"What?" She looked at me, her eyes wide.

"We took the wrong road. I made a mistake. We're on the road that goes to the old hotel. But it'll be all right. We can stay there tonight. We'll be warm."

Amber looked like she was going to say something, but then she closed her eyes, not tightly but just as if she wanted to shut things out for a while, like when you pull a curtain on a window. She kept her eyes closed for quite a long time, and I thought that she was probably trying to clear her mind of all the bad things that had been happening so that when she had to think again things would seem better.

I kept rubbing her arms. They felt thin and frail through the fabric of her coat. Finally she opened her eyes and stared at me.

"Okay," she said. "Let's go."

Before we left the car I took the keys and went back and unlocked the trunk. Inside I found a pair of leather boots and a painter's drop cloth. Wedged against the spare tire was a half-full bottle of Old Crow whiskey. I took it all—the drop cloth and the whiskey and the boots—and went back into the car.

"Here," I said, handing the boots to Amber. "Put these on."

"They're way too big," she said. "And they smell." She made a face.

"It doesn't matter. Just put them on."

Amber took off her sneakers. Her feet were wet and pale and sort of puckered looking. "Wait a minute," I said. I knelt down and started to rub her feet. They were so cold, it frightened me, like stones that have been lying on the bottom of a river. I rubbed and blew on her feet until they got some color back. Then Amber put the boots on, lacing them up as tight as she could.

We were ready to leave the car but there was one more thing I wanted to do. I reached into the backseat and picked up Amber's purse off the floor. I opened the clasp and fished around until I found her Zippo lighter and the package of Old Gold cigarettes. I stuffed them into the pocket of my jacket.

I looked at Amber. "Okay," I said. "Let's go."

We scrambled up the embankment, Amber first and me coming along behind. Amber had to lean forward and put her bare hands into the snow to keep her balance. Then we followed the road, walking single file in the footsteps I'd already made.

The sky was clear now. All the clouds had blown away. A half-moon shined down, casting shadows onto the snowy landscape, shadows of tree trunks and shadows of ourselves, moving quietly through the forest. It was very cold.

"Wait a minute," Amber said after we'd gone only a short distance.

I turned around. Amber stood on the snowy path, stooped over, her hands on her knees. She looked odd with her pink waitress's dress showing beneath her bulky winter coat and her thin bare legs showing below that. She was panting hard, her breath coming out in bursts of vapor that rose around her face.

"We should keep going," I said.

"Wait a minute," Amber said again. She took a few more breaths then stood up straight. "All right," she said. "I'm ready."

When we got to the hotel we climbed in through the broken window. I held Amber's hand to steady her as she stepped through the small opening. Then I led her up the dark staircase to the upper level.

"Jesus," Amber said. "This is creepy." She looked around at the large empty space and the high ceiling with timbers crossing overhead.

"It'll be better when we get a fire going," I said.

I got some magazines from the bookshelves and tore out some pages and wadded them up and put them onto the fireplace grate. Then I went downstairs and pulled four canoe paddles off the wall. I broke them across my knee and placed them on top of the wadded paper. As I set them into place I read the inscriptions; they seemed to be mementos of canoeing trips made by people who had stayed at the hotel, camping adventures that had been the high points of peoples' lives and needed to be remembered. One read: "Tom Wintermeyer, June 29–31, 1943, To Emmet's Point and back." Another read: "Lucile and Oliver Metcalf, September 14–16, 1935, the Autumn Honeymoon." The third one read: "April 4, 1947: Opening day. Four brookies, one rainbow, Howard Vandenberg and son Robert (12 yrs. old)."

I lit the paper with Amber's lighter. After a couple of minutes the fire spread to the wooden paddles.

"Nice going, Sergeant Preston," Amber said. She edged up close to the fireplace and held her hands out toward the flames.

"I think we've got enough canoe paddles to keep the fire going until morning," I said. "If we run out I can go outside and find some dead branches."

"You've thought of everything," Amber said. She smiled at me and I smiled back.

"Let's have a cigarette," Amber said. "It'll be like smoking a peace pipe."

I took Amber's Old Golds out of my pocket and shook out two, one for Amber and one for me. I snapped on the Zippo lighter and held it under the end of Amber's cigarette, the tiny yellow flame dancing above my hand. Amber held the cigarette with two straight fingers. She took a deep breath and blew out a long trail of smoke.

"Do you still think this place is spooky?" I said after I'd lit my own cigarette.

Amber walked over and sat down on the stone ledge in front of the fireplace. She folded her arms and crossed one leg over the other, her foot with the big leather boot dangling out in front. She looked up into the high ceiling with the heavy rafters.

"No," she said. "But it's kind of solemn. It's like being in church or something."

The reflections from the shifting flames played across the walls and ceiling. I thought of the night I'd sat on the sofa with Harriet Walker, when the flame from the kerosene stove had made everything seem to come alive. I'd been afraid that night, but now I wasn't.

"It makes you want to talk in a quiet voice," I said.

"Yes," she said. "Like you want to be respectful of something."

"Are you afraid?"

"No. I was afraid back in the car, but I'm not afraid now."

We smoked for a while without saying anything. I liked blowing out the smoke and watching it curl and disappear up into the rafters. I liked seeing the reflections of the flames dance across the walls and across Amber's face. I liked being in a place that felt safe.

"Are you going to go to Montreal?" I asked Amber.

"Yes," she said, and she spoke without any hesitation. "I decided about it when I was waiting for you in the car."

"That's a good decision," I said.

"I checked last week and that school will still let me in. It costs two hundred dollars a year, but I've got half of that saved up already."

"What about Wayne?" I asked.

"That's all over."

"You'll be all alone up there in Canada."

"I'm pretty much alone already." She turned her face toward me. "Except for you, I mean."

Amber stubbed out her cigarette on one of the fireplace stones, making a black smudge. Then she said she was tired and wanted to go to sleep. She still looked very pale and her face was kind of pinched. Staying in the cold car and walking through the snow had been hard on her.

We lay down on the floor next to the fire, pulling the painter's drop cloth over us as a kind of blanket. Amber was next to the fire and I was next to Amber. The drop cloth was large enough so that we could lie side by side without touching. I didn't want to be touching Amber. I remembered what had happened in the rowboat and I didn't want that to happen again.

"What about a pillow?" Amber said after a minute. "It's not so great to have your head on a wood floor."

"Hold on," I said. I went over to the bookcase and brought back a stack of magazines: copies of *Look* and *Life* and *National Geographic*. "Try this," I said. I knelt on the floor. Amber lifted her head and I slid the stack of magazines under it.

"That's better," Amber said. She moved her head from side to side, like she was testing the makeshift pillow. "It's not very soft, but at least my head's in the right place." She looked at me and wrinkled her nose.

I got another stack of magazines for myself and got back under the drop cloth. Then I lay on my back and stared at the patterns the fire was making on the ceiling. I wasn't really very tired. I was excited about having gotten us out of the trouble we'd been in. I had made some choices, and now everything would be fine. By morning the snowplows would be out and cars would be moving on the highway. I could walk out to the county road and flag down a passing car to take me into town to get a tow truck. Everything would be fine.

I closed my eyes and listened to the noises coming from inside the old hotel: the creak of shifting timbers, the metallic clang of iron pipes expanding and contracting, the whistle of wind blowing through cracked windowpanes. I could hear my heart beating. I could feel my bare hands lying against the rough wooden planks. I could hear the gentle sounds of Amber's breathing. After a while I went to sleep.

Chapter Twenty-Three

WHEN I WOKE UP, THE FIRE was almost out. Just a few embers glowed on the grate. I stared at them for a while. They shimmered in the currents of hot air, like a miniature version of the bombed-out cities I'd seen in World War II newsreels.

Amber was asleep beside me. She had rolled over and was facing in my direction, her head resting on the stack of magazines. She looked peaceful. But then her eyes began to move beneath her eyelids, and she made a whimpering sound.

"Amber!" I shook her shoulder. "Amber, wake up!"

Her eyes came open but only partway. "What is it?" she said sleepily.

"You were dreaming. You were having a bad dream."

"Okay," she said. "I'm sorry. I won't do it again."

Her eyes blinked a few times then closed.

I went downstairs and took down three more paddles. I carried them upstairs and put them onto the glowing embers. After a minute the fire flared up around them. Just before the paddles disappeared in the flames, I read the inscriptions etched into the wooden surfaces:

"Orv and Alice Spector, June 12–14, 1932. Sunny skies all the way!"

"Richard and Dorothy Vyn, July 4th, 1927. The Firecracker Expedition."

"Sam MacIntyre and Biscuit (German s.h. pointer), Oct. 17, 1940."

It felt odd to be burning the souvenirs of other people's adventures. After the paddles were gone there would be nothing left to prove that those adventures had happened. Only the memories that the people carried in their minds, and then only for as long as those people were alive. *Were* they still alive? I wondered. Orv and Alice? Richard and Dorothy? Sam MacIntyre? And *did* their adventures count for anything? Did they make any sort of difference, now or ever? Or were they only a reason to write something on a paddle, a silly memento that someone could use someday to build a fire and keep warm?

I thought about my mother and her decision to go to Chicago, and I thought about my father and his decision to give up Harriet Walker. And I thought about Amber and her decision to go to Montreal and raise her baby there. But did any of *that* matter, either? Would anyone remember those things or care that they had happened? Or were they just another type of adventure—like going on a canoe trip—something that would happen for a while and then be forgotten?

I went over to the windows and looked out onto the lake. The sky was clear now, full of stars. The moon had moved halfway across the horizon. I could see the wash of light that was the Milky Way, that dense band of stars that somehow included the one I was watching from, and for a moment I felt disconnected, as if I were a satellite adrift in space. But then I picked out Orion and Pisces and Cassiopeia, and somehow those familiar shapes seemed to anchor me again and make me feel better.

I shifted my gaze down lower. The thin membrane of ice had expanded from the shore. Now it covered almost the entire lake. It rolled gently with the movement of the water underneath, a slow silent surging, as if some great aquatic beast were trying to break free from its confinement. And then I realized I was seeing something that was impossible—ice bending—and I decided that when I had the time I would study more about the science of water and ice so I could figure it out and understand it.

A wispy half-transparent cloud drifted across the face of the moon, making everything slightly darker. Across the lake I saw the light from our cabin. It seemed to be burning brighter than before. I imagined my father pacing the floor and wondering where I was, and I felt sorry to be causing him concern. But I felt an odd contentment, too, as if I wasn't sure I belonged there anymore.

Behind me, Amber whimpered. Then she made kind of a moaning sound. I went over and knelt on the floor beside her. In the flickering firelight, I saw that her face was flushed and covered with sweat. Strands of curling dark hair lay damp against her forehead. She breathed in and out in quick little gasps.

As I watched, leaning over, her face drew up into a kind of grimace and she whimpered again. Then her eyes fluttered and came open. She stared up at me, her expression blank, and for a moment I thought she was still asleep. But then her eyes came into focus, and a kind of comprehension crept into her face.

"Hello, Sergeant Preston," she said. She smiled weakly. "Is it morning yet?"

"No. Not yet. You can go back to sleep."

She winced slightly. "I don't feel too good." Her words were slurred.

"What's the matter?"

She rolled onto her side so that she was facing the fire, gathering the drop cloth around her shoulders, as if she were wrapping herself in a cocoon. "I'm cold," she said. "Sort of hot and cold at the same time."

I reached around and felt her forehead. She was very hot. Then I saw that she was shivering.

"Can't you stoke up the fire and make it warmer?" she asked.

"I just put more wood on it, Amber. It's going pretty good now."

"I'm so cold. And I have a terrible headache."

Her whole body was shivering under the drop cloth.

"Amber, I think you have the flu."

"That's what I was thinking, too. But I was afraid to say it."

"Don't worry. I've had it and it's not so bad."

"I'm just so cold," she said. "Isn't there anything you can do?"

I sat and watched her for a minute. Then I lifted the drop cloth and lay down and sort of fitted myself against her back. I was touching her more than I wanted to, but it seemed to be all right. I could warm her up. That was what she needed. I put my arm around her waist and drew in tight against her.

"Is that better?" I asked. I felt her hips against my stomach. My face was close to the back of her neck. I could see strands of loose hair and the wound from the fishhook. It was just inches from my eyes, a tiny gouge scabbed with dried blood.

"A little," she said.

She squirmed back against me, as if she were trying to crawl inside my skin. Then her shivering stopped and she grew quiet. For several minutes all I could do was lie and feel the long length of her body pressed up against mine. It was a strange sensation, like doing a thing you'd always imagined but having it be completely different. Then Amber moaned again. But this time it was sharper, more like a cry.

"Do you feel really bad?"

"Yes," she said. Then she said, "I'm a little frightened, too."

"It's all right," I said, even though I didn't know if it was or if it wasn't. "All we have to do is wait a few more hours until morning. Then the snowplows will be out."

"I keep thinking about something the doctor told me," Amber said after a pause.

"What's that?"

"That the flu is harder when you're pregnant. It hits you harder. It's more dangerous."

I didn't say anything. Then I said, "We'll get out of here in the morning, Amber. It's just a few hours from now."

I lay behind Amber with my arm around her waist. I felt her shoulders move with each breath she took, quick jerking movements, as if breathing took an effort or inflicted pain. And then I suddenly realized that my hand was resting on her stomach, and I felt the slight swell, the tiny envelope of life lying just beneath my fingertips, the life she and Wayne had made together.

For a moment I stopped breathing and lay completely still, paralyzed by that thought, as if the bulk of the old hotel were holding me like a specimen beneath a pane of glass. And I think I was waiting for something to happen, some sign to tell me what I could or should do next.

"It's going to be all right," I whispered into Amber's ear.

"I'm not afraid," she murmured sleepily. "It's just that I can't stop worrying about what's going to happen."

And then I told her that I loved her—just like I'd done when she'd been injured by the fishhook—and I said it for the same reason, to make her feel safe, because I thought that's one thing love was for.

I waited for Amber to say something back. I lay very still and breathed very softly. I didn't want to miss her slightest word. But she had already gone back to sleep.

And so I didn't know if she had heard me.

Chapter Twenty-Four

I LAY AND LISTENED TO AMBER'S breathing and felt the rise and slump of her shoulders and the quick beating of her heart and the soft brush of her hair against my face and lips and the slight bulge of her stomach beneath my hand. I watched the moon move across two panes of window glass. The patterns it cast, the gray diminishing rectangles, moved slowly across the floor, as if being dragged by some giant unseen hand. And I thought about Amber having the flu and how there was no place to get help and how I'd been the one who had brought us to this isolated place. And I thought about the other mistakes I'd made, and I began to be afraid.

Please God and Jesus, I prayed (because I couldn't think of anything else to do), please let everything be all right. It was me who told Wayne that Amber didn't love him and me who made us take the wrong road and me who decided to stay in the hotel. So if you want to hurt someone please let it be me and not Amber, who didn't do anything wrong. I know you're the same thing as truth, and I know it wouldn't make sense to let anything happen to Amber, so please don't let anything happen to her, even though I know it's not going to. And I'm sorry about what happened in the rowboat and in the alley with Charlene and the thoughts that came into my head just a moment ago when I realized where my hand lay. But that's all over now, and you can see that it's different now because I'm here with Amber and nothing's happening. I've got my arm around her waist and I'm lying close against her like a lover, but I'm not a lover in the normal way because nothing else is happening. I'm lying here to keep her warm, which is what she wants and what she needs, but please don't let anything happen to her because that wouldn't make sense and it wouldn't be fair.

I went on praying like that for a while. But then I thought I'd prayed enough and so I stopped. I had said everything I could say to God and Jesus, everything that seemed to matter. If anything was going to happen I thought it would happen now.

I got out from under the drop cloth and went over to the windows. Outside everything seemed to be the same—the heavy blanket of snow, the huge black sky studded with thousands of stars, the thin black sheet of ice rolling slowly under the action of the water.

I took the bottle of Old Crow out of my pocket and uncapped it and took a large swallow. It burned going down, just like it had before, but this time I expected it and liked the feeling. I sat on the window ledge, drinking the Old Crow and watching Amber sleep. I think I was waiting for some sign that God or Jesus had heard my prayer. I didn't know what the sign would be but I thought I'd know it when I saw it. Perhaps Amber's fever would suddenly break and she would awaken and smile and say something clever. Or perhaps a bolt of lightning would flash across the sky or an angel would appear in the rafters overhead, bathed in radiant light. Or possibly the sign would be something simple: the sound of a car coming up the trail to rescue us, or the shout of a member of a search party, or the bark of a tracking dog. Whatever it was, I knew I would recognize it when it happened.

Several minutes passed. The shadow of a tree branch crept across the window ledge; then it moved slowly over my leg, as if trying to include me in some larger plan or pattern. Outside, a squirrel scampered up a tree trunk.

I took another swallow of the Old Crow whiskey. And suddenly I began to feel stupid, because I knew my prayer was not going to be

answered—at least not in any of the ways I'd been thinking about—
and it was pointless to expect it. I had made the wrong choice about
telling Wayne that Amber didn't love him and the wrong choice
about turning onto the two-track road and the wrong choice about
taking shelter in the old hotel. And now it was up to me to get us out,
to make other choices that would set things right again. I couldn't
depend on God or Jesus or anyone else to do it.

I got up off the window ledge and looked out at the starry
landscape. Moonlight slanted through the clearing, casting shadows
that reached the old hotel. Off to my right I noticed something
move. Just at the edge of the clearing, a giant buck stepped out
from between two pines trees. It took a few uncertain steps into the
clearing and stopped.

I reached into my coat pocket, where I still had the revolver. I felt
around with my fingertips until I found the safety button; I eased
it off and placed my finger on the trigger. Then I drew the revolver
slowly out of my pocket.

The deer bounded over to a spot near the picnic table, jumping
high to clear the deep drifted snow. I focused on the spot where I
would have to shoot to bring it down—the fold of flesh behind the
shoulder where the heart and lungs were. If I could kill it, it would
help. Amber and I could stay in the hotel, living off the venison and
burning canoe paddles to keep warm. We could lie by the fire and
talk to each other about Montreal and geometry and fly-fishing and
anything else we wanted to talk about. And we could love each other
but not in the way I had loved Charlene but in the other half-love
way that we preferred. It was a crazy idea—completely insane—and
it lasted for only a moment. But during that moment it seemed like
a wonderful plan.

I tapped the gun barrel twice against the window glass. The deer
raised its head and swung its gaze in my direction. For an instant
our eyes met, and a kind of wild intelligence seemed to flicker in its
expression. Then it turned and bounded off into the forest, jumping

high and throwing up of bits of snow.

And then I had another idea. And this was a better idea because it didn't involve prayer or killing a deer or anything that was unreliable or insane. I would walk back out to the highway and find help. That was all I needed to do. If I made it to the highway there was a good chance I'd find a car to flag down. The storm had been over for a couple of hours now, and cars might be out on the roads. At the very worst, I'd have to walk to Amber's house, which I could reach in an hour or two of walking. That would be the worst case—if no car came along to pick me up.

I put down the revolver and went over to Amber and shook her awake. It took a minute but finally she opened her eyes. This time, though, there was no recognition. She didn't say anything. And she didn't smile.

"Amber, I'm going to go find some help."

She looked up at me. She looked confused.

"What? What did you say?" She was very groggy.

"I'm going to walk out to the road and flag down a car."

She raised herself on one elbow.

"But you said there won't be any cars out until after the snowplows come."

"I know. But maybe there'll be one or two. And if there aren't I can walk to your house and tell them what happened so they can get help."

"I don't want you to go."

"But we have to do something."

"No we don't. Just stay here with me. We can take care of ourselves. Lie down and talk to me. That's enough."

"But it doesn't make any sense."

"Just stop arguing. Please just stop arguing."

I got under the drop cloth and fitted myself against Amber's back. This time there was no thought about my hand or anything like that.

"What do you want to talk about?" I said.

"Anything at all," she said. "Just anything."

There was an urgency in her voice that hadn't been there before. I noticed it right away.

"Tell me about fly-fishing," she said. "Or talk to me in French."

"But I don't know many French words. Only the ones we studied together."

"Use those."

"Okay," I said. And then I said the words *maison* and *paysage* and *homme* and *femme* and *mourir* and *naître* and a few others I could remember.

Amber moved, as if a spasm were passing through her body.

"You say them beautifully," she said.

"Are you all right, Amber? *Vas-tu bien?*"

"Just talk to me."

"All right." And I thought about what I could say next, because I'd used up all the French words I remembered.

"When you fish with flies, you need to know what insects are hatching on the water," I said. "And then you choose a fly that looks like the ones that are hatching. That's the most important thing."

Amber moved again. This time it was matched by a quick intake of breath.

"So you have to know what the different insects look like. And there are a lot to know about, like the caddis fly and the mayfly and the nymphs. And you should know when they hatch. The time of year, I mean."

"How do you learn that?"

"You read about it. Or you pay attention when it's happening. Or someone tells you. *On vous dit.*"

She jerked again.

"Amber, are you all right?"

"Say it in French," she said.

"*Tu vas?*"

"Yes."

"And then you have to use a tapered leader."

"What?"

"You tie the fly to a tapered leader so the fish can't see the line."

"That makes sense."

"Yes," I said. "It's called presenting the fly to the fish. Isn't that an interesting expression?"

"It is. It's a wonderful expression. I love it."

"Amber, something's wrong. What is it?"

"Nothing." She squirmed a little. "How can you tell when a fish takes the fly?" There was a tightness in her voice that frightened me.

"You just can. *On sait.* You feel the life at the other end of the line. It suddenly comes alive. It throbs."

"That's amazing," she said. She spoke in a quick breathy voice.

"Yes," I said. "It's amazing."

After that I didn't say anything for a while. I lay quietly, waiting to see what Amber would say next. I waited for a long time. But all I heard were the creaks and groans of the old hotel adjusting to the cold. Then Amber sobbed.

"Amber?"

"I want to go to sleep now," she said. "You don't have to talk to me anymore."

She was very upset. But her breathing seemed to have evened out. In that way she seemed better, but only in that way. She was still feverish and upset. But at least she was breathing normally.

"Amber, what's going on?"

She was crying very quietly.

"I'm going to sleep now," she said. "You can keep talking if you want to, but I might not hear you."

"You've got to tell me why you're crying."

After a long pause she said, "All right."

And then she told me that her baby had just died. She had felt it somehow. She couldn't explain, but something had changed inside of her and she was quite sure of it. She couldn't say what it was, but she knew.

"Amber," I said, "you can't be certain about that."

"I want to go to sleep now," she said, crying softly. "But don't leave me, okay? Don't leave me while I'm asleep. Because I don't want to be alone right now."

"Okay," I said, because I could tell she didn't want to talk about the baby and there was no point trying to make her. It was a settled matter as far as she was concerned. Something she knew and didn't want to talk about.

"I'll be all right," she said after another long pause. "It's just that I wanted to have the baby and now it's gone."

I lay there and thought about Amber. For some reason she had wanted to have the baby and she had figured out a way to have it without her parents or Wayne to help her out. It didn't make any sense, but that's what she had wanted. But none of it mattered now. She was going to be a normal girl again, doing the normal things that girls do.

The wind was rising. It made a low moaning sound as it curled around the sides of the old hotel. I heard the creak of a timber shifting somewhere in the great abandoned building. It was a sharp sound, almost like a gunshot going off.

Outside, the temperature was changing. Becoming warmer. Somehow I knew that. A new front of air was coming in. Things were moving: pipes and timbers and stones. Pressures were building up that needed to be released. It was based on scientific principles, but it was random, too—nothing you could count on or predict.

"I just want to go to sleep now," Amber said again. She spoke in a breathy voice. I could barely hear her above the wind and creaking timbers. Her body seemed frail inside my arms. Beads of perspiration dotted the back of her neck, and the tips of her hair came together in glimmering points.

I was very frightened. I knew Amber didn't want me to leave, but I knew I should. She was very weak, and I was afraid of what would happen. Going to get help was the right thing to do. Then other people could come and take charge of things, people who knew about cold and sick girls and dead babies.

"Okay," I whispered back.

I waited until Amber's breathing became steady. It didn't take long. Then I got up and got some canoe paddles and stacked them near the fire where she would find them when she woke up. Then I left the hotel.

When I reached the county road, the sun was just coming up. It was going to be a clear day. I started walking in the direction of Amber's house, but after a few minutes I saw a snowplow lumbering toward me in the distance, its red lights flashing. I flagged it down and asked the driver to take me to the sheriff's office in McBride. When we got there I told the deputy at the front desk about being caught in the snowstorm and spending the night in the hotel with Amber and about her still being there, needing to be rescued. The deputy listened with a skeptical expression, as if he half suspected he was being made the butt of some teenage prank. But then he promised to send out two officers in a Jeep to bring Amber out.

Chapter Twenty-Five

IN THE MONTHS THAT FOLLOWED that night in the abandoned hotel, my father made an effort to spend more time with me. We went on many hunting and fishing trips together, sometimes for several days at a time, even causing me to miss days of school when that was necessary to be included in some special adventure: a rabbit hunt on a farmer's fields near Cheboygan or duck hunting in the shallow headwaters of the Au Sable River or fishing through the ice for perch with tip-up rigs along the shore of Saginaw Bay. He had concluded, finally, that his dream of living in the north woods had been a mirage, and he was waiting for the right time to change back to the person he had been before, a tool-and-die mechanic who lived in the city with a family who loved him and depended on him. And he was waiting for my mother to change *her* mind, too, and to come back and live with us again, which for some reason he was confident would happen. In the meantime—while he was waiting for that right time to come and for my mother to change her mind—he wanted to enjoy the things that had brought him up north in the first place, the outdoor adventures he had learned as a boy from Harry Sherwood, and he wanted me to enjoy them, too, while there was still time.

Our conversations were different. Rather than examine me about other people's wisdom, he seemed to want to impart his own, at least to the extent he understood it himself. Understood about life,

I mean, and how to live it. But it was still a form of teaching, his never-ending effort to ground me in ideas that would make my life better. Better than his own.

"Try not to think you have to be like other boys," he said once. "Your differences can be your most valuable possessions."

And this: "Every bad thing doesn't have a villain behind it."

And this one, which I believe was the most important, because I believe he had learned it during this time: "The things that are most true are the hardest ones to talk about."

All of this was for my benefit—I understood that perfectly well— to arm me against the pain he believed I was feeling and that he thought he had contributed to in some indefinable way. And it was also to prepare me for a future he did not completely approve of but that he knew I would have to deal with, a future of corporations and large governments and sprawling cities and masses of people bound together for some larger purpose. I appreciated the gesture, even if I didn't agree with all of his advice, or even understand it. In the final analysis—as I said before—he was trying to use his own imperfect understanding of the world to teach me. That was the one constant in our lives together.

One day in early February we sat together in the shadowed darkness of an ice-fishing shanty we'd dragged out onto the frozen lake the previous day. We sat side by side on a wooden bench above a large opening we had chopped through the eight-inch thickness of ice, waiting for a northern pike or a muskellunge to swim by and examine the silver-speckled lure floating just a foot below the surface. My father held a steel-shafted spear with five barbed tines. Daylight entering the ice outside the shanty infused the water with a greenish subterranean glow, making it seem as if the source of it—the light—lay down deep within the lake itself.

For most of the afternoon we had sat without speaking. A thermos of coffee had kept us warm, and we had eaten ham sandwiches and Baby Ruth candy bars. Once or twice my father reached over and absently patted my arm, as if he wanted to remind me that I was an integral part of his adventure. Twice a northern pike had swum by to examine the silvery lure. Both times it had appeared almost magically in the light-infused opening, its long speckled body and stupid jut-jawed head making it look like a creature from a prehistoric time capsule, and twice it had been spooked away by some unapparent danger before my father could throw the spear.

"How was it that you met that Amber girl?" my father asked after the big fish had vanished for the second time. "That's something you never told me." He asked the question in a hesitant voice, as if he understood it was a subject I might not want to talk about.

"It was one of the nights last October when we were practicing golf by the lake. I hit a wild shot and when I went to find it, she had the ball."

"Oh, yes. I remember that night."

"It was the night Mother called and said she wasn't coming back until the house was built."

Down below us, the northern pike swam back into view, its tail moving slowly in the thin watery gloom. The membranes of its fins trembled along the sides of its sleek body.

My father's arm drew back slowly. I held my breath, waiting for him to throw the spear. But suddenly the fish flicked its tail and was gone.

I felt my father's body relax. His shoulders slumped. After a moment he said, "That's interesting."

"What's interesting?"

"That that was the night you met her. Because that was the night you declared a kind of independence, I think."

"What?"

"The Gettysburg quote. What you said about doing something in its own due time. That's the way I understood it."

"I guess I hadn't thought about it."

He was silent for a moment, but I knew he had another point to make. I watched the opening in the ice.

"Try not to let this change the way you look at things, Danny," he said in a quiet voice.

I didn't respond. I was concentrating on the opening in the ice, as if I could bring the great fish back by the sheer power of my thinking.

"Don't let it make you bitter," he continued, "or cynical about trying to do what's right." Without taking his eyes off the opening, he reached over and put his arm around my shoulder in that partial gesture I knew so well.

"I can't protect you from very much, Danny," he continued. "All I can do is try to help you stand up to it."

I sat very still, waiting for the fish to reappear, trying to think of nothing else.

At noon on the day I left Amber in the hotel, my father fought his way along the snow-clogged roads to the sheriff's office in McBride. He came into the interrogation room where I was waiting and sat down heavily on one of the folding chairs lined up against the wall. He was unshaven, and his eyes were bloodshot from the sleepless night he'd spent. He leaned forward with his elbows resting on his knees and began tapping his fingertips together, making and unmaking a sort of cage with his hands. He had just come from speaking with the sheriff.

"Son, I'm sorry you had to deal with that."

"I'm all right."

"Yes. Well, it was good that you were there to help the young woman. I'm sure it was easier on her for that."

"Amber," I said.

I was looking out the window where a sheriff's deputy was shoveling off the sidewalk that led up to the main entrance of the small, yellow brick building. The sun was out now, and the sky was bright blue. The snow had started to melt. Sparkling drops of water fell from the roof across the window space.

"What?" my father said.

"Her name was Amber."

"Yes. Amber, then."

We sat in silence, my father tapping his fingertips together, staring at the floor. The sound of the shovel scraping against the concrete walkway came through the window. I was crying very softly.

Two hours before my father arrived, a young sheriff's deputy with a crew cut and a shy, almost apologetic manner had come into the interrogation room and told me that Amber had shot herself with Harriet Walker's revolver. She'd been found by the two officers who'd been sent to rescue her, slumped against the wall beneath one of the big windows that looked out over the lake. Evidently she had awakened alone in the hotel and found the revolver where I had left it on the window ledge after seeing the deer. She had fallen in the same spot where I had left it, the third window over from the right, as if the terrible idea had come to her and been acted on in a single impetuous instant. That was the patrol officers' conclusion.

"She went a little crazy, I guess," the deputy had said after giving me the news. "Because she was distraught about being pregnant and all the trouble it made for her." He paused. I felt him looking at me. "Is that your belief, too, son?"

"What?" I was crying and had not heard the question.

"That she was distraught. That was why she did it. When she woke up all alone in that hotel." He looked at me. "She didn't mention anything else, did she?"

"She was sad about losing her baby," I said.

"Yes, of course," the deputy said, and he spoke with some impatience. "But she wasn't married. You'd think that losing the baby would have been a kind of relief, actually."

I didn't say anything.

"Well, anyway," he continued, "I guess that's neither here nor there." He folded his arms across his chest. His gaze began to travel idly around the room.

"Do you know anything else about her?" he asked after another moment had passed. "Anything that's worth knowing about."

I didn't want to think about his question because it hurt too much. So I said the first thing that came into my mind. "She was learning French because she wanted to study art in Montreal."

The deputy smiled. "Anything important, I mean."

"They made her quit school."

The deputy gave me a puzzled expression.

"She didn't love the boy she was supposed to marry. She had to pretend about that so her parents wouldn't make her give the baby away."

"Okay, son," the deputy said. "That's enough."

"She wanted me to stay."

He looked at me. Then he reached forward and placed his hand on my arm. "That's enough, now," he repeated quietly.

Just then another deputy came in. He made a sign and the two went off to one side and spoke together in lowered tones. I heard them mention Amber's name two or three times. Then the new deputy came back.

"Do you think you're up to seeing her?" he asked. "Her parents have declined to do that. I don't know why. We'd like a positive identification."

"Yes, sir. I can do that."

The new deputy took my arm above the elbow and led me out of the interrogation room and down a hallway and into a small window-less room where a single bare lightbulb hung from the ceiling. Three walls were covered with wooden shelves filled with police gear: boxes of ammunition, traffic flares, coiled ropes with grappling hooks, electric searchlights—all the equipment for keeping people safe. A table in the center of the room held a figure covered by a white sheet.

The deputy motioned for me to stand along one side of the table. When I told him I was ready he pulled back the sheet.

Amber lay with her arms at her sides, her hands clenched in fists. Her eyes were open, and her head was tilted back, as if she were trying to peer at something far off in the distance. She was dressed in her underwear. Her skin under the harsh light looked like plaster.

"I guess they had to remove her dress to make the examination," the deputy said. His gaze shifted over to me. "I'm sorry if that disturbs you."

"No, sir. It doesn't."

I studied her face, trying to spot something that would remind me of the girl I had known. But everything looked wrong. None of it was the way I remembered Amber.

"Well, son?" the deputy said.

"Wait a minute."

"Take your time."

I reached out and moved a strand of hair away from her face. Beneath the curve of the ear was the ugly wound from the fishhook. An inch or so higher was a second wound, a small opening with blackened edges.

"That's her," I said.

"I need you to say her name. It's for the official record."

"That's Amber Dwyer."

I let the strand of hair fall back.

"Good," the deputy said. He sounded satisfied. He started to draw back the sheet.

"Wait a minute."

I looked at Amber. It was hard but I forced myself to look. If I stood there for a moment I might begin to understand something about what had happened. Something I could take away and keep in my memory. Some answer that would remove the terrible anger I felt for Amber and for myself. But everything was happening much too fast, and my feelings were much too strong. Too fast and too strong for there to be any good thinking to make answers from. And so finally I gave up. I could think about it later, I decided, after things calmed down and the feelings got quieter. Maybe then I could make sense of it and have some memories.

I went to the foot of the table where Amber's dress lay folded in a neat bundle. I shook it out.

"What do you think you're doing there?"

I began to draw the dress up over Amber's body.

"Stop that," the deputy said. He reached forward and grabbed my arm. I pulled away and pushed back against him with my shoulder. He stumbled back a few steps.

"It's not right," he said.

"Get out of here if you don't like it."

I tucked the dress in around the edges. I was crying so hard I could barely see what I was doing. But in the end it seemed that I had made things better. As much as I could, I had tried to fix things. Amber looked better than she had before. She almost looked like I remembered.

My father and I left the ice shanty that February afternoon and began walking in off the frozen lake. The wintry sun—a vague white ball behind the low cloud cover—sat just above the horizon. In a few moments it would dip below the tree line and stop spilling its feeble light into the shallow basin of the lake. I always dreaded that sudden change from bright to darkness—which is unique in the Midwest—and I was hoping we would reach the shore before it happened.

"Why do you think she wanted that baby so badly?" my father asked when we were about halfway to shore. "When it would have been so easy to give it away?" He spoke as if he had been thinking about the question for a while. But then he added quickly: "I'm sorry, Danny. If you don't want to talk about it, that's okay."

I was carrying a burlap sack with two pike in it. They were stiff from lying on the ice outside the fishing shanty and they knocked against my leg like pieces of cordwood.

"Why do people want anything?" I said, which was an attitude I was beginning to try out.

"That's not a good enough answer," my father said. He spoke with some sharpness. "That's the coward's way out."

He stopped walking, and a space began to open up between us. I took several more steps and then I stopped walking, too. But I didn't turn around; I just stared in the direction of the setting sun where only the slightest portion showed above the tree line.

"All right," I said, "how's this? I think she was looking for something to put into her life. Something that would make up for a part that was missing."

"You mean she wanted something to keep busy?"

"No, not that."

"What then?"

The last sliver of sun disappeared below the trees and in just that instant of time the light drained out of the sky.

"She wanted something that would make her feel less alone," I said. "Something that would take her love and give it back—because no one else would do that."

I felt my father's gaze on me. "But you did," he said. "That's how it seemed to me."

"I tried. But I guess I wasn't good enough."

There was a long silence as I waited for my father's next question. Along the shore the wind moved through the bare tree branches, and the soft sifting snow blew like sand across the frozen surface of the lake.

I heard the metallic clang of the steel spear dropping onto the ice. I turned to look in my father's direction. His face was barely visible in the sudden gloom. He walked across the narrow space that separated us and placed his hands on my shoulders and looked into my face. And suddenly I knew he had no further words to say to me.

For a long time we stood facing each other—we just looked at each other—and then he put his arms around me and held me for a while, held me in the darkness as if I were still a child . . . and for a moment I felt calm, and innocent, and at peace.